CHASING
THE
HORIZON

Books by Mary Connealy

THE KINCAID BRIDES
Out of Control

In Too Deep

Over the Edge

TROUBLE IN TEXAS
Swept Away

Fired Up

Stuck Together

WILD AT HEART
Tried and True

Now and Forever

Fire and Ice

THE CIMARRON LEGACY
No Way Up

Long Time Gone

Too Far Down

HIGH SIERRA SWEETHEARTS
The Accidental Guardian

The Reluctant Warrior

The Unexpected Champion

BRIDES OF HOPE MOUNTAIN
Aiming for Love

Woman of Sunlight

Her Secret Song

BROTHERS IN ARMS
Braced for Love

A Man with a Past

Love on the Range

THE LUMBER BARON'S DAUGHTERS
The Element of Love

Inventions of the Heart

A Model of Devotion

WYOMING SUNRISE
Forged in Love

The Laws of Attraction

Marshaling Her Heart

A WESTERN LIGHT
Chasing the Horizon

The Boden Birthright: A CIMARRON LEGACY *Novella (All for Love Collection)*

Meeting Her Match: A MATCH MADE IN TEXAS *Novella*

Runaway Bride: A KINCAID BRIDES *and* TROUBLE IN TEXAS *Novella (With This Ring? Collection)*

The Tangled Ties That Bind: A KINCAID BRIDES *Novella (Hearts Entwined Collection)*

A WESTERN LIGHT · I

CHASING THE HORIZON

MARY CONNEALY

BETHANYHOUSE
a division of Baker Publishing Group
Minneapolis, Minnesota

© 2024 by Mary Connealy

Published by Bethany House Publishers
Minneapolis, Minnesota
www.bethanyhouse.com

Bethany House Publishers is a division of
Baker Publishing Group, Grand Rapids, Michigan

Printed in the United States of America

Library of Congress Cataloging-in-Publication Data
Names: Connealy, Mary, author.
Title: Chasing the horizon / Mary Connealy.
Description: Minneapolis, Minnesota : Bethany House Publishers, a division of
  Baker Publishing Group, 2024. | Series: A western light ; 1
Identifiers: LCCN 2023030985 | ISBN 9780764242656 (paperback) |
  ISBN 9780764242755 (casebound) | ISBN 9781493445158 (ebook)
Subjects: LCGFT: Christian fiction. | Romance fiction. | Western fiction. | Novels.
Classification: LCC PS3603.O544 C53 2024 | DDC 813/.6—dc23/eng/20230711
LC record available at https://lccn.loc.gov/2023030985

Scripture quotations are from the King James Version of the Bible.

This is a work of fiction. Names, characters, incidents, and dialogues are products of the author's imagination and are not to be construed as real. Any resemblance to actual events or persons, living or dead, is entirely coincidental.

Author is represented by the Natasha Kern Literary Agency.

Baker Publishing Group publications use paper produced from sustainable forestry practices and post-consumer waste whenever possible.

24 25 26 27 28 29 30   7 6 5 4 3 2 1

To Elle, Isaac, Luke, Katherine,
Lauren, Adrian, and Quinn

I love you.

1

Elizabeth Rutledge crept out of the alley when she heard the creaking of wagon wheels. The man driving the garbage cart, the same route every night, slowed to a near stop as he turned onto the last lane to take the trash and dump it in an ugly pile that would soon be added to by the garbage created by Horecroft Asylum.

"Sir, can you help me?" Beth was dressed in what looked like mere rags, clothing even the servants in her father's home would disdain to wear.

Her voice was laced with fear, and she put a tone of begging into it. The fear was easy to come by. The thought of what she was doing made her heart pound until she felt it in her ears.

If this failed, she'd almost certainly end up locked away with Mama.

"I've dropped a nickel in a crevice between the cobble-stones, and I can't get it out. I need it, sir, to feed my children."

The garbage man pulled his reeking cart to a stop and jumped down. He rounded the dapple-gray nag and crouched beside Beth. She saw evil in his eyes, even in the nearly pitch-dark of the street, which was lined with crumbling brick buildings.

She'd studied this man and knew far more about him than he'd ever suspect.

He'd help her all right, yet she'd never regain possession of her coin. She felt the weight of the gun in her pocket and hoped the man was just a thief and not something much worse.

While the two of them struggled with a little stick to lift out the coin that Beth had lodged thoroughly in a tight crack, Beth heard a faint rustling coming from behind her.

It was nighttime near a garbage dump. Any rustling sounds were usually made by rats, and this man didn't strike her as very smart.

He didn't see Mama as she climbed out of the back of the wagon and slipped into the night. Beth thought Mama had made a bit more noise than would be expected, but she didn't dare turn to look. That was all it would take for Mama to be discovered, then taken and locked away. Again.

Swallowing hard to make her dry throat work, she saw the garbage man finally dislodge the coin. He held it up with a smirk.

"Oh, thank you—"

His laugh cut her off as he closed his hand around the nickel. "It's mine now."

"No! Please . . ." She had to make a fuss or the man

8

might become suspicious. "If you take it, my children won't have anything to eat. Please!"

He ignored her, clambered onto the wagon seat, and slapped the reins on the swaybacked horse. He laughed as he rolled away.

When his laughter had faded in the distance, Beth whispered, "Mama?"

A shadow shifted in the narrow alley across the street. Beth hurried over.

"Elizabeth." Eugenia Rutledge flung her arms around Beth. Mama smelled just like the man's garbage wagon.

Beth only hugged her tighter. The feel of Mama hugging her thickened Beth's throat with tears. She fought them until Mama burst into tears herself.

Beth clung tightly as she wept. Several minutes passed before she was able to regain her composure.

"Elizabeth, my darling girl—"

"Shh. It's *Beth* now, Mama. And from this moment on, you're *Ginny*. My older sister, Ginny Collins."

Father had never called either of them by a nickname. In truth, they'd never called each other using one. Yet no one would think twice of them if they went by Beth and Ginny, or so Beth sincerely hoped.

Even after three years in an insane asylum, Mama was youthful-looking, her hair still fully brunette with no sign of graying. She was far too thin, though, and Beth had to wonder what the food was like in that house of horrors, Horecroft.

The plan was for them to pass as sisters. Beth prayed for a lack of curiosity among those who encountered them.

"You've given us Oscar's surname? Beth and Ginny

Collins . . . Yes, of course we need new names." Something fell off Mama's head. Beth thought it might be a cabbage leaf.

Another shadow emerged, and Beth grabbed for her six-gun.

"I-I brought someone with me," Mama explained. "She's a friend. I couldn't leave her behind. She helped me find my way out of the asylum. I'd have been hard-pressed to make it without her."

A woman so frail that she looked breakable came to Mama's side.

Beth was speechless. She'd made plans, detailed plans. For two.

"Let's go. I've held us up too long as it is. There's no time to waste." Mama didn't know the plan, but she did know their situation was urgent.

"I'll go by Kat," the delicate blond woman said. She was so small, she looked more child than adult. "I'll do whatever I need to do to stay out of that horrible place." Her determination rang out in her voice, even at a whisper.

Beth didn't have much choice in the matter. Time was limited. She'd plan their next steps on the walk to the wharf. "Let me get my satchel. It has everything I believed I'd need for two women—sisters down on their luck, working their way downriver to Independence, Missouri." She'd have to find additional clothing for Kat that might fit the woman, who was slender to the point of starvation, and not raise suspicion. "And I've got two bonnets that will pull forward to mostly conceal our faces. Kat, you can wear mine." Beth would think of something before Kat needed a change of clothing. She had until they reached Independence, where the wagon train should be heading out of town right about now.

Their transportation to the West.

They'd go and find a place beyond Thaddeus Rutledge's reach, and they'd hide for the rest of their lives. She'd told Oscar not to wait for them. She and Mama, and now Kat, would have to catch up sometime later.

And to get there, they'd be working their way westward.

"A cattle boat?" Ginny clutched her throat with a delicate hand as she stared at the low, flat-topped steamboat floating at dock on the Chicago River "What in the world is a cattle boat?"

The question was foolish because, as Ginny could clearly see, it was a boat that was being, right this minute in the predawn hours, loaded with cattle. A wide gangplank with sturdy railings slanted downward a bit as cattle were driven from shore to boat. The animals followed each other until a man on the boat steered each into stalls along the main deck of the boat.

The lowing of the cattle broke the morning air, along with the splashing of the tide against the shore. Occasionally a cow gave a full-on *moo*, its voice high and indicating fear.

Ginny knew how the poor things felt. She'd lived with gut-twisting fear for three years in that asylum her wretched tyrant of a husband had put her in. She'd lived with fear longer than that because Thaddeus had always terrorized her.

But never had she expected he'd sink so low as to lock her away. Trapped behind walls. Forced to act exactly as she was told in the daytime. Locked into a room shared with two dozen other women at night. Women who were either mad or slowly being driven mad. But she'd found kindred souls in there as well, and she prayed day and night to find a way to escape. And she'd wanted to take all those poor imprisoned women with her.

In the end, escaping had proven so difficult that right this moment, cattle or no cattle, the wonder and relief of walking around free had doused every drop of her deeply felt terror.

Yet there was plenty left to fear. Thaddeus would search for her. Ruthlessly and endlessly he'd search. But to breathe free air. To hug her daughter. To walk by her own choosing rather than being prodded and pushed along like . . .

She watched the marching cattle and knew that what she'd been through had been worse. Much worse.

The cows had no knowledge of freedom. No understanding of any such thing. But Eugenia Wyse Rutledge had known freedom. She'd been stripped of it brutally. And if he had his way, Thaddeus would lock her right up again.

He had the power and the law on his side, while she, an educated, wealthy woman—wealthy in her own right—could only be free by escaping and running. The fury within threatened to truly make her start screaming like a madwoman.

But she'd always fought for decorum and manners, knowing that letting her fury show would only further prove to anyone watching that the asylum was exactly where she belonged.

She was free. If she wanted to remain free, she had to run.

It would not be easy. The pens, the boat, it all smelled terrible. The boat looked overcrowded and apt to tip. And Ginny was going to live on it for the next few days, along with a few hundred apathetic cows and more than a dozen hungry men.

With her attention frozen on the vessel that would be her home for a while, Ginny wondered at her daughter's steady nerves.

"I've got an idea." Beth stayed well back from the gang-plank.

The three of them huddled beside a warehouse with a good view of the boat, but in the hour left before sunrise, hopefully they weren't visible to the busy men. "The trip is four days long, or so the captain told me when he hired me. We have a tiny berth for the two of us. I don't see the captain anywhere, though he's probably in this hectic crowd somewhere. We'll get Kat hidden on the boat, and we can sneak her food. We'll keep her hidden."

"A stowaway?" Ginny said.

Kat nodded firmly. "I can stay hidden."

A long, low *moo* came from the boat.

"They'll soon have the cattle loaded. We ship out at dawn."

Ginny noticed that besides the cattle, men were shoveling coal into the steamboat's tenders.

"We must move now—while it's still somewhat dark." Beth slung an arm around Kat, pulled her close enough that a casual observer might not recognize it was two women rather than one. Beth headed for the gangplank.

"Remember we're sisters, Ginny. And Kat is our . . . um, sister-in-law. My brother Michael just died. From a fall. We don't want any hint of disease. Kat coming along, if she's discovered, was a last-minute decision after Michael's death."

Since Beth was Ginny's only child, it was a bit of a trick to add a son and daughter-in-law so suddenly.

Kat said, "I miss Michael terribly. I told him not to go out on that roof."

Beth snickered and kept moving.

Everything smelled terrible. The Chicago River was polluted until the water was like a cesspool. And of course, all around was the smell of cows.

Ginny was no freshly picked daisy herself, nor was Kat. Honestly, they fit right in with the overall stench.

"Mama . . . that is, *Ginny* and I were hired on as cooks."

"I can't cook, Beth." Ginny felt a warning was in order. She might be a terrible cook, but she kept right up with her daughter as they walked the plank.

"I can. I've learned so much. I'm ready for whatever lies ahead on the journey."

Soon they were on the boat, and Beth led them straight over to a steep stairway.

Talking quietly, Beth pointed things out. "We're walking on the deck right now. This door is the hatch, and the stairs are called the companionway. It leads to our tiny berth. There's not really room for one, but with a single, narrow bunkbed, they call it a room for two. Now three.

The bottom bunk should be off the floor far enough for Kat to hide beneath it."

Ginny nodded, knowing how slender Kat was and also how determined.

Beth had the door closed for only a moment when a firm knock sounded.

Without a word, Kat dropped to the floor and vanished under the bunk. Ginny hoped whoever was at the door hadn't seen them come aboard.

Ginny pressed her way past Beth so that Beth could handle the door. Kat shoved her bonnet out from under the bed. Ginny snatched it up and handed it to Beth. Ginny pulled hers down around her face and looked hard at the floor.

Ginny thought she had their story straight, but she didn't want to put it to the test just yet. She resolved to say little or nothing and fastened her eyes on the floor, or deck, whatever it was called.

Beth tied the bonnet on quickly, then cracked the door open a few inches. "What da ya need?"

Ginny recognized the accent. It was the same as the boy's who cleaned and polished the boots at the Rutledge house.

"Food's been loaded into the galley. Come along, both of ya, and we'll go over things."

Beth followed the man's voice. Ginny hadn't even seen who it was. But Ginny was right behind her daughter, who was posing as her sister. Ginny closed the door behind them and hoped poor little Kat would be all right.

Hooves stomped overhead. The hall was narrow, the smells almost smothering. And they were working in this hulk and would be for days.

All that had been stolen from Ginny hit hard as they walked the narrow corridor toward the boat's kitchen. She tried to focus her thoughts and ignore her temper. It was the same thing she'd been doing for three years in the asylum.

She entered the kitchen, though it was called a galley on a boat. What story had Beth told? Maybe Ginny was supposed to be an old hand at cooking on a boat. Maybe she wasn't supposed to know anything.

The man pointed and talked. Beth nodded, so Ginny did as well. Her anger soon returned, and she was swept up by fury as she thought of what her husband had taken from her and from Beth, and now Beth was making this desperate rescue attempt.

Ginny clamped her mouth shut and looked at the floor so her expression wouldn't show. Ginny knew she should offer to go back. Being locked in an asylum was a monstrous act by her husband, but to save her, Beth was giving up everything.

Ginny couldn't say the words that would give Beth back her life. She just couldn't go back there.

She glanced up, determined to be as much help to her daughter as she could. Fourteen men on the boat, most of them there to handle the cattle. Only two meals a day, but that was meals for the men. Ginny had no idea how often the cattle ate.

Ginny lowered her head and closed her eyes. It was all too much. She missed most of what the skinny man was saying. He sounded grim when he talked of food. Clearly he didn't expect much. Ginny would be little help making meals. She'd never so much as peeled a potato or sliced bread in her life.

Maybe Beth had truly learned some skills and could handle the cooking. Beth had always been unusually bright, so if she'd set out to learn, she would have done it.

Ginny would be her helper. A glance at a large pile of potatoes told her that peeling them would be a big part of this job. She squeezed her eyes shut and drew a deep breath. Surely if a reasonably intelligent person did the same chore hundreds of times, she'd get good at it.

She forced a determined expression onto her face and opened her eyes.

That was when Ginny saw her first rat.

2

"Wagons! Ho!" The wagon master's voice echoed across the line of twenty-three wagons. "Move 'em out!"

A bullwhip snapped in the cool air of the early Independence spring morning, and the first wagon, driven by Parson McDaniels and his wife, began rolling forward.

Jake Holt, in his job as scout, felt his heart speed up. The first morning was always the most fun. A line of folks setting out in search of a better life. He enjoyed helping them. And this was his last journey. The longing he felt for home had grown until he could hardly escort any more settlers across the country. Instead, he wanted to spur his horse and gallop straight for the land he'd homesteaded in Oregon.

He'd homesteaded last September during a previous trip when he'd reached Oregon, spending the winter there. But he needed the money and he'd promised his friend Dakota, the wagon master. A few years back, he'd've had to wait until the mountain trails opened, which could be as late as June. But now with the trails widened and the train tracks cutting through, he'd headed east in the early spring, rushing across the country on the train to reach Omaha, then south on a paddlewheel boat to Independence, Missouri, in time to ride back west one final time.

Dakota Harlan, the wagon master, had plans to team up with Jake and settle down..How many times now had he made this trek? Five? Six? Twenty-five years old and he'd made this trip across the country many times. Wagon-train travel was safer now than it had been when he'd first started doing this. The West was more settled; the trails were better scouted.

Of course, there could still be plenty of trouble. Long, hot days. Disease sometimes swept through the train. Flooding, tornados, the occasional interaction with a grizzly or a cougar or a rattlesnake.

Avalanches and blocked trails could cause trouble in the mountains. Jake had once survived a buffalo stampede. A small herd, but even a few buffalo could prove deadly.

Horses came up lame. Wagon wheels broke. Children could hurt themselves or fall sick. Jake knew all of that could happen and much more because it had happened to him. But even with all that, the trips had gotten safer.

Right now, this morning, the whole group teemed with enthusiasm and optimism. As the months passed, though, they'd all settle down, himself included. The dreary miles, the dry spells. The heat, the cold. The rainstorms that would turn the trail to muck and force them to have to stop and wait, sometimes for days. There were mountains to cross and all sorts of dangers to deal with. Before long, the early excitement would turn into hard work and gritty determination. But for now, spirits soared.

He rode past the line of wagons as each in turn began to roll with the creak of wheels, the groan of wood, the slap of canvas from windblown wagon covers, and finally the cries of the drivers. Jake looked for anyone who needed help. Horses snorted and tossed their heads, and the metal in the traces jingled like Christmas bells.

It was a wagon train of immigrants. Different folks from all over the world. Mostly Irish this time, and a hardworking crowd if he'd ever seen one. But Jake also saw Germans, Polish, Swedes, and Italians. Lots of nationalities. Their own languages flavored the conversation as Jake did his best to communicate with them.

They'd begun gathering three days ago. This train was small compared to the early years of movement westward. Few folks even took this route anymore, yet there were enough that he'd found steady work. And now he was nearly done. He had plans, just as these folks did, to settle down on a homestead, alone.

He adjusted his Stetson on his newly shorn hair. By the end of this crossing, his dark hair would be overlong and tied with a leather thong at the back of his neck, if he bothered to fuss with it that much.

He rode his quarter horse down the line. The critter was a rich chestnut with pretty white socks and a blazed face. The stallion had a black mane and tail. Jake had plans to buy a few mares and breed horses on his homestead. He hoped to expand and gather a herd of cattle eventually.

Following the slow-moving wagons, he reached the hindmost wagon and studied the man driving an excellent team of six cattle. But not the usual oxen, which were, in Jake's experience, always gelded bulls that seemed to never stop growing. These weren't gelded. Five of them were cows. Huge, shining black critters and a batch of beauties. And the sixth was an Angus bull.

Jake recognized fine stock in the six cattle pulling the rear wagon. They'd been thoughtfully chosen The usual wagons were drawn by oxen or draft horses, sometimes mules. Usually four were used to pull the load and two saddle horses came along, and occasionally they'd be switched out to take a turn pulling. By the time they reached Oregon, the livestock would be weary, thin, and worn down. But they would recover and be valuable to sell if the pioneers were so inclined. Or with good care, they'd regain their strength and make decent farm animals.

The last three wagons were of a kind. Large, sturdy, and well loaded, and the man driving the final wagon, Oscar Collins, was the owner of all three, or at least he handled the details of all three. He and his two brothers drove the teams, all of them strong men who'd be good to have along.

Four sturdy Morgan horses, two chestnut-colored, the others a buckskin and a gray, pulled the front team. They were young, healthy critters, and Jake knew horses. The buckskin was a stallion and the others mares. Oscar was driving west with the stock he intended to use to start a farm.

The middle wagon was pulled by more Angus. Six on this team, too. Gleaming black, strong and gentle. All cows. There seemed to be no nonsense between the cows and bull, nor the mares and the stallion. Jake guessed that the stock might have been together long enough for them to be carrying babies, and that might help to keep bulls and stallions calm when they might otherwise act up, intent on breeding. It was a smart decision, and with the rest of the wagons in the train pulled by oxen, or in one case, mules, it would probably work.

It was just that Jake had never seen such a thing before.

"What made you think of trainin' Angus cattle to pull your wagons?" Jake rested his gloved hands on his saddle horn and relaxed as if the wagon train didn't need his attention anymore.

He'd talked to Oscar a few times and liked the man. He wasn't an immigrant like the others. Oscar had said there were other members of his family coming along—his sisters and someone bringing them. They'd been delayed but would catch up. It was as irregular as the Angus.

It all added up to Oscar and his three heavily loaded wagons being a puzzle, and Jake had a liking for solving puzzles.

The missing pieces of the puzzle might bring the picture into focus.

Jake was looking forward to meeting Oscar's sisters.

3

Getting Kat on the boat had been simple. Hiding her had been ridiculously easy.

The woman crawled under that bunk and stayed there. A space so narrow only someone as thin and fine-boned as Kat could have fit.

If she shared the space with rats, she made no mention of it. Kat didn't even speak again until Beth and Ginny came back from making the first meal on the evening after they'd set out.

"I've brought you a plate of food, Kat." Beth heard the exhaustion in her own voice. Mama hadn't been fooling when she'd said she couldn't cook.

That left Beth scrambling. Mama, or Ginny, tried, but she had no idea what to do. And the woman couldn't peel a potato to save her life.

Kat slid out from under the bunk. Bringing food to the cabin was forbidden for several reasons, the most obvious of which was that Kat was a stowaway.

Beth sent Ginny ahead, with Beth only a pace behind

carrying food. They didn't bring a plate because Beth couldn't think of a way to hide it. Instead, she wrapped up what could be handled in a cloth and tucked the cloth inside her shirtwaist. No stew for Kat.

Another reason taking food out of the galley was forbidden was that scraps of food drew vermin. Since the ship crawled with rats, bold as you please, the rule was a wasted effort. Even so, the rules were set down, and Beth was breaking them.

And above all else, Beth didn't want to do anything to get herself and Ginny, and now Kat, thrown off this boat.

Ginny hurried into their berth. Beth heard the steady thud of feet coming down the ladder.

Ginny as good as dove into the room with Beth hard on her heels.

"Cook, hold up there."

Beth yanked the food, two biscuits made into beef sandwiches, out from under her shirtwaist, thrust it at Ginny, relaxed her expression from fear to weary boredom, and turned to face Captain Walsh. He had a full white beard. He was tall and unkempt, but he had a good way with giving an order, and so the men obeyed him, and fast. Beth did the same.

"What was your name ag'in, miss?"

"It's Beth, Cap'n Walsh." Doing her best to slur her words, Beth leaned heavily on the doorframe, with the door open about a foot. Mama was very smart, and Beth knew she was busily hiding the food right now.

Kat was making herself as still and silent as possible under the bunk. They were all worried that the captain might insist on inspecting their berth.

"I wanna tell you ag'in how good the food is. One meal into our trip and the men are noticing, mentioning it to me. I'd like you to consider signin' on for the return voyage. We go up and down the river real regular. I'd double your wages. It'd keep my men happier."

"'Preciate it, Cap'n, but nope. Cain't. Gotta get to my family south of Independence. Glad the food's good, though."

"Triple your wages, then. No better payin' job for a woman anywhere on the waterfront."

"Mighty fine offer. I'd do it if'n I could. But I cain't."

The captain narrowed his dark brown eyes at her. He glanced into the cabin over her head. Frowning like a man who'd never heard the word *no* before, he said, "You consider it, Miss Beth. You consider it real hard."

Beth didn't want him to stay longer so she nodded. "I'll do just that. I will."

The captain frowned again, then turned and walked back to the companionway and climbed up to the main deck.

Beth swung the door shut and leaned her back against it with a sigh of relief. "He's gone."

Kat stuck her head out from under the bed, sat up with her legs still under, and Ginny handed her the biscuits.

"You *are* a fine cook, Beth." Kat chewed fast as if being out in the open as she was terrified her, and only hunger kept her in sight.

Beth saw that she'd used the chamber pot, but she'd done so privately. Her determination to make her escape was etched in every move she made. Every word she spoke . . . or didn't speak.

Beth wanted to get to know the young woman. That phrase caught her. Young woman. Kat probably was no younger than Beth, who was twenty-one. But for all her determination, Kat seemed young and frail, while Beth was a tall woman, much like Ginny.

Mama . . . Ginny. Beth tried her best to think of her mother only as Ginny, afraid she'd slip up. Ginny was dark-haired without a hint of gray. Though the last three years had been hard on her, she was a youthful, pretty woman in her early forties. Beth had been born soon after Mama had married, and she'd been the only child born to the wealthy Rutledge family.

Ginny's blue eyes and dark hair, her height and build were all similar to Beth's. They had the same sharp cheekbones and straight noses. They had the same firm chin and long necks. Calling Ginny her older sister was believable.

Kat looked as different from them as was possible.

Thin to the point of being frail. Wispy blond hair that straggled out of the bun she tried to keep at the base of her neck. Her eyes were so light blue that, in the dim light of the room aboard the ship, they looked gray.

There was no resemblance between Kat and Beth. Beth had known sisters who looked nothing alike, but it seemed that their story of Kat's widowhood was a good one. But possibly they wouldn't have to tell it. The boat, the stinking, mooing boat, had three more days before it docked in Independence, if the trip went well. Kat had to stay under the bunk until then.

Finished with the biscuits, Ginny thrust a cup of water at Kat. She gulped it down gratefully. "I should probably take that job. A good chance Father would never find me

26

here. This might be a better hiding place than a wagon train."

A cow mooed overhead, and Ginny said, "I think one trip on this boat will be enough."

Kat handed back the cup and ducked under the bunk. "It'll be enough for me."

Beth set the cup on the floor by the door so they wouldn't forget it when they went back to the kitchen.

"Enough for all of us, I'd say. And as for my great talent at cooking, I smuggled salt in my satchel onto the boat. I think that's the secret of my success."

"The food must have been terrible before if salt causes this much enthusiasm." Ginny leaned against the ship's wall. "How are we going to keep this up, though, Beth? I can't cook. I'm sorry, but I'm worthless."

Beth said, "We'll get by." But she was afraid. Cooking for all those hungry men had been all she could manage, and the meal had been sparse.

"What are we going to do? You saw all those potatoes. I'll do my best, Beth, but I have never cooked in my life. What a spoiled failure of a woman."

From under the bunk came Kat's quiet voice. "I can cook."

Beth's eyes met Ginny's. Then they both looked at the crawl space under the bunk. "Come out here." Beth had to wonder.

Kat stuck her head out but stayed in a good position to hide quickly. She asked, "Did anyone really see Ginny? I mean, she's been wearing that bonnet, and she stayed in the galley and kept her eyes down."

Beth covered her mouth with one knuckle. "Let me

think. Did you talk to anyone, Ginny? Did you ever remove your bonnet?"

Ginny shook her head.

Kat crawled out. "I'm honestly a decent cook. My ma died when I was sixteen, and I cared for my pa's household, and I doctored with him until I married."

"Did your husband toss you into Horecroft Asylum, too?" Ginny frowned and crossed her arms.

"Nope, my husband died, and my greedy uncle-in-law decided my wanting to inherit his share of the family company meant I was crazy."

The women scowled as Beth tossed around the risks of switching Kat for Ginny. "It's honestly about the only way I can see us managing. Ginny, it's more than a two-person job. Do we dare to let Kat take over for you?"

Ginny said weakly, "I'm skinny enough to fit under that bunk."

Sure enough, Ginny fit, and Kat took her place in the galley, and no one seemed to notice the difference.

Jake drew his horse up beside Oscar Collins's wagon. It was just after sunrise on their third day. "When are your sisters going to catch up with us?"

Oscar frowned. His face, three days without shaving, had a serious scruff of beard. "No idea. There was no help for it but to head out." Then Oscar's face went from serious to grim. "I trust 'em to catch up, but if they don't, it'll mean something happened to stop them. I'll have to turn back."

Jake studied the man. Oscar looked to be about forty

years old. No gray in his beard or in his hair. Few if any lines on his face. His nose was bulbous. He was stocky, but it looked like pure muscle and no fat. He was six inches shorter than Jake's six-foot-three.

Oscar's two brothers, Bruce and Joseph, each driving their own wagon, looked like him. Same dark hair, similar build. But Bruce was younger enough it showed, and his hair was long enough that he kept it tied back. Meanwhile, Joseph was a couple of inches taller than his brothers and leaned more toward lanky. It was all a matter of slight differences, though. The brothers were of a type.

Oscar, who'd been an easygoing man so far, suddenly looked like he had a heavy weight on his shoulders. "There's no way my sisters could pass us or take the wrong trail, nothing like that?"

Shaking his head, Jake said, "I'd say the road we took is the only one getting any travel heading west. Nope, if they haven't gotten here, it's because they were slow setting out."

Oscar looked down at the reins he held, frowning. "My sisters and I have been separated for a while. I'd surely like to see those girls again, and soon."

Jake nodded and looked back down the trail. He could see a long way out, and there was nobody in the distance—no other wagons or horses behind them.

4

Beth gathered up her few possessions when they docked in Independence, most especially her gun, and went out to scout the hallway for a sight of the captain.

He'd treated them decently in his gruff way, and Beth didn't like that they had a stowaway with them. But Kat had more than done her share of the cooking. And they'd all eaten less, hoping a third share wasn't more than Beth and Ginny would have eaten. And now they were all hungry.

Beth had money to feed them—lots of it. She'd sewed rows of pockets carefully into the lining of her skirt to the point the money was heavy to carry. But spending it in excess might draw attention.

The coast was clear. The captain was busy directing the wider gangplank for the off-loading of the cattle, now in progress.

Rushing back, she whispered, "Now, let's go quick. I'll go first, but once we're on deck, Ginny, you and Kat get ahead of me. There's a red warehouse right along the dock. Hide behind it and wait there."

Beth led the way. When she reached the deck, she looked around, then waved Ginny and Kat past her. They walked fast to the gangplank and across it, hitting the dock in full daylight. Beth watched them, her eyes darting to the captain, who stood toward the back of the boat. Once Ginny and Kat were on dry land, they soon vanished behind the warehouse building. Beth ran after them.

"Hold up, Cook!" The captain strode toward her.

He was a rugged-looking man. The term *old salt* came to mind.

"As I mentioned before, I'd be mighty interested in having you stay on with us." He tugged on the brim of his blue sailor cap. His beard, streaked with gray and untrimmed for years, covered most of his face. "Your vittles were the best we've had on this ship in a long time. Same stock of food as ever, but you made it taste better'n can be believed."

"Thank ye, Cap'n Walsh. I've considered your offer, but I've plans ahead I cain't change." Plans to run far and fast.

"The young lady you brought along was a fine cook, too." A sharp intelligence flashed in his dark eyes, and no cruelty.

Beth hesitated. She was caught and knew it. "I have a coin or two I can give you for passage, Cap'n."

"I'm inclined to have you arrested and sentenced to cook on my cattle boat." Then she noticed his mouth beneath the thick beard curled into a smile.

"I'd best be on my way now." Beth heard the tone of her

voice. She had fought to speak as a less educated woman might, but just now she'd slipped.

His eyes narrowed.

Beth decided it was time to go and turned for the gangplank. She hurried but didn't run, half expecting the captain's hands to grab her and drag her to a stop.

Seconds later she was on the dock, then on the solid ground of the shore and moving fast. She reached the back of the red warehouse and turned back. The captain was back to directing the off-loading of the cattle. Beth sincerely hoped she hadn't been memorable. She regretted how skillfully she'd cooked. Adding that salt had been a mistake.

She found Ginny and Kat with their backs pressed to the side of the building. They smiled with such genuine relief, Beth felt like the world was opening up. She'd given two women their freedom. Not a bad use of her time. She had a sudden urge to rush back to Chicago and set every woman in that dreaded asylum free. Oh, there was no doubt that some of them were truly a danger to themselves and their families. There were those with badly broken minds who needed a safe place to live. Yet those poor souls were very likely not being cared for any better than Ginny had been.

Beth said, "We must hurry. Oscar bought horses for us and a packhorse apiece. They're in a livery stable nearby. Of course, he bought four horses, two of them intended as pack animals, and supplies to load on those two. But we'll see if there are other horses to be had. Let's go."

Moving briskly, with only Oscar's slim directions to guide them as he'd had no way to know just where the cattle boat would land, they found their way through the throng of sailors until the worst of the crowd had thinned. They left the docks, the high-pitched cry of gulls, the splash of the tide rushing in and retreating, and entered a run-down neighborhood along the docks.

The street was lined with bars and worn buildings packed tight. It was early in the day, and no one much was about. As they hurried forward, Beth searched for street signs and businesses that Oscar had described. She spotted a large building ahead and a sign with dark blue lettering saying it was the headquarters for this district. It was exactly as Oscar had described it. The livery stable should be close by.

"We're almost there," Beth said.

A low moan sounded from a crack between two buildings, too narrow to be called an alley. Then just above a whisper, "Help. Please."

Beth froze. Mama did not. She headed straight for the tiny opening, barely wide enough for two people to enter. Beth feared it was a trick, but Mama—Ginny—had already darted into the black crevice.

"She can't stop herself from helping. That's how I weaseled my way into her escape. We can do no less." Kat followed Ginny.

Beth thought they could do much less but didn't say so. Since both women were now out of sight, that would be pointless.

She reached the darkened space between the miserable buildings to find Ginny crouched on the ground behind a well-dressed man. He was slumped over, sitting on the hard stone of the space. His hands clutched his belly. Beth saw the red.

"You're bleeding!" Like a shot, Kat was beside him.

He had blond hair, neatly trimmed, and shining blue eyes with thick lashes. His black boots were scuffed, but they looked new and well made. His face had chiseled features that were now twisted in pain.

He spoke hoarsely, "Take this." He fumbled in his inner suit coat pocket and produced a leather packet. Kat took the packet and handed it to Beth as Ginny gently pushed the man's hands away from where he held himself.

"No, go on," he insisted. "I'm finished. There's an address on the letter in there. Please send it on. I've been shot. The man who shot me may be close by."

Ginny tugged the man's hands away from his wound.

Kat gave Beth a hard look and snapped, "Hand me something I can use to staunch the bleeding." Beth jumped at the cracking voice from the demure little blonde. "One of the dresses, anything."

Beth dug out a gingham dress, clean but tattered, from the satchel she carried. She held it out, and Kat snatched it and went to work on the man's wound.

There was a rip of fabric.

The man groaned in pain. "A man is after me. You've got to go. Get out of here. That packet—"

"Quiet." Kat cut him off. "This wound isn't mortal."

Fabric ripped again. Kat made a bandage of one of the strips, then with others she wrapped the man's belly. Her hands moved with skill. Beth didn't quite believe the quiet woman, who'd hidden so completely and had barely spoken, was so commanding.

Kat looked over her shoulder. "We'll be a while finishing this. Find those horses. Bring them here. You talked of buying another one. See if there's a cart and a horse to pull it. We'll throw something over him to hide him, then get him out of here."

Beth thought of ten reasons to protest, but Kat's eyes had a light in them that kept Beth from doing anything but obeying her. She turned from the alley and ran.

The livery stable, a derelict place in the run-down neighborhood but functioning nonetheless, had her horses waiting. Beth carefully slipped a few silver dollars from the pocket of her skirt. She had gold sewn into her pockets, but that would draw attention. Even the silver coins were a bad idea considering how poorly she was dressed, yet she had no choice but to use them.

She bought a solid cart and the best horses available, including a draft horse that looked old enough it might want to hop into the cart and be hauled along. But the hostler she dealt with claimed the draft horse was sound. Besides the four horses Oscar had waiting, she bought two more horses to add to their collection. She almost had a herd. A few were packhorses, though there were no packs for them to carry.

The hostler chewed on a piece of straw while they dickered. Beth got him down on his price a bit but decided being too sharp might bring the man to gossiping about the woman he'd dealt with. She hoped she'd be forgotten.

She paid his price and bought shabby leathers. The man helped her hook up the cart and then load the supplies Oscar had stored there. Beth accepted every bit of help the hostler offered, but there wasn't much Oscar hadn't taught her or that she hadn't learned from books. She'd studied and worked and learned. Now all that was left was to hope and pray she was ready.

She led her little cavalcade of horses back to the alley where the others waited. She was terrified she'd find the man, along with Ginny and Kat, attacked and killed by whoever had shot this stranger. Instead, Kat helped the man to his feet with firm commands. He rose, acting as though he was helpless against her strong will, with her arm slung around her waist and with Ginny holding his other arm around her neck. He let himself be loaded into the cart.

"Head down the trail the way you'd planned to go." Kat, in charge, climbed into the back of the cart with him. It was a small cart with low sides.

"We're taking him with us?" Beth drove the cart.

"Yes. His name is Sebastian Jones, and that packet of his is important. A man tried to kill him for it."

Ginny rode horseback and led the string of horses.

What a fine situation. This man, barely conscious, had no interest in heading for the American frontier, and they didn't have food for him if he did want to go. And as if they didn't have enough troubles of their own, he brought danger along with him.

But he didn't demand to be delivered anywhere. Glancing back, she could see he was quiet because he'd fully passed out. With a sigh, she slapped the reins on her horse's back and headed west.

They rode for a time getting out of the city, and they were just on the edge of it when she feared she was running out of chances and rushed into a mercantile to buy what supplies she could find. The others went ahead as she bought cloth to make Sebastian a shirt that wasn't blood-soaked and a blanket to cover him. Her next stop was at a grocer's, where she bought food enough for two unexpected guests for a week. She had no idea how far down the trail the wagon train had gotten and wasn't sure what they'd do if it was too much longer than a week.

She also bought a pistol, a Colt revolver. She had one in her pocket, but decided a second pistol for Ginny might be called for.

Determined to drop Mr. Jones off once they were away from town—like a Good Samaritan, she'd find him a nice inn and give him a little money—she set out west and soon caught up with the group, who were moving slowly.

Beth was an intelligent woman. Educated. She led this group with her eyes wide open to the dangers, the distance, and the struggle. But to get beyond her father's reach, she didn't dare travel in any comfort. He'd have the train stations watched. He'd wire towns far and wide, alerting the law. He'd want Mama, and he'd want Beth. And not just because they were both wealthy, which they were, but because nobody thwarted Thaddeus Rutledge. The man owned half of Chicago, his cronies splitting up the other half. They ruled like titans. And never had Thaddeus accepted the word *no*.

He wouldn't this time either. She thoroughly expected him to search for her for the rest of his life. Which meant she had to go nowhere she'd normally go while she left him far behind. She'd change her name and appearance.

Then once she got far away, no matter how far, she'd need to find a good hiding place.

Beth had no doubt there were Pinkertons searching for her already.

If Thaddeus found his runaway wife and daughter, he'd crush them.

5

Pounding footsteps jerked Ginny awake.

Thaddeus!

Her husband rushed out of the night, straight for her. His ugly cruelty distorted his face, his hands outstretched like claws to grab her.

"No!" Ginny kicked her blanket aside, and it wound around her legs. Fighting to stand, she tripped and fell, as if the blanket were on her husband's side.

"No! Leave me alone." She screamed the words and heard high-pitched shrieks and wrenching sobs as she struggled with the clinging blanket.

Then she saw Dr. Horecroft, his intense expression, the one he always had as he judged her to be a madwoman. Arrogant, infallible in his own mind. All his tortures handed out "for her own good." He was a pace behind, carrying a straitjacket, his jaw clenched, his eyes burning like a demon.

Her screams hurt her own ears. She stood, then fell, then shoved herself backward along the ground, desperate to be free of the binding blanket so she could run. Run for her life. Run forever.

Thaddeus's hands clamped hard on her shoulders and shook her. "You're furiously mad. You're insane!" He roared it in her face, so close that she felt his hot breath. She felt spit spray her face.

She struck at him. "I'm not. I'm not!"

So many times she'd remained calm, wanting to do nothing to give the appearance of madness. Now she'd lost all control. Slapping and scratching, she knew she'd failed. There was nowhere left to run. All was lost.

And her daughter. Would they take her, too? Lock her away?

Poor Beth. Ginny fought against Thaddeus's hold and screamed.

She screamed doubly when she saw Dr. Horecroft head for the blanket where Beth slept. He jerked Ginny's precious daughter to her feet, shoving her arms into the awful restraining jacket he used as punishment.

Ginny clawed at her husband, wishing she had a weapon. Why hadn't she armed herself?

Thaddeus laughed in a way he never had before. Thaddeus was grim and cold to her all the time. His contempt lashed her like a whip, but he never shouted, never struck her. Never put his hands on her.

Now he did.

Screaming, clawing, fighting, Ginny felt an ice-cold dash of water soak her face. Her eyes opened, only this time she saw night. Felt cool night air. She lay on dew-soaked grass.

Thaddeus had vanished. Dr. Horecroft had vanished.

"Mama, please wake up." Beth knelt above her. Not

bound. Not taken prisoner. Beth shook her. It was Beth's hands on her shoulders.

Claw marks on the side of Beth's face, red and wet. Then a movement behind Ginny drew her eyes to Kat. Standing, her expression grim and knowing. Kat held a dripping washbasin in her hands.

Ginny's mind still carried the horror of Thaddeus being there. A nightmare, but so real. So terrifying. Awful enough to make a woman never go to sleep again.

She looked up and realized it wasn't full dark anymore. Dawn would soon lighten the sky, giving way to a new day. Blinking, Ginny said, "I'm awake. I'm all right."

Beth studied her with the saddest expression Ginny had ever seen.

Ginny rested one hand on Beth's bleeding face. "I did this. Oh, please forgive me. God forgive me. Beth. My Beth."

Beth pulled her into her arms and hugged her so tightly, Ginny could hardly breathe. But it felt wonderful. Her arms wrapped around Beth's back.

Ginny looked past her daughter, tears burning her eyes for all she'd put her daughter through. She saw Kat and the washbasin and said, "Thank you."

Kat nodded silently.

Ginny looked Beth in the eye and whispered, "It was a nightmare. A terrible nightmare. Thank you both for pulling me out of it."

"I've had a few of those myself," Kat said. "I'll check our patient."

Ginny glanced at the cart and saw no sign of Mr. Jones awakening.

Kat left Ginny to hold on tight to the daughter who'd

rescued her. Rescuing all three of them. So much weight on such slender shoulders.

"I'm so sorry about this." Ginny's voice broke, but she fought back a sob. She had to pull herself together and not be more of a burden. "I love you, my precious girl. I hate that I've caused you so much worry these last few years."

Beth pressed her hands to Ginny's face. "I'm sorry for what you went through. You're a strong woman to have survived it." She lifted her chin and said to Kat, "Both of you are. I'm so glad we're away from there. And I'm glad I have two strong women at my side as we make this trip." Easing back, she sat on her heels and asked Ginny, "Do you have nightmares a lot? I haven't been awakened by one before."

"I think the nights have been too short, and the work of the day too long and hard. I must've gotten a night of truly deep sleep. I had bad dreams at Horecroft some, but I'd hoped getting away would soothe my fretful mind."

"We'll pray it does. And pray Kat doesn't suffer from them either."

"It's no use trying to sleep more." Ginny noticed her hands shaking and fought to gain control of herself. "I'm too afraid of what sleep might hold. Let's get started on the day a bit early."

Beth stood, spry like the youngster she was, and extended a hand. Ginny caught hold, and Beth helped her to her feet.

A groan escaped before Ginny could stifle it, but she ignored her discomfort and said, "Let's get on the trail. We've got a wagon train to catch."

As Ginny hobbled about getting the horses ready to

ride, she fought back the pain of every muscle and bone in her body. Somehow she found the strength to make her joints and limbs work as she led the horses to water, then strapped them into their leather.

Yet it was harder to fight back the terror she carried of her husband and his viciously cruel minion Maynard Horecroft, who were out searching for her and wanting to make Ginny feel very sorry for her gaining her freedom.

Which was one more thing she'd be carrying west with her.

6

Thaddeus Rutledge felt his jaw tighten. He fought to control it, disgusted with himself for the lack of mastery over his reactions.

Eugenia was gone. Elizabeth with her. They needed to be retrieved.

He lowered the paper that Hemler Blayd had just handed him.

Blayd was the man who knew more about Thaddeus's business than anyone and who kept things running smoothly.

"How long ago did she . . . vanish?"

"He said it just happened. Last night. He reported it to us immediately." Blayd, a tall man, broad shoulders, eyes so cold he could make a woman hand over her rent even if it meant her children went hungry.

"I don't believe it." He didn't trust Horecroft. In fact, he was certain the good doctor wouldn't have contacted him if Elizabeth hadn't vanished. Thaddeus had immediately suspected it was connected to her rude, impudent, stubborn mother and had gone to check on her. Elizabeth was almost as bad as Eugenia. Thaddeus regretted he hadn't sent the girl to boarding school in Europe to get her away from Eugenia's influence. But then how his daughter grew up hadn't interested him much. Not enough to go to the trouble and cost of sending her away.

He'd fully intended to let her grow to adulthood, marry her off to whoever wanted a connection to Rutledge Industries, and be done with her. Perhaps hope for a grandson since his worthless wife had never produced a live child after Elizabeth.

And Thaddeus had found the perfect match for her. Walter Lindhurst, who was one rung below Thaddeus in the Chicago business world. Ruthless and intelligent. A man who loved buying real estate and collecting rent money. And Walter wasn't inconvenienced by a lot of moral scruples to stop him from taking advantage of a promising business deal when he saw one. It was a mindset that Thaddeus respected.

Walter had one son, who was as much a disappointment to him as Elizabeth was to Thaddeus. His wife recently and conveniently died. Thaddeus envied that stroke of luck—though *luck* might be the wrong word if her fall off a horse had been assisted.

Yes, Walter would make an appropriate husband for Elizabeth, but not if Thaddeus couldn't locate his daughter.

And that meant he had to find Eugenia because most certainly they were together somewhere. No, Horecroft wouldn't have said a thing if Thaddeus hadn't demanded to see Eugenia to see if his stubborn wife had any knowledge of Elizabeth's whereabouts.

Horecroft hadn't been able to produce her. Claimed he

just discovered her missing and she'd been right there the night before. Thaddeus doubted that, as it seemed Elizabeth had gone missing several days ago. The servants said she'd gone to stay with a friend. The friend had no idea there were any such plans. More lies from his rebellious daughter. He'd find the truth, because if Eugenia had been gone for days, that would give a better idea of how wide to cast his net.

Because he *would* find both of his ridiculous women. Two wealthy women with tidy sums carefully tucked away in elaborate trusts that Thaddeus had never been able to touch.

He'd never really needed their money, especially because Eugenia had brought a handsome dowry to the marriage. But what was theirs was *his*, and so he would find a way.

Thaddeus crumpled the paper in his hand with a vicious curl of his lip. Again he pushed aside the anger. Nothing was ever accomplished in a fury. He knew better and was a bit surprised at himself. Usually he handled situations like this better. He was known for keeping a cool head when things were going wrong. He'd always found it simple to do so.

This was different, however.

Blayd stood ready to do as Thaddeus wanted.

"Contact the Pinkerton Agency. Tell them I want their top agent here within the hour."

"What if their top agent is out of town?"

Thaddeus locked his gaze on Hemler Blayd, his right-hand man. His head of security. The man who enforced Thaddeus's rules without question. Blayd made sure all those who rented his boss's apartments paid their rents on time.

"Within the hour, Blayd. I'll accept no excuses from you or from them."

With a jerk of his chin, Blayd turned and left.

Thaddeus liked to instill fear in his employees, and why wouldn't they fear him? He paid his men well, but he'd fire them on the spot if they got in his way or failed him. It put fire under their steps.

But no such fear existed in Blayd. Instead, he read Thaddeus's mood and made sure to pass it along.

Thaddeus cast the crumpled letter onto his desk, then considered where his women might have run off to. If they were smart, and he doubted they were, he expected they'd run far and fast.

The train. That's how someone would go if they wanted to get far away. But how many days ago?

Finding that out was the Pinkertons' first job. Horecroft understood money, so he would agree to tell all he knew. Not because Thaddeus would bribe him, but because if he didn't, Horecroft well knew Thaddeus had the wherewithal to destroy him.

As for the Pinkerton Agency, Thaddeus was preparing to pay many agents, all across the country, to do their very best work. And if they didn't do it well, he'd take pleasure in destroying them, too. He was very much in the mood to destroy anyone who got in his way.

"Beth, you have to stop. His fever is raging, and he can get no rest with the wagon rolling."

Kat coming along on this journey was wearing Beth out. That went double for Mr. Jones. On the other hand, the delicate little despot was trying to save a man's life.

Beth saw a break in the trees ahead and what looked like the mouth of a canyon. A quiet creek flowed out of one side of that mouth. The sun was low in the sky. Beth had hoped to press on and drive well into the dark tonight. She had to catch up to the wagon train. They were supposed to be riding horseback—a much faster way to travel than pulling a cart. Their supplies were already running low, and Beth felt the rising fear inside her. She'd somehow taken the wrong trail. No, not possible. Oscar had talked of landmarks, and Beth had seen them just today. The trail was clear, the passage of animals and wagons obvious.

But when day after day passed and the wagons she kept hoping to catch sight of didn't appear, it was easy to make up things to worry about.

She'd hoped for another long day, yet she wasn't going to get it. As if the day wasn't long enough. They'd been moving at first light for the fifth day in a row. Or maybe sixth. Or fourth? The trail, the rolling cart, the dreadful beef jerky and hardtack they could only swallow because they were starving all became a blur.

No fire at night. No chance to sit and talk. She still hadn't talked to Ginny about Horecroft, the place that had given her such nightmares.

And their nights usually ended with Ginny's screams, which made the day start brutally early. Kat had a few, too. Beth felt the weight of what the two women had been through, as if she wore a collar around her neck, like the horse pulling their cart.

It was a terrible way to wake up. Beth's heart ached for her mama and for Kat. What in heaven's name had they gone through in that place?

"We'll stop just ahead, Kat." Beth guided her horse off the trail. Every night she'd found a place near water with plenty of grass.

Beth guided the horse toward the water. Ginny, leading the string of horses, turned off soon after. Ginny had toughened up after five days on the trail. The pale, drawn look on her face, the stiffness she tried so valiantly to hide and the way she slept, like she was more unconscious than asleep—all of that was easing now.

Kat was sunburned, mostly riding in the cart, not a properly covered wagon, but just a small rolling box barely longer than Mr. Jones's body, whom Kat tended as best she could.

Mr. Jones, whose name Beth was right this minute changing to Sebastian Collins. He was now her brother. Collins was the name they were all going by on the wagon train. They would claim to be sisters of Oscar Collins, and now Sebastian was his brother. She'd speak cautiously when they caught the wagon train until she knew what Oscar had told everyone, so that their stories matched.

The sunburn banished Kat's pallor from the asylum, which was, Beth hoped, at least a bit of a disguise. Kat's hair was scraggly, her nose peeling, her dress filthy. She and Ginny badly needed washing up, but the water Beth had found wasn't enough for bathing. And they worked so hard all day, they preferred to sleep at night. Since Ginny's nightmares seemed to come in the predawn hours, they needed to get every moment of sleep they were allowed.

Her women, Ginny and Kat. Her sisters now. Well, sister-in-law for Kat, as the wounded Mr. Jones was now Ginny and Beth's brother.

When Beth had any spare time at all, she wondered what was in that packet that someone was willing to shoot Mr. Jones for. Or *had* they shot him for it? Maybe he'd interrupted a burglary and been shot, and his wanting the packet mailed had nothing to do with the shooting.

She'd held it. It wasn't gold. It felt like a thick sheaf of papers. Not paper money either. It was more the size of writing paper. Not much that small had any great value, and money was usually at the root of crimes of this sort. As Mr. Jones was either unconscious or delirious most of the time, Beth didn't bother the man to find out what exactly was in the packet.

After watering the horses, she staked them out to graze, and then got out the meager food she had left for supper. She was grateful that Ginny and Kat were helping her because the day's chores had used up every ounce of her strength, and she needed her fellow travelers to bear part of the burden.

7

B eth, he's awake."
Beth pulled the cart horse to a halt. It was time
for a break anyway. Days on the trail plus the worries that they hadn't caught up with the wagon train yet
had begun to take their toll.

Worries because she knew by now that her father was
searching hard.

Worries because their food supplies were running low.

Beth glanced back at their mostly unconscious passenger, who'd distracted her from the catastrophe of her own
life. Which wasn't to say she welcomed his being awake.
Not exactly, but she did want to have a word with the man.
She set the brake, pivoted on the seat, and looked down
at Sebastian Jones. "Are you feeling better?"

Beth wasn't sure why he got to feel well when the rest
of them were exhausted and filthy and smelly and, well,
the man had been shot, so Beth did her best to sound
genuinely concerned for him.

Sebastian's blue eyes were wide open. He stared at Beth,

then slid his eyes to the side to stare at Kat. Then he looked at Ginny. "Who are you ladies? And where am I? I thought I was going to die, but this isn't even close to heaven."

Beth arched a brow at him. "You tried to get me to mail something, remember?"

"Mail something?" His expression sharpened as he thought for a moment. "My plans—where are they? Did you send them off?" He sounded nearly frantic with his last question.

Beth surmised that if her answer was yes, he wouldn't be happy about it. "You're sleeping on top of them," she finally answered.

Sebastian fumbled beneath him and drew the packet out from behind his back. He hugged the fat leather packet to his chest, then winced.

Beth suspected his ribs protested.

Kat piped up. "Your request seemed to be based on your belief you were dying, and we were intent on that not happening. So we kept them for you."

"At some point we'll draw near a town," Beth went on. "You can send the plans off in the next few days if you still want that."

Beth wouldn't do it, though. Staying away from towns figured prominently in her strategy for escaping her father. But Sebastian could toddle right on into the next town with a train station and take a train wherever he chose. She'd gladly give him enough money for a ticket.

"I-I don't think we need to mail it off now, after all. You're right that I thought I was done. I was shot, then fell a long way. I think I must've landed on a freight wagon or something that was moving. Falling from a rooftop is the last thing I remember until I woke up in that alley. I didn't even know what part of town I was in."

"We found you near the docks."

He frowned. "I was nowhere near the docks when I . . . uh, ran into trouble. When I heard you walk by, I'd accepted it and was thinking how to get the . . . the packet into the hands of someone I trusted."

Beth really couldn't resist asking, "Plans for what?"

He clamped his mouth shut. When he opened it again, he firmly changed the subject. "We're going to Oregon, did you say?"

"In that general direction. We're not sure where we'll end up." And now she clamped her own mouth shut. She should have just said yes. Of course, a group following the Oregon Trail was going to Oregon. Surely Sebastian would be long gone before they reached their true destination.

"C-can I go with you? I don't have a change of clothes. Not a bite of food." He shoved his hand into his pants pocket and produced a wallet. He flipped it open, and Beth saw a fat wad of paper money. "I still have my money. I can help pay for any supplies we'd need. My presence will be a drain on your food stores." He thrust the wallet at Beth.

Ginny, sitting on horseback, studied the wallet. Kat stood on the ground, looking over the edge of the cart. Beth didn't see how going to town to buy more food would work if no one wanted to be seen in town. Still, Oscar should have supplies enough for one more.

No, two more. Beth almost snorted in disgust at all the people she was bringing with her. She got down to what was most important. "In the next few days"—*please, dear*

God, not too many more days—"we'll be catching up with a wagon train where there will be plenty of food." She hoped. "Maybe when you're stronger, you can go to town and catch the train. Oregon couldn't fit with your plans. For now, keep your money. You may have need of it."

"How badly hurt am I?" Sebastian asked.

Beth turned to Kat. "Well, how badly hurt *is* he?"

Sebastian's eyes flew to the end of the cart. "You've been caring for me, haven't you? I came around a few times and you were tending me."

"Please call me Kat." She smiled. "Yes, I've been the one mostly tending your wounds."

She sounded gentle yet strong, completely at odds with the demure, frightened woman who'd jumped out of the garbage wagon with Ginny. It might be wise to remember that not everyone in Horecroft Asylum had been falsely accused. Even so, the smile was nice. Beth didn't think she'd seen that expression on Kat's face before.

"You were shot. The bullet went through, so I wasn't called on to remove it. I cared for patients at my pa's side when I was growing up, and I didn't think we needed to take you to a doctor. It tore up the muscles low on your belly. It shouldn't have hit your ribs, but a bad fall would explain that pain. You've got bumps on your head, which is why you've been sleeping for days. It's hard to be sure what all is causing you pain. The bullet was off to the side enough that I don't think it pierced any vital organs. The fact that you're here and alive is evidence of that. But you're going to hurt for a long while. You've been running a fever for days. It's down now. I'm hoping it's gone for good."

His eyelids drooped again. This time he had to fight to open them.

Kat said, "You're worn out. Sleep some more. We'll continue our journey and discuss this more when you're stronger."

He nodded as he quit fighting sleep.

Beth studied the man for a few moments. It flickered through her mind that he was falling asleep at a very convenient moment. He had certainly not given them any real answers about why in the world he was willing to take an unplanned trip all the way across the country.

A mystery surrounded Sebastian Jones. A mystery that had nearly gotten him killed. Just one more thing Beth didn't need.

Midmorning on the seventh day of the wagon train journey, Jake saw a group approaching from behind. Hopefully the sisters had arrived. He felt a wave of relief. Oscar was becoming increasingly worried. The train was making good time, and Jake hoped to reach Nebraska soon.

They could do better. Twenty miles a day wasn't out of the question. But it averaged out to more like ten due to weather or breakdowns or, God have mercy, if sickness swept through the train.

Yet the trip had gone well so far. The spring weather had been dry. They'd made a few creek crossings, and it wasn't a spring for flooding . . . so far. If all went well, they'd reach Oregon in three to four months. If all went normal, it would be five.

He had hoped those sisters would catch up with them before Oscar abandoned the wagon train to go back for them.

And here they came.

They approached briskly, but the wagon train was moving, too. So they were a while catching up. A ruckus at the front of the train pulled him away before they got here, so he was denied his first look at them.

"It's the wagon train." Beth felt like crying.

The relief that swept over her was almost uncontrollable. And she knew it was her wagon train because the last wagon was being drawn by the Angus cattle Oscar had convinced her to buy. Animals he had personally trained to pull a wagon.

She hadn't seen the black cattle, but she and Oscar had planned out everything. Those were her cows and her wagons, and that was her Oscar! She drew a shuddering breath. A man she'd known most of her life and who'd been more of a father to her than Thaddeus Rutledge ever was.

The wagon train didn't stop. Though she wished they'd stop, she knew better. Everything about a wagon train was set up to push onward, to cover as many miles a day as possible. Just as they hadn't waited for her in Independence, neither did they wait for her now.

Sometime later, they finally caught up with the rear wagon, and Beth saw Oscar looking back, watching them. When they came close enough, Oscar reined in and leapt off the wagon. He rushed back and hugged Beth so hard, he lifted her off the ground.

"I was close to turning back for you, girl! You made it."
Then he turned to Ginny. "And you." He hugged her, too.
More gently, but for longer. "You're free, Mrs.—"

"Hush. It's Ginny now. And yes, I'm free." Tears ran
down Ginny's face as she pulled Oscar close again. Never
in her mama's life had she gone so far as to touch one of
the people who worked for her at the Rutledge house. But
this moment transcended all those from before.

"I've prayed until I've worn out the good Lord's ears
hoping you'd get here." Then Oscar added, "Come along
now. Let's get on those wagons and keep rolling." Oscar
looked past them, and Beth explained it all quickly.

Mama's name—well, everyone's names. The extra
woman, also an escapee from an insane asylum. A
wounded man whose fever was up again today. His fic-
titious relationship to them seemed to be all right with
Oscar. She also told him about the extra horses and how
their supplies were running out. While they talked, Oscar
unhitched the cart horse, then rigged the cart to the back
of his wagon so it wouldn't need another driver.

He found a clean shirt and swapped it for the bloody
one Sebastian wore. They helped Sebastian into the rear
wagon, hoping the cover would give him shelter and keep
curious folks away.

Kat hopped into the back of the wagon with Sebastian.

Oscar strung the horses they'd brought along to the
back of his wagon, telling Beth to run to the front wagon
and climb up there to sit with his brother Joseph. Ginny
would ride with him.

They were rolling in only a few minutes, and although

the rear wagon had been left a bit behind, Oscar closed that space quickly.

Beth, riding up high on the wagon box, introduced herself to Joseph and asked if she could take the reins. She wanted to sharpen her skills with a team of six before another day passed.

She knew how to guide them, but Joseph was very skilled and gave her helpful pointers until the last wagon was back in line and the train was steadily moving along without any great fuss being made of Beth's arrival.

By the time Jake, Dakota, and Parson McDaniels had calmed the oxen, whose thrashing had caused a bit of mayhem while not stopping the train from rolling, Oscar's sisters had joined the wagon train and settled in.

Jake rode back to meet them. A young woman sat up on the box of the group's lead wagon, which was the lead of these three. She had a bonnet pulled so far forward, it cast her face in shadows. Still, she nodded at him.

She wore a faded blue calico dress, so worn it didn't match with the obviously prosperous Oscar and his brothers. Her bonnet was a drab brown.

Joseph Collins, Oscar's brother, said, "Jake, this is Beth Collins. My sister. Beth, this is Jake. He's scouting for the wagon train."

Beth and her bonnet nodded again. "Howdy, sir."

Jake tried to see her face. Though the bonnet shadowed her features, he saw a smile and the gleam of pearly white teeth. A few dark curls had escaped and fluttered around her face. He thought her eyes were blue but couldn't swear to it. It occurred to him that she might not be all that young. She moved like a young woman, though. He just wasn't quite sure what that even meant since she sat on a high box and didn't move much at all.

"I'm Jake Holt. I'm ramrodding this wagon train. That means I'm in charge when the wagon master, Dakota Harlan, is busy with something. I scout for him, do some hunting to keep us in fresh meat, and help out where I can. If you need anything, let me know."

"Thank you kindly," she replied. "Oscar's my older brother, as are Joseph and Bruce. Ginny, my older sister, is riding with Oscar."

Ginny, she'd be in the third wagon.

The woman sat beside Joseph, who'd been driving, but she had the reins. A hitched-up team of six Angus cattle took some skill to handle, and it looked like Beth had that skill.

A gust of Kansas wind flapped at the ruffle of her bonnet, and for a moment he saw her. Blue eyes for a fact. Beth grabbed at the fluttering hat . . . grabbed just a bit too desperately and drew it around her face. Like maybe she wasn't keeping her face in shadow by accident. The sun wasn't bright enough to burn, so that left her not wanting her face to show.

And what a face it was.

Fair skin and blue eyes so bright they all but gleamed. Eyes rimmed with long dark lashes. Her nose was a straight little thing, her cheeks pink as wild roses. Her eyes blinked as if she were worried he'd seen her. And that worry was laced with a sharp intelligence that no bonnet in the world could hide.

Hide. That word fit. Beth Collins was hiding from something. Or someone.

"Another pair came with us at the end—my brother and his wife. He had plans back in St. Louis and a job to hold him there, but he got injured. Then he got fired and decided to throw in with us. He's not seriously injured, though. Cracked ribs mostly. He's healing after a week on the trail but still being careful. Sebastian's injury slowed us down some. He had to ride in a cart when Ginny and I planned to ride horseback to catch up. They're in the back wagon, resting. At least my brother is. I'm not sure about Kat."

It all came out in one big breath. So they were leaving trouble behind. So be it. Many who headed west were doing the same. Just so long as they didn't bring trouble with them, Jake would be happy to have them. And he had a strong urge to help her anyway he could. And that urge went far beyond helping her hitch up the team in the morning. In fact, it seemed mostly to have everything to do with those blue eyes and long lashes.

Which he knew was just pure stupid.

Setting aside his stupidity, he settled on believing it was all part of the puzzle.

The Collins family. She was a whole lot younger than Oscar and looked nothing like him.

He thought of his redheaded ma, who lived in Fargo, North Dakota. Twice widowed, she now had a third husband and young'uns with each of them. Jake resembled neither her nor any of the men she'd buried, including his own pa. Ma had seven children last time he'd checked. Their ages were spread as wide as Oscar and Beth's.

Well, the wagon train had months to make its passage, so there'd be plenty of time to solve any puzzle he wanted solved.

"Welcome, Miss Beth." Jake touched the brim of his Stetson and then headed toward the last wagon to meet Ginny Collins, as well as the injured Sebastian and his wife, Kat.

8

Beth turned to Joseph, Oscar's honest-to-goodness brother. At least someone around here was telling the truth.

Whispering, she asked, "Do you think he believed me?"

Joseph was a quiet man, younger than Oscar by a few years, but a seemingly hardworking man if the last hour of acquaintance was to be believed. He looked at her and shrugged. "Reckon he'll keep his mouth shut about it if'n he don't believe us so long as we cause no trouble."

Beth felt her brow furrow, as it tended to do when she was worrying, thinking, or frowning. Considering that the last three years had been nothing but worrying, thinking and frowning, she was doomed to have a wrinkled brow at a young age. "Why would he do that?"

Joseph tugged on the front of his wide-brimmed hat. It was badly worn and stained, and Beth wished Oscar had spent more of the money she'd sent him to get Joseph a good hat. Probably not a wise thing as they wanted to blend in. The three wagons and all the supplies were bad enough.

"It's the West, miss."

"Call me Beth. A brother doesn't call his little sister *miss*."

Joseph nodded. "A man don't pry into another man's business out here. It ain't polite. A man—and that goes for a woman too—is what she can make of herself. The West is for the strong, Beth. Ain't much law, though things are better'n they used to be. You can spread out and make of yourself as much as you want. Jake will give you leave to mind your own business, and he'll mind his. It's the best way to git along."

Beth smiled at Joseph and gave a firm nod of her head. That sounded like a life that would suit her fine while also helping her to hide.

Jake rode past the second wagon, being driven by Bruce Collins, and as he reached the third, he saw Oscar listening to the woman beside him. It was clear from the look on Oscar's face that he loved his sister and wanted to hear every word of their journey.

This woman matched with Beth. He had only gotten that one glimpse at Beth, but now he felt as though he knew what she looked like. A good bit older, more of an age with Oscar, but those same blue eyes with their corners tipped up, that same straight nose, those rosy cheeks.

She saw Jake coming, stopped talking and beamed at him. Just beamed. Jake felt like he'd been hit with rays of the sun. This woman was happy to be here.

"Ginny, this is Jake. He scouts for the wagon train. Does some hunting and is second to the trail boss. You'd best mind him when he speaks." Oscar sounded falsely stern, and Ginny smiled.

"I most certainly will." Ginny tapped Oscar on the arm. "Howdy, Jake. There's too many of us Collinses. You'd best call me by my first name. I've got my sister-in-law, Kat, in the back there. She's tending our brother, Sebastian. Truth is, I s'pect they're both sleeping. More folks named Collins."

Jake liked the woman immediately. Not the same way he liked Beth, but she seemed friendly and cheerful. She'd already eased the furrows of worry from Oscar's forehead. While Jake still needed to meet Sebastian and Kat, that could wait for now.

He welcomed her to the train, exchanged a few words about her journey, and said, "Reckon we'll talk more later, Ginny. We've got a creek crossing coming up ahead, one of about a dozen. I'd better see to some duties." He turned his horse and trotted to the front of the train.

~~~~~~

Beth watched the scout ride toward the front of the wagon train, handed the reins to Joseph, and hopped down.

Nearly all the women and children were walking. Odd to think the wagons rolled along at the pace of a walking man, woman, or child. Joseph said it saved the horses' strength to lighten the load, and the rattling wheels on the rough trail made it miserable to ride in the wagon if it could be avoided.

A few folks rode horseback. She'd have liked that, too. She ached from the days of sitting on that rough-riding cart. But she'd climbed up on the seat and taken the reins when she'd seen Jake coming, mainly to stay a bit farther away from the handsome stranger. She was hoping to stay as far from everyone as possible, for as long as possible.

She shuddered when she thought of how her bonnet had flapped in the wind. He'd gotten a good look at her. She'd seen those dark brown eyes focus right on her.

He said he was here to help. She wondered if he could be trusted but knew it didn't matter. She didn't dare trust anyone. She also wondered why a handsome man like that was riding along on a wagon train. Where was his home? Joseph had said something about Jake having traveled this route many times. What kind of man would do that?

What made a man rootless? Wandering to Oregon and back east, then out to Oregon again, over and over. It seemed like an odd life. Joseph's wagon passed by her, and she smiled at the red-spotted cow and its playful baby.

She stood still and waved at Bruce as the second wagon passed. Another cow, but no calf at her side. She let the third wagon approach, and Ginny was scampering down from her seat beside Oscar by the time the last wagon drew even with Beth.

Ginny was beaming and threw her arms around Beth's neck. Beth still hadn't really talked to her. They had just never been truly alone. Now here Ginny stood, so happy. So free.

Maybe it was best not to speak of all Ginny had gone through. Maybe speaking of it would only make Ginny unhappy. Bring the nightmares back. For now, Beth decided to leave it alone, let Ginny decide what she wanted to speak of.

Oscar called out, "Don't lag behind the final wagon. Stay close."

Kat and Sebastian were in the back end of this wagon, so talking about anything serious would have to wait.

Oscar's wagon, pulling the cart, passed them. A string of horses plus one more milk cow walked alongside the cart, right near the cinched-up wagon cover. Beth saw Kat clambering down. The three of them together, that was something Beth never intended.

"How's Sebastian?" Beth fell back to let the cart pass, along with the cow and horses tied to the cart.

"He's sleeping. No more fever. He's going to be fine, though his chest pains him terribly. It's going to be a while before he can be any help."

"I must admit I hadn't considered putting him to work. What does he think about our heading out west?"

Kat shrugged. "He seems a bit addled still. A concussion no doubt."

"Concussion?" Beth had never heard the word. "You said your pa was a doctor?"

"Yes, a concussion is what happens when you take a blow to the head and are knocked unconscious. Double vision, nausea, dizziness. There are several symptoms. He just needs time to heal. He's certainly too feeble to be on his own."

"Maybe we'll cross the railroad tracks somewhere on the trail, and he can decide then if he wants to return home." The man had been more asleep than awake the whole journey. She didn't expect to learn about his wishes anytime soon. But they would soon be driving parallel to the Transcontinental Railroad. He could go into most any town, buy a train ticket, and strike out on his own with little trouble.

Beth walked a bit wide of the wagon train so she could see it all strung out in front of her. She hadn't had time to truly study the situation.

"I count twenty-three wagons. That's quite a small train. I've read it wasn't uncommon to set out with a hundred wagons, or even two hundred. But you'd think that would make it hard to graze the livestock. The first train of the year would eat down the grass, and another train would come along before it could grow back."

"Oscar said we're the first wagon train to head west this year, and since the train opened all the way west this spring, overgrazing won't be the problem it once was."

Beth turned to Ginny, listening. "You've been studying, too. I thought it was just me."

Ginny smiled sheepishly. "There were some books at Horecroft. I was very careful not to pay close attention to any one subject for fear someone would remember." Ginny gave Kat a nervous look. "Was it obvious? Could you tell when I paid special attention to any books about the frontier and wagon trains and such?"

Kat shook her head. Then she glanced around. Dropping her voice, even though they were a good distance from anyone, she said, "I didn't know you had any plans until that last night. I caught you slipping down a hallway after we were to be locked in our rooms."

Ginny nodded. "I learned to pick my lock. It took me six months to master it."

Beth gave her chin a firm jerk up and down. "Good work." Then, looking back at Kat, she asked, "And what were you doing wandering?"

"I was different from you. I could pick my lock by the end of the first month. But I never gave them the trouble you did." Kat's wan face lit up with a smile. "That's what I loved most about you. You had the courage I lacked. Instead, I obeyed. I kept the outrage and rebellion in my heart and never let it show." Kat's smile faded. "But I felt it. I felt it until it was a terrible sin. I wanted to fight. I wanted to hurt everyone who'd locked me up. I-I think that place was slowly driving me mad. I wasn't in there because I was insane, but if I'd stayed much longer . . ." Kat's throat worked as if it were full of unspent tears.

Ginny reached for Kat and held her hand.

Kat cleared her throat and went on. "If I'd stayed much longer, I-I would have been. I knew it was brewing inside me to take some terrible, desperate action. Instead, I just sneaked down the halls at night, snooping."

"That's how you knew what doors you could get through. You had a better plan for getting out than I did."

"I found my way around the asylum and saw what they did to anyone who objected to their dreadful treatment. Walking the halls at night was my rebellion. I could only disobey the rules on the sly, while you stood up to them with honesty and courage and grace. I'm a weakling and a coward, Ginny. You saved me. Beth saved me."

Shaking her head, Ginny squeezed Kat's hand. "Don't condemn yourself for seeing the truth and fighting down the urge to do something futile and dangerous. You were a steady presence in our reading group and Bible study. I knew you were a strong, intelligent young woman. That's why, when I ran into you in that hallway, I knew I wouldn't be able to evade you. Which is why I brought you along. Not that you gave me much choice." Ginny drew Kat into a warm hug. "I'm so glad I did."

Beth saw that the three of them were still out of earshot of the other women walking. She said, "I know our plans are to go into hiding, but I've done a lot of studying on the laws about insanity and asylums. There is a way for you both to be free of the danger you're in."

Ginny grabbed her arm. "You mean go back? No!"

Kat's eyes grew wide, and she shook her head violently. "No, never. I'll run away. I'll—"

"Please just let me explain."

Both women looked at Beth as if she'd sprung a pair of fangs and was ready to bite. But they quit saying no.

"The law that locked you away isn't a hard-and-fast rule. If we find the right state, with good insanity laws, you'd need to go before a judge. He could declare you to be fully sane and revoke the ruling Father used, and whoever locked you away used, Kat. You wouldn't be able to be locked away. The only way it works honestly is if it's done quietly. No ruling is made, no judge or doctor declares you insane. You just—"

"So you're saying," Ginny interrupted, "I'd need to go before a jury of men and hope they'd declare me sane? And if I couldn't prove I'm sane, I could be locked away again? That sounds an awful lot like I'm guilty until I'm proven innocent."

"What I've heard is that in the West, men are much

kinder to women than the men back east. Women are rare and protected out here. Yes, the jury would be men, the judge, any doctors would be men. But, Ginny and Kat, you are both women of propriety, decency, and sanity. Men out here, far from Father's influence, or whoever did this to you, Kat, could be trusted to find you sane."

"That's if Thaddeus doesn't get here with that awful Dr. Horecroft and testify to my insanity, and if he doesn't spread money around to the jurors or know someone who knows someone who knows the governor or the judge. You know he's fully capable of doing that, Beth."

"I just want you to be thinking about this. I've brought paper along. You could write out your experiences. Write out what led to your being locked up, which you know comes down to you just refusing to agree with every word Father says. You'd win this case."

"And if we don't, what happens then?" Kat quietly asked.

Bedelia McDaniels chose that moment to walk over, smiling at them. "Good morning, ladies." Her husband was a parson, and they were lovely people. But the conversation was over about how a woman went about declaring herself sane.

Guilty until proven innocent seemed to sum it up pretty well.

Ginny let Kat go and turned to hug Beth. "And you, my . . . my little sister, I am impressed anew each day, each hour, by how smart you are. Heaven knows I've got a lot to learn."

Fiona O'Toole joined them, along with her grown

daughter and two little ones at her side. "What's this about a lot to learn? Sure glad to be of help."

Ginny smiled. "I don't have the skills I need for this trip, and right now I'm riding in the wagon instead of getting out and helping pull. I mean that literally, despite being here on my feet walking. I'm determined not to be a drag on this group. I'm only realizing now how ignorant I am. I vow to you, I'm going to learn."

Beth had seen a few of Ginny's attempts at cooking. She controlled a shudder. But the company of Bedelia and Fiona had put an end to their conversation. "There will be plenty of time to learn, Ginny. Everyone will help you. Now, to practical matters, all of us need a bath."

Bedelia laughed. Fiona nodded with a comic expression of concern on her face.

Ginny looked around. "And where is the bathtub? Did you bring that, too?"

"And our clothes need to be washed. We'll see to it the next time we find a stream deep enough."

The Angus cow leading their third wagon mooed suddenly and tossed its head. Beth rushed to the animal's neck, grabbed the leather halter, and soothed the critter. It never missed a step, but it could have stirred up the others in the traces.

"Fine work . . . Beth."

Oscar obviously wasn't used to using her name. He'd called her Miss Rutledge all his life. But Beth had discussed it with him, and he was learning. A big brother would say Beth and not hesitate. It'd be the same with Ginny because of his admiration and respect for the mistress of the house. Still, he was getting there.

"What's going on?"

The shout came from the wagon bed, Sebastian waking up again. He seemed to come in and out of consciousness. And even when he was awake, he wasn't quite fully lucid. They'd talked that one time, but other than that, he'd spent the journey here in the cart, at times with a low-grade fever, more asleep than awake—or pretending to be.

Kat came running and swung up into the back of the wagon. "Hush now, Sebastian."

He was now Sebastian Collins, Oscar's youngest brother and Kat's husband, suffering from cracked or broken ribs. There would be no mention of a gunshot. Beth hoped Kat could explain that to him for the twentieth time and get the man to cooperate. If not, he was going to cause them all a lot of trouble. And Jake Holt was a sharp-eyed, savvy character.

As she walked alongside the nervous Angus cow, patting its shoulder, she realized she could learn from Jake. Oscar was very knowledgeable about the West, but there was always more, and Beth intended to learn all she could.

A week on the trail and Beth had her hands full keeping Ginny alive.

Ginny hadn't been joking when she'd said she knew nothing. Now her bright-eyed determination to learn was going to get them all killed.

"You're taking too much of the peel, Ginny. Here now." Oscar took the potato and knife away from her before she harmed herself.

"No, give that back. I have to learn."

Oscar sighed with poorly concealed exasperation. "You have to learn, yes, but we don't have enough potatoes for you to cut away half of each when you're peeling them. Beth?" The last word was just below a shout.

Beth watched Jake as he rode down the line of wagons, passing out a joint of the venison he'd brought along to each wagon. Not enough on a deer for everyone to get full, but he'd cut the haunches down smaller so there was enough to flavor a stew.

Beth wanted to go to him. She wanted to help him cut up the deer, do any chores he needed to do. But she knew that tone in Oscar's voice and hurried to Ginny's side. "Let's work on building the fire."

"Nope." Oscar was peeling potatoes at a blurred speed, as if afraid Ginny would come back and demand to help.

"Yes, setting fire to kindling is—"

"Spread to the grass yesterday. You gotta weed out a good-sized area or you'll start a prairie fire."

Beth looked at Ginny, who'd crossed her arms and narrowed her eyes. "I'm not going to remain so useless."

"All right." Beth grabbed one of Oscar's potatoes and a knife. "This potato needs to be diced."

"Cut herself just yesterday. Had trouble stopping the bleeding." Oscar peeled faster.

Jake moved closer.

Beth whispered to Ginny, "Jake won't believe you've reached adulthood without learning to cook, not in a family such as the Collinses. So why don't you fetch a bucket and get water from that—"

"She'll fall in," Oscar hissed, sounding like a pot of boiling water.

"I'll go along." And not get to talk to Jake, and not do much to help with the evening meal. "Let's go." Beth caught Ginny by the arm and carried the bucket, walking away as Jake came alongside Oscar.

"Beth, I've got to learn. I didn't fall into the stream this morning. I slipped on a stone and got my feet a bit wet is all."

Beth kept walking, trying to think how to teach Ginny all she needed to know without hurting her feelings overly. They fetched water, as did folks from the other wagons, skirting the herd of cattle and horses that had been watered and staked out to graze.

"What can I do first, Beth? I do need to learn."

No fire. No knives. No potatoes to spare.

"Um, you can wash dishes. I think Oscar will allow that. In fact, you can dry dishes." Everything was either tin or cast-iron. Short of dropping a pot or pan on her toe, she'd be fine. Ginny wrinkled her nose, which made Beth smile. "I didn't learn to cook overnight. Neither will you. But you'll learn, and in the meantime, there's work enough for everyone. We bring the livestock inside our wagon circle overnight; in the morning we let them graze again in the hour it takes to eat breakfast and tear down the tents. You can help with the water, the animals, and the dishes. In a few days or a week we'll add more chores—once you get the hang of things."

The Collins family built its own campfire at night and cooked its own meal, just as each wagon did, but she'd seen Jake walk between campfires, talking easily with the pioneers. Often he'd leave a haunch of venison or a couple of rabbits. He was particularly mindful of the wagons with children. The O'Tooles, who had two wagons and four children, though two of them were old enough to be considered adults, were not far in front of the Collinses' wagons.

Jake had something for them most days. He answered questions, worked hard to help when help was needed, and offered encouragement that the long journey ahead would be well worth it. It was impossible not to compare him to her father and his cold greed and tyrannical cruelty.

She'd asked for her father's help exactly once in her adult life. She'd learned very young not to ask for it as a child. When she'd gone to him after she'd learned what happened to her mother, she'd been outraged and demanded Mother be brought home. His icy disdain cut like a razor. He didn't lay a hand on her, but she left his office battered and frightened to cross him in any way. She never asked him for anything again.

That day she'd realized if someone was going to save Ginny, she'd have to do it herself. And she'd set to work planning. Meeting secretly with Oscar, hashing out one wild scheme after another until they'd settled on this desperate dash—a very slow dash—for freedom.

Oscar had taught her so much, and she'd studied fervently, but she wasn't foolish enough to think she knew everything. And she also had a firm belief in seeking wise counsel.

Yes, she'd strike up a conversation with Jake and learn from him. She'd see if he'd help prepare her for the life ahead. She found herself a bit overly eager to talk to the man. No idea why.

But she had to be careful. Jake Holt was not a man easily fooled, despite Joseph's assurance that western men didn't poke and prod into someone else's past.

Her past was too full of danger for her to trust anyone.

9

~

ure enough, if every one of my cows has a baby
every year, the Angus plus the milk cows, I'll have
me a herd before too long."

Jake gave her an odd look. He did it too often, and
she wasn't sure why. But she kept talking to him. She was
learning a lot, and he didn't seem to mind. In fact, after
she'd sought him out with her questions about the West
the first time, he'd ride back to her wagons on a regular
basis, swing down off his beautiful chestnut quarter horse,
and walk beside her.

A short shriek from the wagon ahead drew their attention.

"Get it off me!" Ginny, on the wagon seat beside Oscar.

Beth did her best not to roll her eyes.

Jake said, "Wonder what it is this time."

"Probably one of the horses . . . uh, splattered her."

Such things happened when a person sat behind a draft
animal.

"Or maybe a bug." Jake shook his head. "Not a very

tough woman, Ginny. Lots of times, when you reach her age, and you've been living a rugged life full of brothers and animals and such, you get used to some . . . indignities."

Beth let that hang in the air because she couldn't think of a response. Nope, Ginny wasn't exactly used to a rugged life. "When you fired up that forge . . ."

Jake turned and paid attention. He was going to let her change the subject.

"How can a fire get hot enough to melt iron down to being bendable by using bellows, but not when . . . ?"

He'd let her watch the next time they fired up the forge to repair a wagon wheel. He'd left a pair of grouse for her to butcher. Oscar insisted he'd handle it, but Beth was determined. She wanted to know everything she needed to know.

They talked blacksmithing for a while, then turned to the subject of her Angus cattle and the herd she envisioned.

"It takes a long time to build up a herd, Beth."

It had taken her days to get him to stop calling her Miss Beth and just call her Beth. The *Miss* made her feel a bit too . . . too something. Upper class or snooty? As if she were *above* everyone else. And with her terrible accent, she had to wonder if he was suspicious that she was mocking others with a similar accent, which she wasn't. She hated the idea of her birth and wealth keeping her separate from others. Because of her father, she'd always been kept separate from those less fortunate, but that was all over now.

Beth nodded with excitement. "A cow gives birth once a year, right? And a calf has to reach the age of, what, two before it can have a baby? I should have dozens of cattle in just a few years."

"Unless your calves don't all survive," Jake said.

She gasped at the terrible thought. "How sad."

"Or you get in a pinch and need to eat beef over the winter."

She looked at the nearest black Angus, harnessed and working. She couldn't imagine eating her. More than that, she couldn't imagine how a person turned a cow into food. Oh, she knew they did it. She ate beef and assumed it was like butchering a deer, only heavier work. Even so, the details of preparing the meat were daunting and a little heartbreaking.

"Or mountain lions or wolves pick off a calf or an older cow."

Fighting for her cattle would apparently begin the moment they stopped moving.

"Sometimes a cow doesn't breed back."

"B-breed back? What's that?"

Jake smiled. "That means she doesn't get a calf growing inside her. Older cows often reach a point when they don't breed back."

She blushed at such talk and wished she hadn't asked.

"Sometimes lightning and thunder stampedes your herd, and you lose half of them. Sometimes one falls and breaks a leg and must be put down, but those ones can be butchered so you don't lose the meat. Cattle rustlers can—"

"I know things can go wrong, Jake," Beth said, cutting him off. She turned to him with a frown. "And I need to learn about all of it. But maybe listing them all right now isn't necessary. We'll face each of those things when it happens."

"Folks in the West need to face things ahead of time to be ready when there's trouble."

She wanted to add in blizzards and freezing cold, cliffs and avalanching snow, but those were mountain troubles, and Jake was expecting her to go all the way through to Oregon. He figured they'd be settled in Oregon long before a blizzard could bury them in snow.

But Beth's plans didn't include Oregon. She gave a firm nod. "You're right. I want to know as much as I can before there's any trouble."

"You seem to already know a lot, and you're eager to learn more. That will serve you well. You really think you can build a log cabin?"

"We were a couple of years planning this trip. My skills aren't like a truly talented builder, but I could build a log cabin if I had to. I could for sure chop down a tree. I can do plenty that might not be taken as work a woman should do. But we'll need everyone working hard. Of course, Oscar and his . . . uh, *my* brothers will be adding their skills to mine, and I know Oscar has built a cabin before."

Jake gave her a sharp look as she stumbled over claiming Oscar's brothers as her own. His eyes narrowed as he leaned close, too close, and whispered, "Your accent slips when you're upset."

Beth pulled away from him, thinking fast. Before she could come up with some bumbling excuse, he said, "I'm just giving you a warning. Not threatening to expose you as something you're not. Now, about building a cabin . . ."

"I've got a lot to learn, but I've been trying to prepare for this trip as best I can."

Jake nodded. "What would you like to learn today?"

"Teach me about hunting. What animals will you hunt for as we ride west? You've brought in deer a few times. Grouse. What else should I look for, and how do I hunt them? And yes, Oscar and my brothers will do most of that, but I'm still interested. Will mountain lions really eat my calves?"

"They will."

"How about grizzly bears? I've seen a bearskin rug, and it's hard to believe bears get so big. Are they mostly in the mountains, or do they wander onto the flatland?"

"I've been on this trek a lot of times. Do you know where you plan to settle in Oregon? Different parts of the state have different wildlife."

Since Beth intended to leave the wagon train long before they reached Oregon, she was afraid all he told her would be of little use. "We are thinking eastern Oregon, closer to the mountains."

Ginny squealed again. Jake looked at Beth with one arched brow, then shook his head and didn't comment.

"I've seen a few grizzlies . . ." Jake went on to tell her stories that fascinated her. His eyes sparked with the adventure and humor of it all. The man was a storyteller for a fact, and Beth found herself asking breathless questions and hanging on his every word.

Thaddeus slid open his top desk drawer and pulled out a notebook, along with slips of paper. The investigation into Elizabeth's and Eugenia's whereabouts was taking a very strange turn. He'd hired Pinkertons, but Thaddeus wasn't a man who wanted to let anyone get the overall picture of his machinations.

So, yes, the Pinkertons, but he'd hired other investigators, as well. He'd hired staff who worked for him alone. He'd pushed Blayd and the others on Thaddeus's security team hard, and they'd gotten more done single-handedly than the other investigators combined. Blayd had quietly consulted a few lawmen Thaddeus owned, and they'd done searches for Elizabeth, following her activities before Eugenia had vanished.

All the information he'd gathered amounted to something strange and interesting. It stirred up his anger because it was a puzzle, and he couldn't put the pieces together. In fact, some of the pieces didn't seem to fit into the puzzle at all, and he wondered if he should disregard them.

Reading his notebook, he studied the slips of paper he'd written out with all that Elizabeth had been up to. His investigators said they found great reluctance to discuss Elizabeth. Thaddeus had to wonder at how many folks had claimed to have no knowledge or hadn't been found at all. Because Elizabeth had gone to great lengths to be discreet. Several folks who'd talked to his men didn't know her as Elizabeth Rutledge. He wondered how many aliases she'd assumed.

Cooking in a diner.

He stared at that one note. Why in the world would his brilliant, wealthy, and very busy daughter get a job in a diner, miles from home? She'd done it and worked there under the name Ann Wilson. According to the folks who owned the diner, she'd come in knowing little, but she'd taken a pathetically low wage and worked with great earnestness, bending to each task, no matter how menial.

He set that note, jotted on a five-inch square of paper, on his desk. He laid down the next one.

Harness and care for horses.

This one he'd found out right away because she'd done as much in his stables. Elizabeth had gone to the stables and expressed a particular love for a new horse and wanted to care for it.

The men in her stables had appreciated her interest and worked with her to learn to brush the horses, ride them, walk them to cool off. After some pressure from her, she'd learned some doctoring. Then she'd learned to saddle the horses and eventually even hitch them up to the Rutledge carriage and buggy.

Gardening.

He didn't know what to think of this. He laid the note in the row, not sure if it belonged. She'd worked with the Rutledge gardener, focused on the kitchen gardens, tending vegetables and fruit trees.

This was an interest a young woman of good breeding might honestly have, though usually she'd tend a rose garden rather than vegetables.

One of the Pinkertons had brought in news that she'd worked briefly in the office of a sawmill. She'd worked under the name Ann Johnson. But what she'd done there was a mystery. None of the men working there would talk about her and seemed, in the Pinkerton's words, "hostile of anyone who'd ask questions about the lovely Miss Johnson."

There were other notes: *a seamstress, a baker, volunteering at the local school.* All these he lined up and pondered. Some of them he could put down to his daughter learning to take care of herself, with a long-term goal of striking out on her own. Cooking, sewing, gardening. Plain things. Goals that suggested she'd go to ground somewhere.

He turned to the most recent note. The details had come in slowly due to hours and hours of investigation. He was tempted to just let Elizabeth and Eugenia go, and good riddance to both of the wretched, ungrateful women.

But that would mean he'd failed, and he couldn't stand the thought of it.

He stared at this note. Blayd had gotten his information from the bank that held Elizabeth's trust, and that trust hadn't come to him. The trust from Eugenia's parents to their only grandchild was tightly sealed. And the man who owned the bank felt it was a calling from God to prevent Thaddeus from accessing that money. Thaddeus had no idea how much money was in there, but he knew it was sizable.

Eugenia's parents had been wealthy. It was very likely a fortune.

The banker did have employees, though, and one of them was overly fond of horse racing and gambling. Even then Thaddeus had to pay a premium to learn that Elizabeth had withdrawn a lot of money from her account, all of it in cash. The man wouldn't say how much or when, nor how much was left. But he did say none of it went to a company with a bill seeking payment. Twenty-dollar gold pieces. A lot of them. And Elizabeth had carried it away in good-sized chunks over the course of two years.

That meant his daughter had planned this disappearance with her mother. Thaddeus had known that as soon as he found the two women gone.

But where had they disappeared to? He stared at the notes and considered the puzzle before him.

Thaddeus hated puzzles.

10

The whole wagon train was in a jovial mood.

Beth understood it and did her best to include herself in the enthusiasm, but always she felt her father closer, closer, closer.

Twenty-three wagons in the train and hers were the last three. The folks right in front of her were a pair of Italian bachelor brothers: Luigi Da Luca, called Lou, and Antonio, who went by Tony. Neither of them spoke much English, but they were good-natured and hardworking and always had a kind greeting for the Collins family.

Nice though they were, it was hard to get overly friendly with them, as each man drove his wagon alone. The O'Tooles were ahead of them. Good folks who had a longing to own "a piece of the sod," as Mr. O'Toole liked to say. Mrs. O'Toole, Fiona, and her husband, Shay, were eager and friendly, full of talk of what lay ahead and what lay behind.

Fiona walked with Beth, Ginny, and Kat most days. She had a grown daughter, Maeve, who had bright red hair and a patchwork of freckles to match her parents and her younger brother, Conor, and little sister, Bridget. The children loved to run, and though Fiona was a kindhearted mother, she always kept a hawk eye on them and could be stern at times, making sure her children didn't wander away from the wagon train.

The couple owned two wagons, and their eldest son, Donal, liked to hold the reins. Fiona and Maeve minded the two younger children, with the family often at Beth's side. Which kept her from talking to Ginny about the harm that had been done to her in the asylum. It seemed there was always a reason not to talk of her harsh memories.

Ginny still woke up screaming every few nights. Beth had come to sleep right beside her and was awakened when Ginny began to moan and stir. Beth kept a basin of water at hand and used a cool, damp cloth to apply to Ginny's forehead to help calm her following a nightmare. Beth had found this to be the fastest way to pull her out of the dreams.

Talking about her nightmares and what had caused them might help, but that wasn't possible because Kat slept in the tent beside them, and the Collinses and the Da Luca brothers nearby might overhear them in the night. All Beth could hope was that with Ginny being free now, her painful memories would begin to subside a bit as time went by.

Yet Ginny wasn't the only one with bad dreams. Kat had them, too. And some nights Beth herself awoke feeling her father's hot breath on the back of her neck.

They'd left the rugged country surrounding Independence behind them. They crossed so many creeks that Beth, who'd studied trail maps with great interest, had completely lost track. Jake had announced a few days back that they were in Nebraska now. Dakota, the trail boss, and several of the pioneers talked excitedly of making this next step into the western wilderness.

They covered ten to twenty miles a day, and it was a thousand miles still before they reached Oregon. One thousand divided by twenty was fifty days until they made it to the end of the line. Except they all rested on Sundays. The families on the wagon train were people of faith, so they honored the Sabbath as Parson McDaniels led them in worship.

Oscar had told an impatient Beth that although the Lord had asked man to rest on the Sabbath, it was the draft animals that desperately needed the day off. And just possibly if the animals needed a day of rest, and man could see that, then maybe God could see that man, and even Beth, needed rest, too.

So, four weeks into their journey now, they'd left the bluffs and hills of Missouri behind, traveled across the northeast corner of Kansas, and entered the endless expanse of grass that was Nebraska. It was the perfect land for their travel. The cattle could graze at night, first outside the circled wagons, then inside for their own safety overnight, then again for an hour or two until it was time to hitch the critters to the wagons each morning.

The grass made a soft bed for the weary travelers. Every mile looked the same, except for when they came across a creek once every day or two. It was a comforting sameness, however.

Beth could see her mother growing sturdier, her chin less likely to be lowered, her eyes not so often downcast.

She had almost mastered peeling potatoes and building a fire, though it made Oscar nervous to see her with a knife.

Sebastian had finally regained a bit of strength. He didn't talk much, but it was clear he understood that he was now a Collins brother. The only truly odd thing about him, besides clinging to that packet night and day, was that he didn't seem to mind riding west on a wagon train. Not a choice anyone would reasonably make on a whim. But he seemed content. He was learning to care for the animals and even took turns driving the wagon, since driving a slow-moving wagon over flatland with the occasional gently rolling hill required little strength or skill.

His gut still pained him, which was obvious if you watched his face for a time, and Beth did as she tried to figure the man out. He never complained, but helped the others whenever he could. Except for the mystery that came with him, he seemed like the ideal man to bring along on this trip.

"How's Conor, Fiona?" Ginny asked. Fiona's youngest boy had fallen hard and sprained his ankle badly. He'd submitted to being carried in his father's wagon, but only because Fiona and Shay gave their seven-year-old ball of energy no choice.

"That boyo is fair to driving me batty with his complaints. He wants out, but there'll be no running on that ankle for a time, and it serves him right for his recklessness."

Dakota, the wagon master, came galloping up to them. Another handsome young man. Beth wondered about him and Jake and their strange life of constant travel. "Creek up ahead. I want to get across it fast. We're into June now, and that means lots of rain coming. Most of the creeks are shallow and crossing them isn't a problem, but this one will keep us on our toes. Ladies, I suggest you ride in the wagons until we're across."

Maeve smiled at Dakota. "Aye, sir. You've made this journey many a time before?"

"That I have, Miss Maeve."

Beth wasn't sure, but she thought the girl gave Dakota a look of admiration, and a blush tinted her cheeks. Maeve was sunburned, though, so it was hard to tell.

"You've a great knowing of the land." Maeve made it a definite compliment, and Beth suppressed a smile when Dakota looked a little smitten.

Dakota tugged the brim of his hat. "Its banks are steep, and the water's a bit deep in the middle, and very deep if you get off the ford. But we'll make it, Miss Maeve."

"Bridget, let's load up. You ride with Conor. He has a time of it sitting still with that ankle." Fiona's order was met with groans. The wagons were overly warm with no breeze getting past their canvas covers. No one chose to ride inside one if they didn't have to.

"Maeve, your da and I will drive the lead wagon. You and Donal take the back one."

Maeve headed right for the wagon while Beth went for her lead wagon. Its high seat, beside Joseph on his right, had become her designated spot. Ginny rode beside Oscar. Sebastian now rode next to Bruce in the middle wagon. Kat climbed into the back of the third wagon. They did all this as the wagons kept on rolling forward, not stopping for anything or anyone.

Beth peered ahead and saw what looked like a row of

bushes. But as they drew nearer, she noticed they were tree-tops. "Dakota was telling the truth about the steep banks."

Joseph rested one hand on the brake to his left. The trail curved a bit, and Beth watched as the first wagon inched downward until it was out of sight.

They maintained a few yards between the wagons, and a minute later the next one went down the bank. Dakota was next to go down, riding his mustang. Before long, each of the wagons up ahead, one by one vanished from sight.

When it came their turn, they crested the bank. Gasping, Beth said, "It's treacherous."

"It must've rained recently." Joseph pointed at the bank as they rolled slowly down, weaving to the left. All the grass was swept onto its side and coated in mud. "You can see how high the water came."

Nodding, Beth shuddered to think of getting caught in such a storm at the bottom of this creek. They were on a muddy trail, lined with trees on the uphill and down-hill sides so they couldn't tumble off the edge of it. They brushed against branches that reached out into the trail, and their wheels took a beating as they churned through the mud. The trail, with its winding from side to side, helped in reducing the sharpness of the descent. Even so, Joseph pulled back on the brake and leaned hard on it to keep their wagon from picking up speed.

The brake squealed as Joseph fought for control. Sweat broke out on his forehead as the team of Morgans skidded forward, unsteady in the mud. One of them was about to sit down when Joseph yanked on the reins and prevented the horse from doing so.

The trail made a final curve to the right, and soon the

bottom of the creek was visible, wider than what they'd seen since starting the journey. Probably one hundred feet across when most had been twenty feet. With a sigh of relief to see they were almost down, Beth watched wagon after wagon crossing. The water was brown with mud and moving fast. The wagons jarred as they hit underwater ruts. Beth saw the first wagon finally gain solid ground again. The oxen team pulling it leaned into their leathers, and with the rattle of wheels they began the steep ascent up the bank.

Soon another wagon made the crossing, followed by a third and a fourth, and the tension started to drain, her shoulders relaxing a bit. It was much like the other creek crossings, even though the stream was wider and deeper and so rough that the wagons seemed to want to break apart. But one by one they made it to the far shore.

The O'Toole family with their two wagons rolled into the ford. Beth's turn was coming after the Da Luca brothers. She saw the front wagon was driven by Shay, the second by Donal. Fiona sat beside her husband, and her two eldest, Donal and Maeve, were perched on the seat of the next wagon.

Bridget poked her head out of the back end of one wagon and waved and grinned at her big brother and sister. Conor, in the first wagon, must be resting with his leg injured.

Shay was halfway across. Beth had seen each wagon strike something hard right where Shay was when a loud snap sounded from the O'Tooles' front wagon. One of the back wheels split in half, a chunk of wood floating downstream. The wagon canted sharply to the side.

"Whoa!" Shay pulled his team of oxen to a stop and plunged into the creek. The water was waist-deep.

Jake, who rode between the two O'Toole wagons, waved his arms at everyone following and shouted, "Hold up!"

They were on a muddy slope when Joseph pulled the team to a stop and locked the brake. It was no place to leave a wagon. A cry from Fiona drew Beth's attention from the wagon. It tilted until the corner of the back end dipped underwater and the wagon bed began to flood.

"Broken wheel." Jake sounded calm. This was one of those delays that was all too common on a wagon train.

"Fiona," Jake said, "get your youngsters out of the wagon and send them back to the shore. We'll need all the weight off the wagon we can manage. Then we'll—"

Fiona's cry cut him off, and she disappeared underwater.

"Oh no!" Beth stood to go help.

"Stay where you are, Miss Beth," Joseph said. "You'll only be in the way."

Shay cried out in alarm and waded toward the back of the wagon.

"Stay back, Shay." Jake dismounted.

Fiona hadn't reappeared. Seconds later, Shay, ignoring Jake in his rush to help, reached the spot where she'd gone down. He vanished underwater.

Dakota came galloping through the water, his horse kicking up a spray. "What happened?"

"Stay back! It must be a sinkhole. Fiona and Shay went under and haven't resurfaced." Jake pulled himself along the edge of the wagon and then suddenly dropped from sight. But his hand clung to the wagon box. He dragged himself back up. "Narrow hole, but deep. The wagon straddled the hole, and the oxen walked to the side of it. Quick, throw me a rope."

Fiona's son, driving the second wagon, leapt off his high perch and charged for the spot in the creek where his parents had disappeared.

"Stay back, Donal!" Dakota roared at the young man as he tossed the end of the rope at Jake. "Don't go near there without a firm grip on something."

Donal slid to a stop, fell, and his head sank under the water, but he was up again instantly.

Only smooth water flowed over where Fiona and Shay had vanished.

Jake lashed the rope around his waist, then dropped underwater. He went under just as the current shoved the tilted wagon over. Children screamed from inside the wagon. The youngest boy, the injured one, was in there, along with a sister.

"I'm going down there, Joseph." Beth reached for the side of her seat. "We have to rescue the children."

His hand clamped on her arm. The wagon rolled until its top was submerged, its wheels turning in the air. Then the wagon tongue snapped, causing the floundering oxen to break free. Immediately they started swimming for the shore.

Tony and Lou, the Italian bachelors, charged for the teetering wagon. Beth gave Joseph a furious look that made him wince, but still he hung on to her. "Let the men do their job. You can't swim in that skirt."

As the last wagon ahead of the O'Tooles reached the far bank, shouting men came rushing toward the drifting, tumbling wagon that was breaking apart. The wagon and its supplies were being battered in the current. It rolled again and started floating downstream.

The shouting stopped.

Then, as suddenly as he'd grabbed her, Joseph's control broke. "Stay here," he said, then let go and jumped to the ground.

Jake surfaced with Fiona in his arms. She was unconscious, limp and white. Donal dove into the water, chasing the wagon.

Jake staggered toward the shore, shedding the rope around his waist. Dakota jumped off his horse and sprinted toward the upside-down wagon.

Maeve wailed from her wagon perch and leapt to the ground. She ran to her mother.

"Go!" Maeve yelled at Jake. "Save the children. Save my da."

Maeve wrested her mother out of his arms and floated her on her back, holding her head up against the fast-moving water. The Da Luca brothers waded off the ford and swam for the wagon. Joseph reached Maeve. He plunged past her as Jake turned back to where Shay had fallen. Joseph cast one frantic look between the hole where Shay had vanished and the tumbling wagon. A dozen men were in the water, trying to get to the drowning children.

Jake hurried to Dakota's abandoned horse, tied the end of the rope to the horn of the black mustang's saddle, and wrapped the other end around himself. He dropped out of sight underwater.

Beth, seeing Maeve nearing the shore, climbed down and sprinted and skidded the remaining fifty feet of the steep trail past the Da Lucas' wagons. She reached the edge of the creek just as Maeve got Fiona to shore.

Oscar caught up to her and said, "Don't you go in that water. Help Maeve."

Beth nodded, but she didn't like it. "Joseph has to drag Jake out."

"I'll see if I can help." Oscar ran as best he could in the thigh-deep water while Bruce headed for the wrecked wagon.

Joseph held the reins of Dakota's mustang. "I'm a good swimmer!" he shouted at his brother. "You handle the horse."

Oscar swung onto the horse. Joseph took off toward the destroyed wagon.

"Da! The young'uns!' Maeve turned toward the creek, tears streaking her face as she clung to her mother.

Fiona showed no signs of life.

Ginny came running, as did Kat and Sebastian. They helped get Fiona fully on land.

Kat dropped to her knees. "Roll her onto her stomach." Kat took charge just as she had when they'd found Sebastian.

As soon as they had Fiona turned, Kat began pressing hard on her back.

Sebastian whirled away, headed for the wagon. He shouted in a way that drew Beth's attention to Jake, who emerged from the water hole with Shay slung over one shoulder.

Oscar was on Dakota's horse, backing the animal away, drawing on the rope, dragging Jake from the hole.

Jake stood, gasping for breath, then sank to his knees, his head still above water, his arms locked on Shay.

Shay's head went under again. Oscar leapt from the horse and got to Jake and helped get Shay's head out of the water. It looked like the only reason Jake had surfaced was because of Oscar. Shay looked to be unconscious, not moving at all. He'd been underwater a long time. Too long.

Sebastian turned to the overturned wagon, then to Jake and Oscar.

The oxen were scrambling to shore, the children quiet, unseen. "Go help with Shay, Sebastian," Beth said. "Both he and Jake are all in. Oscar needs help getting them both to shore."

Sebastian did as he was told.

Beth took a hard look at the wagon, its wheels barely above water, the men surrounding it diving under. Boxes and barrels were floating away. Donal emerged from the water with a young boy in his arms. One of the Da Luca brothers latched on to Donal and towed him to the side of the creek. There was no going upstream against this current.

"I'll help Donal when he gets to shore," Beth said.

Ginny gave a firm nod. "Go."

Maeve looked desperately from her brothers to her father to her ma. She stayed by Fiona while Kat pressed on her back, trying to force the water out of her lungs.

Beth slogged her way down the muddy bank that was clogged with scrub brush. She reached the place Donal was heading for. Donal was near collapse, but when Tony Da Luca tried to take the boy, Donal fought him.

Instead, Tony just towed them both along.

"Give him to me." Beth tried her best to penetrate Donal's dazed eyes, which were locked on his brother. Donal was gasping for air, and under all the dripping water, Beth saw exhaustion and tears.

Beth wrenched the boy away and laid him down.

Tony turned back. Beth knelt beside the boy and said, "Help me turn him onto his stomach."

When there was no help coming, she looked up to see Donal rushing back to the overturned wagon. The current pushed him downstream, and he was barely able to fight the current.

Tony took off running toward the wagon. "Donal, no! Come back!" But the young man went on regardless.

Beth said a quick prayer, then went to work trying to get the little one to breathe. She rolled him over and started pressing on his back as Kat had done.

11

Sebastian lowered Shay into the water and floated him along on his back. Oscar slung an arm around Jake's back, drew one of Jake's arms across his neck, and the two of them staggered to shore.

Jake saw Kat pressing on Fiona's back at the exact moment Fiona vomited up a bellyful of brown water. Fiona coughed violently.

"Keep doing what I was doing." Kat grabbed Maeve's arm, and the girl, frantic to help, worked on helping her mother.

Kat said, "Get Shay on the ground. Facedown."

Jake had barely positioned him when Kat went to work reviving the man. "Jake, go help Beth." Kat pointed downstream. Beth was working on one of the O'Toole boys just as Kat was working on Shay. "Oscar, you go with him. Ginny, you help Maeve."

"No, I'm going for the wrecked wagon," Oscar said.

"Look, someone's bringing the other one out."

Jake saw Dakota swimming with the girl. Jake strode

toward Beth, his knees trembling with fatigue, but he plodded on.

"We've got them all!" Joseph shouted as he swam toward the shore, with Bruce helping him. They looked near collapse. All the men did.

The children had been under for too long, but maybe it wasn't too late to help them. Maybe it wasn't too late to help Shay.

Fiona was coming around now.

"Make sure everyone is accounted for," Dakota said.

Jake hadn't even thought of the others in their wagon train, all risking their lives for one family. Sickened with worry, Jake picked up speed to reach Beth.

Raised voices from behind him drew his attention, and he saw several of the women wading across the stream to help. He thought of the sudden way Fiona had vanished. "Go back to the shore! There's a hole. Stay back."

The women froze, then turned and hurried back the way they'd come.

He finally reached Beth. "How is he?"

"Did you see how Kat was pressing on Fiona's back? Can you do that with the other child?"

"Got it."

"No!" Oscar said. "Stay with Beth." He jabbed a finger at Beth, whom he treated more like a daughter than a little sister. "I'll go and show Dakota what to do. No one should be working on anyone alone."

Jake stopped, exhausted enough to obey a direct order.

Oscar hurried toward the second child.

Jake noticed Beth didn't answer his question about the boy's condition. She'd been working on him for several minutes, and Jake saw no response. He dropped to his knees across from Beth. "Let me take a turn."

Beth must have been in an obedient mood because she let Jake take over. "Joseph has the little girl. This one's Conor."

"This is Conor?" Jake pressed on the boy's back, right where his lungs were. "I haven't yet learned everyone's names."

"I should've gone and left Oscar with you. I saw what Kat was doing. Every second counts."

Ginny came to their side from where she'd been helping Fiona and Shay. "I got sent to help with the others." She kept moving, never breaking stride.

Dakota said, "I've got to be certain that all the men made it back to shore."

"Be careful in that current, Dakota," Jake warned. "You're as beat up and worn out as the rest of the men."

Nodding, Dakota looked down at the child Jake was trying to get to breathe. He shook his head. "Not all of them." Then he strode back to the ford, shouting orders.

Beth shook her head glumly. "It's no use. They're all dead."

"Maybe not," Jake said. "Mrs. O'Toole looked gone when I brought her up, but then Kat got her breathing again doing this."

Beth sat up straight. "She did? Kat got Fiona started breathing?"

"Yes, we're not giving up."

Determination firmed Beth's chin. "I should be helping—what can I do?"

"Pray," Jake answered. "We need a miracle."

"I will." Quietly, Beth quoted from Psalm 23 of the Bible: "'The LORD is my shepherd; I shall not want.'"

Her voice sounded beautiful, a bit husky but strong. She didn't go on, and Jake wanted her to. He glanced up at her.

Meeting his eyes, she repeated the words "I shall not want" and shook her head. "How can that be right, Jake? There's so much wrong in this world. There's no end of things to want."

She was looking down at Conor. But he heard more. What terrible wrong had Beth faced? What did she want so badly? "Go on, please." He needed to hear the words.

"'He maketh me to lie down in green pastures: he leadeth me beside the still waters.'"

Jake never stopped pressing on Conor, hoping the effort would start his lungs to breathing again, his heart to beating. He saw anger on Beth's pretty face as she looked at the water flowing behind them. It was anything but still.

She continued, "'He restoreth my soul: he leadeth me in the paths of righteousness for his name's sake.' The next verse is right. 'Yea, though I walk through the valley of the shadow of death, I will fear no evil: for thou art with me; thy rod and thy staff they comfort me. Thou preparest a table before me in the presence of mine enemies: thou anointest my head with oil; my cup runneth over. Surely goodness and mercy shall follow me all the days of my life: and I will dwell in the house of the LORD for ever.'"

"Thank you, Beth. That's a beautiful prayer." An almost overwhelming wave of tiredness swept over him, as surely as the water had swept over the O'Toole family. "Now catch your breath because you have to take a turn."

She nodded. "You were in the water too long. All of you men were. I did nothing but watch. You need to rest now."

Jake thought she sounded as if she felt guilty. "Your accent is gone again." Beth's head came up. She didn't quit trying to pump life back into Conor, but she looked scared. Jake had to wonder why. "I'm not going to say anything, but you might need to be more aware—especially today, if the accent is important for some reason."

"I-I thought folks in the West didn't worry about where others had come from or what they'd left behind."

"I *don't* care." Honestly, he cared a lot. Or maybe it was that he was very curious. There were all sorts of folks from all walks of life in the West. Jake had a good ear, and he heard education and money in her voice. Fine manners and, he'd wager, the northern Midwest. Probably Chicago. Yet he wasn't going to push for information she clearly didn't want to give. "But it's obvious that *you* care. I won't mention it to anyone. It's just, if you're wanting to hide your tracks, you might want to be a bit more careful."

Nodding, Beth said, "Thank you."

"And, Beth—" he paused long enough that she looked up and met his eyes—"if you need help, if you need protection, you can trust me."

Their gazes held, and the seconds stretched out. He saw the grief and the kindness in those vivid blue eyes of hers. He felt as if he tore something when he forced his eyes away from her and out toward the creek. "The rest of the men are getting to shore. Some to this shore, some to the far side."

Conor suddenly heaved, and water spurted from his mouth and nose. He began coughing violently.

"Oh, Conor! Jake, he's alive!" Beth reached for Conor's shoulder and rolled him onto his side. His eyes blinked open. Dazed, but yes, he was indeed alive.

The men strode toward Jake. "Dakota, look. Conor is going to make it."

A shout went up from downstream, and they both glanced over to see Bridget stirring and coughing. Jake and Beth both smiled at the sight. They helped Conor sit up. The boy seemed to be asleep where he sat, but he was breathing, coughing, alive.

Jake turned to Dakota, who was drawing near, carrying Bridget O'Toole. With a firm jerk of his chin, he said, "These two will make it. I'm thankful for it."

Beth knew it had been too long. These two reviving was a gift straight from God.

Dakota looked at the other men and at Ginny, coming along behind him. "I need a head count, men."

"Fiona came around."

"Mrs. O'Toole made it, Conor and Bridget as well. And Donal and Maeve." He looked down at the little girl in his arms.

"What about Shay?"

They all peered upstream, where Seb and Kat were working on the man. He'd been out of the water longer than the children.

"Let me take her," Oscar murmured.

Dakota slid the little one from his arms to Oscar's, then pulled a pocket watch from his vest pocket, flipped it open and looked at it. "Broken." He flung the watch into the stream with a violent motion that belied his calm. Staring at the water, he breathed in and out for a few moments before turning back to Jake.

"Let's go see how Fiona is doing," Jake said.

Dakota nodded as he headed toward the line of wagons, still taking charge. "First, let's get these children across the creek. No one walks. Not a single one of you. I'm tying Jake's horse and mine onto the wagon and riding in the wagon myself." His voice dropped to a near whisper. "We'll get to the other side . . . and then we're going to have a funeral."

12

B eth saw Jake steady himself with the little O'Toole boy in his arms. Kat knelt across Shay's body from Sebastian, tears welling in her eyes.

Maeve sat on the ground beside her ma, who was breathing but unconscious.

Maeve saw Sebastian quit and burst into tears. "No, not Da. No!" Maeve reached for her ma, weeping.

Ginny went to Maeve and pulled her to her feet.

Maeve realized who had her, and Beth thought with a tragic kind of pride that her mama had the strength of ten women. She'd survived three years in an insane asylum. She had plenty to help hold this young woman together.

"Let's get across this blasted creek," Dakota said.

"Load everyone in our wagons." Lou and Tony went to pick Shay up while Jake and Oscar headed for the Da Luca wagon, along with Conor and Bridget.

Three men, very gently, lifted Fiona and carried her to

the front Da Luca wagon with Conor and Bridget, with Shay in the second.

When Maeve saw her mother and the little ones being carried, she squared her shoulders and followed. Then, sudden as a bolt of lightning, she asked, "Where's Donal?"

"Don't fret, Miss O'Toole," Dakota said. "Half the men went to the far side of the creek. We'll find him when we reach that side. Now let's get you in with your ma." He helped her into the back of the Da Luca wagon.

"Jake," Oscar said, "your horse and Dakota's are tied to the back of my lead wagon."

"Good. Like Dakota said, no one rides horseback or walks across the creek. Reckon the team and the wagon wheels straddled that hole. Dakota and I were lucky our horses didn't go down when we crossed."

"That's right," Dakota agreed. "I'll drive Maeve's wagon across."

"I'll ride with you," Jake said.

The two men waded out to where the wagon stood in the water with the team of oxen and climbed onto the wagon seat. Dakota grabbed the reins and began rolling across the creek.

Beth took her usual seat beside Joseph and followed the wagon ahead. She realized she was gripping the seat with white knuckles as they passed the spot where Fiona and Shay had vanished. She prayed that Fiona would recover. Maeve was crushed and needed her mother. At least they had Donal. Caring for the little ones and her ma would give Maeve something to hang on to. The two of them could watch over their family and comfort each other.

Water splashed against the wheels. Beth turned to look at the wrecked wagon, now pushed downstream and nearing a curve. Soon it would be out of sight. Joseph rolled on until they got fully across. The wagons ahead saw them coming and continued on to the top of the steep bank. One by one they left the water behind but carried a heavy grief with them.

Once they were all on level land, prairie grass blowing in the wind around them, Dakota shouted, "Everyone, stop! We'll camp here tonight."

The wagon train came to a halt. It had been midday when they'd reached the creek, and now the sun was halfway down in the western sky. Given the tragedy they'd suffered, they'd stop a bit early today. The rough creek crossing had worn out the oxen and horses; the animals needed to graze and rest up.

Folks set to putting up their tents and preparing the evening meal.

Beth considered asking Dakota if they could go farther and put some distance between themselves and the place where the O'Tooles had lost their father. Of course, what they'd lost would travel with them. But by the time the grave was dug, and with them exhausted from the rescues, they needed to stop for a while and get some food in their stomachs.

The wagons formed into their usual circle. Maeve leapt out of the Da Luca wagon and ran for the O'Toole wagon, calling, "Donal, come quick! Ma's awake." She reached the wagon only to find Jake and Dakota driving it.

"He must've ridden with another wagon, Maeve," Dakota said.

Beth got to the ground in time to see Maeve's brow furrow. Then Donal emerged from a group of men who'd surrounded him. His head came up when he saw Maeve, and he rushed toward her.

"Conor and Bridget made it, Donal. And Beth said you brought Conor in. Ma is going to be all right."

"And Da?"

Maeve shook her head, tears streaming down her cheeks. Donal pulled her into his arms, and the two of them stood there weeping.

Finally, Maeve said, "Enough now. Come and see Conor, Bridget, and Ma. They're going to need us, and we're gonna need them."

Donal slid his arm across Maeve's back, and they walked to the Da Luca wagon where their family slept. "What are we going to do now, Maeve? Da had all the strength and wisdom. He had a way about him that lifted me so high. We were all going to homestead out west. We'd've been landowners, and Da would have taught us the way of it."

Beth had heard Fiona talk of her husband's younger years on his father's farm, before the potato crop had failed year after year. Shay had left the farm and found meager work in town. He'd married and raised a family while they all lived on mere crumbs. Until finally the dream of owning rich, fertile land had guided their feet to a ship and to America.

Now their source of knowledge and wisdom was gone, which left Fiona as the head of the family but with no real understanding of how to farm. Donal and Maeve looked lost as they headed toward the wagon to check on their ailing ma and little brother and sister.

Beth watched them for a long moment, then got to work. They had the camp to set up and a grave to dig.

Shay's body was wrapped in a pretty blanket, but no one could bear to lower him into the ground with no protection, as if he weren't beyond that now.

Maeve tended her family, Donal at her side. Conor was subdued but seemed clearheaded and on his way to full strength. Bridget slept, her breathing steady. Fiona faded in and out of consciousness with her children at her side. Maeve urged sips of water into her confused mother's mouth. Coughing racked Fiona's body often. It was proof of how bad Fiona was that she hadn't asked about Shay. She hadn't noticed that he wasn't with her, and she didn't seem to understand how close she'd come to drowning. Because she'd gone down before the wagon had rolled, and before Shay had gone under, she wouldn't know.

Donal lifted Conor out of the Da Luca wagon. When Beth came up to help, Donal whispered to her, "I'm afraid of what he'll say. We don't want Ma to know about Da when she's feeling so poorly."

One of the women worked over a campfire to warm up some broth for Fiona. Something hot would help her.

Or so they all hoped.

As Jake approached the Collins wagon, Beth saw the pain in his eyes. She handed him a bowl of stew. He took a seat, shaking his head, not bothering to lift a spoon.

"Eat your food," she urged.

"I can't find any appetite for it."

Beth slid a hand to rest on Jake's back between his shoulder blades. She found herself leaning against him. And he leaned back. Realizing this had gone on for too long, she straightened and said, "You'll need your strength tomorrow. You should eat something whether you have an appetite or not. And remember: we had a terrible loss today, but we had a miracle, too. Conor and Bridget must be very special children. God's not done with them yet."

He managed a small smile, then picked up a spoon and took a bite of stew.

It was sunset when they held the funeral. A vivid red sunset lit their group, as if God himself was telling them Shay was with Him now in glory.

Maeve stood weeping, Donal at her side. Conor managed to stand with them, even with his sore ankle. Bridget and Fiona couldn't leave their beds. Parson McDaniels recited the twenty-third psalm from memory. Beth heard the comforting words she'd spoken earlier repeated in the parson's strong yet gentle voice.

His wife, Bedelia, sang with her beautiful soprano voice. She often called the wagon train to worship on Sunday mornings with music. For the funeral, she sang "Fairest Lord Jesus" and "Amazing Grace." The hymns uplifted Beth, but Maeve's and Donal's heads were bowed, and they barely seemed to notice what was happening. Conor sank to the ground and sat. No one tried to get him to his feet.

Dakota briefly spoke of Shay O'Toole—of his strength

and joy, and of his willingness to work hard and dream of a better life. The parson prayed for restored health for Fiona, Bridget, and Conor. And for strength for all of them on their journey ahead.

They all so desperately needed that strength.

13

The occupants of the wagon train fell into a deep sleep. Jake suspected half of them, the men mostly, were closer to unconscious than asleep.

He'd come close to dozing off before he'd had a meal, even though now he was hungry enough to start gnawing on his foot. He wouldn't have eaten if the Collins family hadn't had a hearty stew ready to offer him.

Jake, his belly full, had forced himself to make sure everyone was settled in for the night and the draft animals were brought into the wagon circle. Ginny had stationed herself by Maeve and even slept beside her. It was the last thing Jake noticed before he rolled himself up in his own blanket in the cool prairie night and dropped into a deep sleep.

Just minutes later, a scream ripped him out of sleep. Jake was on his feet, gun drawn, running toward the sound before he was fully awake.

Maeve. He ran toward the tent behind the O'Toole wagon. Poor Maeve. When he got there, he shoved the tent flap aside to see Maeve, sitting up and trembling in fear. She was looking down at Ginny.

Beth came running to the tent. Dakota charged up, as did the Da Luca brothers, others, everyone.

Dropping to her knees, Beth crawled into the tent beside Ginny. "She has nightmares," Beth said, then shook Ginny's shoulders. "Wake up! Ginny, wake up." Looking up at Jake, she said, "A damp cloth wakes her up faster. Can you get one?"

"I'll go." Dakota ran toward the barrel of water on the O'Toole wagon.

"What is it? What's going on?" Fiona sat up slowly. The screaming had been nearly in her ear. Maeve slept on her ma's left, Ginny on Maeve's left.

The tent was crowded enough that Beth and Kat had slept in the backs of two different wagons.

Dakota returned with a soaked towel. Beth snatched it away from him and pressed the cold dripping cloth to Ginny's face.

The screaming cut off.

"Wake up now, Ginny. Wake up. Please," Beth urged.

Jake noticed a crowd of folks from the train standing outside the tent. They watched on, looking real worried.

"Jake," Beth said, "tell everyone to go back to their wagons. She'll be all right. I sleep beside her, and I usually keep a wet cloth close to hand to pull her out of her nightmares. I hear her before the nightmare gets a solid hold. But I forgot all about it tonight."

Ginny took the cloth from Beth. Jake saw her hands shaking as she awoke from whatever dream had tormented her. He nodded and went to tell the others in the wagon train to head on back to their bedrolls. Jake hoped the nightmares weren't contagious.

Maeve hugged Ginny tightly. She turned to her ma, who was sitting up but not fully conscious even now after all the screaming. Maeve said quietly, "Go back to sleep, Ma."

"I'm sorry, Fiona," Ginny said. "You need more sleep. The nightmare has left me now."

Maeve gripped Fiona's shoulders. "Lie down now."

With Beth's help, Ginny got to her knees. "I'll move away so I don't disturb you."

The next morning, Dakota went to Donal and Maeve, who'd worked over Fiona. Bridget was awake now and seemed fine. She'd been told about her father and now clung to Maeve like a limpet.

"Maeve," Dakota said, crouching beside her, "I'm going to give the order to hitch up the wagons. We need to move on. Your ma can rest in your wagon while we're on the move."

"No, I want to wait." Maeve's eyes turned a stormy gray. Her jaw went taut with stubborn resistance.

"Waiting does no good. We need to push on. I'm sorry, Maeve, but it serves no purpose to wait here."

The taut jaw trembled, and Maeve gazed beyond the circle of wagons to her father's grave. They'd fashioned a cross out of branches from the trees along the creek. Crude but beautiful in its stark simplicity.

"No, I won't be leavin' Da's grave alone on this prairie. I can't just let life tear a hole in my heart and then ride away. Not yet. Let's take another day of rest while Ma heals. Just one more day. I want her to wake up. I want her to have a chance to say g-goodbye to . . ." Her voice broke.

Beth saw the struggle on Dakota's face. The war he waged within himself. His compassion for Maeve. His concern for Fiona. Maeve's eyes were locked on her da's grave, and Beth wished the young woman could have seen Dakota's turmoil.

Then his shoulders squared and, sounding gruff, he said, "We're pulling out. I understand that it's hard for you, but it won't harm your ma, so it serves no purpose. It's midweek. Hopefully by Sunday your ma will be feeling better, and we'll take our usual day of rest."

"No!" Maeve clenched her fists and whirled to face Dakota. Both of them kneeling, face-to-face, her chest heaving, her fists looked as if they might swing on their wagon-train boss. No one could miss Maeve's rage.

Donal had led his animals to water. When he heard Maeve shouting, he came at a run.

"Sure, and it's you I'm blaming for this." Her brogue grew deeper when she was this upset. "You should've known that ford might have sinkholes. You should've kept my family in the wagon."

"No, Maeve. You know that's not true." Donal said the right words, yet he glared at Dakota.

The wheel had broken, and the wagon had rolled over. Staying inside had almost killed Conor and Bridget. But Maeve needed someone to blame, at least right now.

Dakota's shoulders looked like they were used to bearing heavy burdens. He didn't defend himself, but neither did he relent. Instead, he rose to his feet and called out, "We're moving out! Let's get hitched up." He gave Maeve one last look of regret and pain, then turned on his heels and strode to the outside of the circle, where the herd had been grazing for the last hour before beginning the workday.

Maeve collapsed forward until her head rested on her knees. Donal drew her into his arms. Conor, the active little boy, came and sat silently beside them. Bridget leaned against Donal's back and wept.

Beth saw the family all leaning on Donal. He wasn't a full-grown man yet so this was a heavy burden for him. She looked up and met Jake's eyes, which showed his concern. A lot passed between them without a word spoken. Beth thought another day would do no harm but knew neither would it do any good. And the wagon train always kept rolling. Forward progress was the only way to reach their destination.

Jake gave a sad shake of his head and followed Dakota.

Ginny knelt beside Maeve and drew the girl firmly into her arms. Kat came to cradle Bridget. Beth went to Conor and helped the limping boy toward the wagon.

Fiona, still addled, was helped into the back of the one remaining O'Toole wagon. Donal got to work hitching up his team. Everyone in the family, save Fiona, cast mournful looks at that single, lonely grave.

~

Donal now drove Maeve's wagon alone, with Maeve in the back with her ma and the youngsters. The Da Luca brothers pulled out ahead of Donal so the Collins family could stay near the O'Tooles and help.

117

Ginny and Kat took turns climbing into the wagon and helping care for Fiona and comfort Maeve.

Fiona was fully in the care of women. Beth thought it odd that they'd become separated from the men this way. Even Conor had taken to riding up in the front by Donal. But Maeve seemed to nurture her rage against Dakota in particular, but she didn't glare at him exclusively, so the men, except for her brothers, stayed clear, not wanting to give Maeve anything more to be angry about.

The third night since the terrible accident came, and Beth steered her wagon into the circle. It was Saturday night. Tomorrow they'd rest. They were a good distance into Nebraska now, with a few more days until they reached the Platte River and turned to head west.

When the circle closed, Jake rode up to the back of the wagon, his expression grim. He dismounted. "I'll help get Fiona settled for the night." They needed to lift her out of the wagon and move her into the tent.

Before Beth could thank him, Maeve stuck her head out of the gathered canvas opening right beside Beth. "We don't need or want your help." Her voice snapped, as cool and crisp as the evening air. "Leave us alone."

Beth looked at Jake. He'd known he'd get this reaction, but he also knew all the women had been working hard to care for Fiona, and they weren't sleeping well. Beth felt near collapse.

Jake said, quietly and calmly, "Maeve, look at me."

"I said I don't want—"

"Maeve!" His voice cracked like a whip as he cut her off.

Beth jumped. She'd never heard such a tone from Jake before.

Donal hopped down from the wagon seat and hurried to the rear of the wagon. "You leave Maeve alone. She said she doesn't want—"

"Listen to me, both of you. I had a little brother who died when he was about six—close in age to Conor."

"Conor is seven." Maeve's eyes were wide, as if she feared speaking in anger to Jake again.

Donal hung his head and shoved his hands into his back pockets.

"My little brother, Billy, was riding a horse. The horse shied when a grouse flew across its path, and Billy fell and broke his neck. He died on the spot. I was there." Jake ran his hand over his mouth as if he wanted to stop the words, as if it still hurt to speak them. "I was eight. I had two little sisters, still too young for school age. Billy and I were just down the trail from our house, riding together to school. We were a few miles away from the schoolhouse, and we often walked there. But it was a cold North Dakota morning, and the walk was going to chill us to the bone. I wheedled Ma into letting us ride that morning."

"I'm sorry about your brother." Some of the anger and the fear faded from Maeve's face, replaced by a grief so big that it hurt Beth's heart.

"At first I was heartbroken, but soon it flipped over, what I was feeling, into anger. I was so furious. I blamed myself. Somehow I blamed my stepfather; my own pa was dead and gone by then. More than that, I blamed my ma because she was the one who had nagged us about schooling. Billy and I didn't want to go."

"Why would you blame your ma and da?"

Jake shrugged. "I got real mad at Billy, too, for not

hanging on to his horse better. And I was so mad at the horse, my stepfather took possession of the family's rifle, afraid I'd kill the poor critter. I was mad at God, too."

Jake dropped his chin, and Beth saw him swallow hard. His chest rose and fell as he drew a calming breath. "The thing is, Maeve—and you, Donal—you're mad as all get-out because of all this. You've gone through something so terrible. The anger you're feeling is normal, I'd say."

Jake's head came up. His eyes shone with kindness, and he held her gaze. "Still, it's not right for you to aim what is a natural feeling at every man on this wagon train. Most especially you're aiming it at Dakota and me. We all, every man here, risked our lives saving your family. We weren't fast enough for your pa, but we saved the rest. I won't shy away from helping you or helping with your ma just because you're unfairly angry at me. I'm so sorry this happened. I'm sorry I couldn't save your da."

Donal looked up, some of the anger gone from his gaze. "Your stepfather? So your pa died, as well?"

Jake nodded. "I was so young when he passed, I only remember a few things about him. He was father to me and Billy. My ma's second husband was father to the little girls. After he died, Ma married again to a man I've never met. I heard she had more children, though I've yet to meet them. We all carry loss in our lives. And yours comes at a hard time when you needed your pa real bad. Again, I'm sorry for it." He paused for a moment, then said, "Now, let me help get your ma out of that wagon." He looked at Beth. "I got a couple of deer today, and I've brought you a haunch."

Beth saw Dakota, who was tough, steady in times of

trouble, watching from a distance. He looked worried and full of regret.

Jake added, "Maeve, you get the blankets. I'll get your ma."

"Let me help," Donal said quietly. "I've left too much to the women."

Jake clapped him on the shoulder. "You've taken a lot on your shoulders, Donal. You've been working hard day and night."

Donal nodded. He and Jake reached in, one on each side, and eased Fiona out of the wagon.

Beth was relieved to have the help. She, Maeve, Ginny, and Kat had been transferring Fiona each night, and it took all their strength to make the awkward move from the wagon to the ground, then later to the tent.

They did this while Donal cared for the horses and put up the tent, built a fire and carried water. They'd done their best to bear as much of the weight as they could, so Donal didn't have to take more on his young back.

Beth took a stack of blankets from Maeve. Beth and Maeve made up a pallet for Fiona on the ground. Then Jake and Donal knelt and gently settled Fiona on the blankets. Oscar was building a fire while his brothers unhitched the teams and led them to a nearby spring. Donal rushed off to do his own chores.

"Maeve," Beth said gently, "you and your family have been cooking your own supper. Starting tonight, you sit at our fire and eat with us."

Maeve looked down at her mother, and then her eyes went to Donal unhitching the team. With sad eyes she nodded. "Thank you."

Ginny walked with Joseph and Bruce to get water for her pot. Kat had fetched the venison and was slicing away at it, preparing it for the stewpot. Sebastian pared potatoes and had beside him a few carrots and some wild onions they'd add to the pot.

Maeve stood over her ma. When Jake rose from the ground, she rested one of her small hands on his arm. "I'm sorry. You're right that what I'm feeling isn't fair, but I can't quite stop feeling it. Thank you for helping with Ma."

He turned to her and tugged at his Stetson. "I don't fault you for your feelings, Maeve. Just for aiming them at all of us. Especially because you won't let us help you."

"I will from now on. And I think you're right when you say you were mad at God. I think I'm blasting away at you and Dakota because that seems . . . safer than being furious that God let this happen."

"Talk to Him, Maeve. Don't do no good to lie to Him. He already knows everything you're feeling. Give Him a chance to comfort you. And trust God to be strong enough to handle your anger."

She nodded, patted his arm a couple of times, then took a basin from Ginny, who'd returned with water.

Maeve knelt by her ma to help—and, Beth hoped, to pray.

14

The next morning, a Sunday, found Maeve, Ginny, and Beth kneeling over Fiona as the sweet lady opened her eyes. They were clear for the first time in days.

Maeve gasped and leaned close. "Ma! You're awake."

"M-Maeve? Is that you?" Fiona's hand, trembling and weak, lifted toward her daughter.

Maeve caught the hand and drew it to her lips. "Aye, it's me." Maeve's eyes came up, and Beth reached for a pail they kept close and poured a full cup of tea. It was cold.

"Maeve, my pretty lass." Fiona, sitting up, supported by Maeve, fumbled to pat her daughter on the shoulder. "Where's your da? He should be helping with the care of me, not leaving it all to you. Is he helping mind the little ones? Sure, and they're a handful, they are."

Maeve pulled her mother into a deep hug. Her eyes

rose to meet Beth's as if pleading with her to tell Maeve what to do.

Moving her lips more than speaking, Beth said, "Later, Maeve."

Relief swept across Maeve's face as she hugged her mother tightly. "Ma, it's good to hear your voice. We've all been in a state, worrying for you. We need you to get better. Now, no more of being a slugabed." Maeve did her best to sound teasing and lighthearted when her heart must be heavy as stone.

"Ah, me girl. Me precious Maeve. 'Tis a fine lass you are, tending me. I'm slowing you down, but thankful I am that I've got you to care for me."

Maeve raised her voice as she called, "Donal, Bridget, Conor! Come talk to Ma."

Sunday morning was the only day they didn't reheat whatever was left over from the night before in their rush to get rolling. On Sundays they baked biscuits and fried bacon. Today there was corn mush with molasses.

Beth went to meet Ginny, who held a cup of coffee, and sat down near the fire, letting the crackling warmth ease into her bones on the cool Nebraska morning.

The smell of the coffee lifted her spirits. They watched the fire, and she took in the smell of burning wood. Oscar had gathered as much as he could when they were at the stream where they'd lost the O'Tooles. It wouldn't last much longer, and unless they happened upon another creek—a possibility that made Beth tremble with fear—they'd be back to burning buffalo chips and twisted cords of prairie grass.

But for now, Beth enjoyed the aroma of the fire and the

sounds of the other pioneers stirring, cooking, talking. The bolstering warmth from good food kept her sitting upright.

Into that mix of sights and sounds and aromas, a soft voice began singing: "'Praise God from whom all blessings flow . . .'"

It was Bedelia McDaniels.

Parson McDaniels led the group in a simple worship service each Sunday morning. And that would come, but later. Right now, Bedelia, his wife, was lifting her voice in song. And her voice seemed to reach up toward God with its crystal purity.

"'Praise Him, all creatures here below . . .'"

Bedelia often sang as they rode along. Often it was hymns, but she was an Irishwoman and, like the O'Tooles, she knew by heart the old Irish folk music that made a person's heart ache at the same time it healed every pain.

It struck Beth that this was the first time she'd heard Bedelia's voice since the funeral after the terrible creek crossing and the O'Tooles' accident.

"'Praise Him above, ye heavenly hosts . . .'"

Beth moved her lips along with Bedelia but didn't truly sing. She just let Bedelia lift them all up to the extent it was possible. Beth hoped Fiona could hear it. She hoped Maeve had it in her to praise God in the midst of this storm. Then Beth hoped she had it in herself to let the music inside.

"'Praise Father, Son, and Holy Ghost.'"

Beth found she could praise the Father, the Son, and the Holy Ghost. She not only *could*, she had to.

Bedelia went on. She sang "Old Hundredth," which was

Psalm 100 sung to the same melody as the doxology. She sang "All Creatures of Our God and King" and "Amazing Grace," reminding Beth of the recent funeral. The music went on as everyone moved about, but silently, letting the lyrics fill their souls.

She ended with "A Mighty Fortress Is Our God." And that was one Beth needed to hear. She needed God as her fortress. Maeve needed it right now even more. Beth turned to look at Maeve, and the girl was bending over her mother with a cool cloth, but Fiona was singing. Weakened from days with little food and water, the O'Toole family surrounded her now with love and care. Fiona looked to be recovering, and she'd soon demand answers about her Shay. But right now, she was getting stronger, and Beth could see the sweet lady would be all right.

When the breakfast was eaten, the cooking remains cleared away and the dishes washed, Parson McDaniels walked to where Fiona lay resting but, Beth saw, awake.

He knelt beside them and spoke quietly to her and Maeve. Yesterday, Maeve would have run him off. This morning she listened. Beth saw her reply. She couldn't hear the words, but she saw the expressions. She saw Fiona's grief and knew the parson was telling Fiona about Shay. Yes, she wept, but it had to be done before they could begin to heal. It gave Beth hope that Maeve would be able to survive this tragedy without being permanently furious at God and everyone else.

Parson McDaniels took Fiona's right hand in both of his and spoke to her at length. Then he rose to his feet, turned to face the pioneers, his eyes fiery with passion for his faith, and said, "Come near. We'll have our Sunday service where Fiona can hear what is being said."

They all gathered. Some brought blankets, spread them on the grass, and sat on the ground. Jake came to stand by Beth and her group . . . her family. She supposed by now they really were a family.

The morning service was full of Bible verses about strength and hope and loss. God's love was woven generously through it all.

15

The weeks that followed slid into a pattern. Their trail occasionally took them near a town or near the railroad tracks. Once, Beth heard the train chuffing and clacking along as it followed its iron trail.

Sometimes they'd camp near a town and a few folks would go in if they needed something. Jake usually rode in, but he never stayed for long.

Whatever the other families did, the whole Collins family avoided the towns, fearful that men dispatched by Beth's father would follow the train tracks. Sebastian and Kat avoided towns, too. Kat was probably afraid she was being sought after.

Sebastian, who could say?

And then the day came when Sebastian did say. He came up to Beth as she walked along behind the wagon, looking around as if afraid he'd be overheard.

Kat was nearby. Sebastian gave her an impatient look, then said, "You might as well hear my question, too."

Kat arched one brow at his tone, and maybe she should

have walked away. Instead, she drew closer. They all considered Sebastian to be a mystery.

"I wonder if . . ." Sebastian stared at the distant line of trees that signified the Platte River. A train had passed by not long ago. He dropped his voice to a whisper and continued, "The thing is, I want to stay with the wagon train, but I need a few things. I'm in danger, or I must be. The gunshot tells me so. I don't want to go to a town. I have some money in my wallet and, well, I had a notion to not go all the way to Oregon. To travel out west for a time, then turn aside and find some land, someplace where I could hope to be safe and—" he glanced around again and whispered even more quietly—"work on . . . what I was working on. I think my work is why I was shot. I need to go on with it, but in secret."

Beth pulled back from him, and she knew a smile snuck across her face.

"Me being shot for my work is funny?" Sebastian, usually so aloof it was worrisome, was clearly upset.

"No, no, that's not what I was smiling about." She looked between Kat and Sebastian. "I'll tell you my secret now. The Collins family has land out west. Not all the way to Oregon. We're turning aside. We don't want anyone to know exactly where we're going."

Kat knew they were running, but Sebastian didn't. Even now Beth didn't tell him why they were turning aside. Why they didn't want anyone to know.

"So I could go with you?" Sebastian sounded relieved. "Not strike out completely on my own?"

Beth smiled. "We'd welcome you."

"But the reason I have to go to town is that I need some

very special supplies for my work. I thought with that train racing back and forth across the country, maybe I could order what I need in a town here and have it sent ahead and it would be there by the time I reached whatever town is down the line somewhere."

Beth nodded. "That's a really good idea." A distant whistle drew her attention, and she saw a smokestack. The three of them turned to watch a train racing along on the rails.

"It makes me feel foolish to be taking such a slow wagon west when that train goes so fast." Beth couldn't tear her eyes away from the iron horse. "But we figured this method of travel would be a better way to be . . . secret."

Kat and Sebastian both nodded in agreement. They had their own reasons, which Beth could surely understand.

"I don't want to go into town either," Beth admitted. "None of the Collins family does. Jake could maybe make your orders for you. And Oscar said we'd turn off from the Oregon Trail west of Fort Bridger. Maybe you could have your supplies sent there. Would the supplies be too heavy a load to be carried in our wagons?"

Sebastian shrugged. "We're lessening the load by eating our supplies, and nothing I want is too huge, though I do need a forge and bellows and some . . ."

"We have a forge along. You could use ours. And it might be best to discuss this with Oscar. Maybe with that cart along, we'd be able to carry everything, and if not, maybe we could add a wagon and a new team, though I'm sure those would be very high priced at Fort Bridger."

"I might be able to pay for that."

Somehow the expression on Sebastian's face made her

wonder just how much money he had because he didn't look all that worried about it.

"Let's talk to Jake about the possibility of ordering in a nearby town and having it sent to Fort Bridger, and then talk to Oscar about whether we can add to our load."

"Thank you, Beth." Sebastian glanced at Kat. "And you've been a fine wife for this journey."

She blushed a bit, then shook her head and giggled. "I keep forgetting about that."

Sebastian chuckled. "That sounds like the kind of wife I'd have."

Beth laughed along with him and Kat. Then Sebastian went to talk things over with Oscar.

Each day was the same. They woke, they ate, they packed the wagons, and they hitched up and rolled out.

Beth, wishing she could reach the hiding place Oscar had found for them, did her best to lighten everyone's load, as they all did for each other.

Ginny slept beside her, and Beth slept beside Ginny. Kat fit into their tent, too.

And so the days rolled on.

The O'Toole family functioned but were loaded down with grief. Mama with her nightmares. Beth feeling hunted. Adding the O'Tooles to their group had one good effect. Fiona noticed Ginny and her complete lack of cooking skills. Oh, there was a lack in many places besides cooking, but Fiona noticed the cooking first.

Beth and Ginny were leading their horses back from the stream one night when Fiona caught up to them and slid an arm across the back of Ginny's waist. "And how, my good friend, did you reach your grand age without learning how to peel a potato?"

Ginny's cheeks pinked up, and Beth held her breath, hoping no truth would slip out. "I suppose my own mama did too much of the work. I had no love for cooking and so managed to avoid it. But I'm regretting that now."

Fiona looked skeptical of the excuse as she said, "You've fallen into the hands of a teacher, Ginny. You must learn these skills to survive, and it's not too late—though it's mighty close."

Maeve was a better cook than Beth, as was Kat. Yet Beth could make a passable meal. Now Ginny had no escape from the work of leading horses and cattle to water and such.

"Jake, can I have a word?" Beth was used to walking with Jake and learning about the West, only this time she needed help.

People tended to let them walk on their own. Beth appreciated it because her questions were so detailed. She also liked the time alone with Jake, even knowing there was no future in her admiration for him.

"What is it, Beth? Hunting? Building? Tending cows and horses?" He smiled as he swung down to walk beside her.

Keeping her voice low, she asked, "Is there a town coming up where we could restock a bit?"

The smile faded as he looked around. "You're running low on things now with more mouths to feed?"

"I am, and I have enough coins, but I don't want to go into town. I don't want the O'Tooles to think they're a burden. I'd like you to buy enough food to keep us going but not make it noticeable when you hand it off to me. We're so close together in the camp at night, I know it's hard to slip anything past anyone."

Jake rested his hand on her arm and left it there. "You've got a good heart, Beth. I'd be glad to help."

Beth, looking around sharply, pulled a handful of coins out of her pocket. She'd opened one of the seams in her specially made dress and taken out a few twenty-dollar gold pieces. Now she reached her hand out to him, hoping it wasn't noticeable. He opened his hand and took the money.

One quick glance at what he held had him raise his brows to nearly his hairline. He quickly dropped the coins into his pocket.

"How often will we stop at a town? Maybe you could buy a bit at each stop or whenever you normally ride in."

"You're not cutting the heart out of your family's savings, I hope."

"Money isn't our problem." She gave him a rueful smile, for she knew she was admitting they had a problem, just one of a different kind.

"I'd listen if you ever wanted to talk."

Their eyes met and held. And held some more.

She wished she could pour it all out and let him help bear her problems on his strong shoulders, but she didn't dare. Her father's reach was too great. Finally, she said, "It's not that I don't want to, Jake."

His nod was full of disappointment.

If only she didn't know that once they went to their hiding place, she'd never see him again. She was sorely afraid she'd miss Jake Holt for the rest of her life. But to tell him secrets he'd need to keep would give him a burden he'd always have to bear. It might even put him in danger if Father searched as long and hard as she knew he would.

"We'll be near a town in a couple of days. I always ride in if any of our travelers go. But this time I'll ride in for sure. I'll bring what I can and pick the right moment to hand it off. Does Oscar know about this?"

"Yes, as do his brothers. So, you could give it to any of them without worrying they'll ask questions.

"Now, can you tell me what plants out west work well for medicine? Do any of them give food a pleasant flavor?"

Jake smiled and said, "Would you recognize a willow tree? Because their bark . . ."

The first night that Fiona and Ginny did the cooking, the whole family gathered around, Beth with some fear.

Jake had brought in several rabbits and given a whole one to the Collinses.

They had a good-sized group around their campfire at night. All three Collins brothers, Ginny, Beth and Kat, Sebastian, and now Fiona and her four children. The O'Tooles were hard workers, but they knew they were in trouble with half their food stores gone.

Beth did her best to reassure them there was plenty without making them feel like they were accepting charity. She knew she could afford to replace her supplies, but she had no wish to tell the O'Tooles that.

Ginny scooped up a stew thick with rabbit meat, potatoes, and wild onions Jake had found on his daily hunting trip. She handed the first plate to Oscar.

With twinkling eyes, he asked, "Is this some honor you're bestowing on me or are you experimenting on me?"

"A guinea pig," Sebastian said with a smile.

Ginny frowned at him. "Oscar is not a pig."

Sebastian laughed. "Sorry, no, he's certainly not. But experiments by Louis Pasteur and Antoine Lavoisier, to name a couple of them, used guinea pigs—a large rodent—to experiment with, observing the reaction of the animals and considering how those reactions would apply to humans. You'll hear inventors who work in chemistry and medicine in particular talk about 'human guinea pigs.' That's Oscar tonight."

Beth tilted her head, probably hoping at some level that what Sebastian was talking about would make sense. "Pasture? Pigs? What?"

Sebastian, normally a quiet man, came out of his good-natured teasing and looked around. His eyes widened as he realized everyone was staring at him. "Not pasture. *Pasteur*. He's the one who found out how to pasteurize milk." He swallowed hard as they continued to stare.

Maeve said, "We put the cows out to graze every night. To graze on grass in what I suppose could be called a pasture. So we . . . uh, pasteurize them? Some man invented turning cows out to graze?"

Sebastian narrowed his eyes as if forcing himself to be silent and not react further. He jumped to his feet and said, "Let me help scoop up that good stew, Ginny."

Beth wondered what the man was going on about. She looked at Kat, who sat beside her. Their eyes met. Kat shrugged and scrunched up her face, clearly as lost as Beth.

The one thing for sure was that they didn't know Sebastian at all.

Sebastian handed the plates around so fast you'd've thought Fiona was shouting at him and Ginny kicking him to speed him up.

Soon they were all eating.

When Fiona had her meal in front of her, the last to sit, she cleared her throat in a very attention-getting way. "My family has made a decision about this journey. We've lost enough supplies that food has become a concern for us. We've decided we're not going all the way to Oregon. Jake told us there's a huge fertile valley in Idaho just north of the trail that's open for homesteading. We should get there by August. He said we might be able to get a few vegetables, the early spring type like beets and peas, and a few other things that we have the seed for, to bear a crop before winter sets in. We're doing that. We thank you for all that you're sharing with us."

Ginny patted Fiona on the arm. "Now you're sharing with us, too. You've got enough food with what Jake brings in."

Ginny knew Jake had brought in supplies just today. Yes, he'd gone hunting, but he'd also found a town along the railroad tracks and managed to sneak a gunnysack full of canned fruits and vegetables and a bag of potatoes and carrots into Oscar's wagon. He'd disguised what he'd found by bringing in wild onions and the rabbits.

Beth thought Jake was a master of subtlety. But then Fiona wasn't to know that, and she understood her own supplies were low.

"Fiona," Oscar said, his stern voice drawing everyone's attention.

Beth saw him look at her directly, and she nodded, giving him permission to go ahead.

"We've decided to turn aside in Idaho, too. In fact, that's been our plan from the first. My brothers and I went out a year ago. The train traveled far enough that the trip wasn't too strenuous with our traveling light, and we claimed land there and lived on it through last summer and fall. Then we rode the train back to pack up our households and collect our sisters. We managed to buy up land in our sisters' names, as well. It sounds like we'll be neighbors then, and we'll be glad of it."

Fiona beamed. "I had no idea you had such plans."

"We've been quiet about it. The rest of the wagon train would've had to know when we left, but, well, there's a bit of trouble on our back trail. Not trouble with the law, just an old enemy we want to leave behind. So we'd appreciate it if you didn't speak of our plans to anyone."

Fiona turned to her plate and ate a few bites. After swallowing, she said, "Your secret is safe with us, Oscar. We'd be happy to have folks nearby who know us. Maybe we shouldn't speak any more of turning aside until it's time to find a land office and stake our claims. Maeve and I with our homestead and—"

"As will I, Ma." Donal sounded firm.

"You need to be twenty-one, boyo, and you're—"

"I'm a man grown. I barely know what year it is, and I doubt you remember the exact year I was born."

Fiona fought back a smile with only a bit of success.

"Why, now that you mention it, I don't rightly know what year it was."

"Surely it was more than twenty-one years ago. Those homesteads are to go to adults who will make promises and keep those promises. I've got a plan, too. We'll claim land that abuts in such a way that there's a three-corner spot. We can straddle three claims with one house and live in it all together while fulfilling our promise to the Homestead Act. We'll be forced to build a house. It's supposed to be, what, twelve foot by twelve foot?" Donal looked to Oscar.

"If you build a three-room cabin that straddles the property line and each room is twelve by twelve or so, that ought to suit a land agent. I doubt they'll be stopping by with a measuring stick. I think to get your land claimed up right, you need neighbors to go in and swear that you've been living on the land for five years. Those neighbors won't bring a measuring stick neither."

Donal smiled and nodded his head.

Oscar went on. "There's a head of household rule, too. Donal, being the oldest man, you'll qualify as head of the house no matter your age, so no need to forget the year you were born. And Fiona and Maeve can each stake a claim. It's a fine plan. I'd say there'll be a regional land office at Fort Bridger where you can get things set up, but maybe there are little towns popping up along the railroad tracks and you can go farther down the line. Jake will know."

It was a genial gathering that Saturday night, and there'd be no early start the next day. An Irishman near the front of the wagon train pulled out a fiddle and started playing it. Joseph joined in with his harmonica, and they all gathered around to sing and dance.

Beth danced with all the Collins brothers and Sebastian. Later, as the long summer day faded to dusk, she danced with Jake. In the moonlight they enjoyed a pretty song in each other's arms.

Beth was left sighing and wishing and wanting.

They rested on Sunday, when the fiddle, along with Joseph's harmonica, turned to hymns.

Their travels continued in such a rhythm, with Beth talking to Jake every chance she got, trying to learn the ways of the West. Mile after mile, as the days and weeks went by, Nebraska passed beneath their wagon wheels.

16

Maynard Horecroft strutted into Thaddeus's office. "I've found something."

The man had been cooperative, but Thaddeus was accustomed to a little more deference, and that was deference from everyone—from his employees to his fellow business cronies to the governor of Illinois.

The unwise Dr. Horecroft seemed incapable of it, however.

Thaddeus exchanged a long look with Blayd, who stayed close whenever possible. He was an excellent listener, and Thaddeus liked to know what the man's impressions were after a meeting, especially one like this.

"It's about time," Thaddeus said.

Horecroft went straight to the chair centered in front of his desk and sat without waiting for an invitation. The man was rotund. He had a full head of white hair and wore a dark gray suit that looked like he'd spent all the money he charged Thaddeus on his clothes. "I found a woman who spoke with Eugenia and occasionally eavesdropped when Eugenia would talk aloud to herself." Dr.

Horecroft shook his head with regret. "I fear your wife is still dangerously insane, Mr. Rutledge. She needs more time and treatment at my asylum."

His wife's insanity was a thorn in Thaddeus's side. The woman had defiant opinions she knew differed from Thaddeus's own, and she spread them far and wide. She had no control over spouting every thought in her head. Her insanity had reached the stage where she was a constant embarrassment to him, and he'd had to take steps. And she'd inherited a great deal of money and thought it was right to keep it from him. Which was madness in itself.

And now he might be able to find her and bring her back. Thaddeus leaned back in his chair, his skin prickling with excitement. He'd take great pleasure in looking Eugenia in the eye when he locked her away again. "Where is this woman who talked to Eugenia?"

"I have her in solitary confinement. She's quite mad. Because of her erratic state of mind, I'm not getting a full story, but I'm sure she knows something, and she'll tell it to me if she wants to eat."

"Bring her here. She'll talk to me."

Horecroft shook his head. "I'll handle it. It's a delicate business talking to Mrs. Hannon."

"I can ask her in a non-delicate way that will wring the answers out of her." Thaddeus watched the hungry expression on Horecroft's face. The man looked like he'd enjoy watching someone else abuse his patients. Thaddeus had to respect that.

He felt Blayd's tension. There was a man who knew how to get information out of someone. Though Thaddeus enjoyed doing the abusing himself when someone wouldn't give him what he wanted or wouldn't get out of the way so he could get it for himself, he sometimes had more to do than one man alone was capable of. In such cases he'd send Blayd.

Blayd shifted so he was a bit closer to Thaddeus. He'd been casually, at least outwardly casually, reading a report. Now he leaned against a table, his arms crossed. Looked like maybe he'd like a few minutes alone to persuade Dr. Horeroft to bring the woman in.

Horecroft continued, "We have a special room away from the asylum for matters like this. She's at risk of running away. Bringing her here would possibly be . . . uh, very *embarrassing* for you—I mean if she gave into the ravings of her mind while we're trying to bring her in. She's attempted to get away many times. And yes . . ." Horecroft held up a staying hand.

Thaddeus was tempted to break his arm.

"Yes, I can get attendants and surround her and keep her under control. But do you want me to parade Mrs. Hannon in here with hulking men around her? Or into your home?"

That gave Thaddeus pause as he pictured it. What if the woman screamed for help? If she was furiously mad, the whole world might hear of this. What if they had to gag her and bind her arms and legs and carry her in? Such a scene was distasteful to Thaddeus. His home was no better than his office. No one he employed would dare to question him, but that wouldn't stop the gossip. Word would get out. He'd be a laughingstock.

Without waiting for Thaddeus to reply, Horecroft added in a smug tone, "I thought not."

"Where then?"

"I would respectfully ask you to give me just a few more days. I hope I can get the full story out of her with my technique of restricting food and administering ice-cold baths. It's a remarkably effective way to temporarily clear the thoughts of a madwoman. If it doesn't work within the week, because I know you are anxious to get your wife back, then you can come. By the end of the week, Mrs. Hannon will have calmed down to the point I believe she'll tell me what we want to know."

A week. Thaddeus's jaw tightened. It had already been months. He was spending a fortune now with the Pinkertons. They were scouring the train stations. They were checking on carriages that had left Chicago in the last week. But then, Thaddeus thought with a cool smile, he had a fortune to spare, didn't he?

"One week, Dr. Horecroft. Then I'll see if she won't talk to me."

That hungry look again. A cruel man. That was one of the things Thaddeus liked most about him.

Horecroft jerked his chin down and up, stood from the chair, and said, "We'll have the answers before then. I very fervently hope." He hurried from the room.

Thaddeus watched the door close and considered what else could be done about his errant wife and daughter. He wasn't a man to strike a woman, though he'd resorted to caning Elizabeth when she'd misbehaved as a child. For the most part, his women were very careful how they acted around him, and punishment hadn't been necessary. Until Eugenia had lost her mind. Terrible shame. She'd been a decent enough woman to marry. Extremely wealthy.

143

Her parents gave them, as a wedding present, a luxurious house, long before Thaddeus could afford it. In the finest neighborhood in Chicago.

Eugenia's mother had outlived her husband by nearly a decade. Thaddeus had gotten a nasty surprise to find they'd left Eugenia a tidy fortune in a tightly controlled trust fund he couldn't get his hands on. They'd left the bulk of their money to Elizabeth, with her listed to inherit what was left of her mother's money upon Eugenia's death. He'd gotten plenty, too. But his wife's and daughter's money, beyond his reach, was a slap in the face. It should have been his.

All that money had furthered Eugenia's madness. She was a difficult woman when she didn't need anything from him.

Thaddeus suspected Elizabeth had taken a good chunk of her inheritance with her on this ridiculous escape. Because of the way it was written, Thaddeus couldn't even see if any money had been withdrawn.

His hatred of his in-laws was a cold and vicious thing, and they were lucky to be beyond his reach. The only way for him to ever get that money was if both women died before him, and Elizabeth never had a child.

He considered a possible talk with a raving woman. It was all a great nuisance, and it twisted an already sharp blade in his anger.

Thaddeus saw the sense in both his women pre-deceasing him.

~~~~~

They rolled into and across the prairies of Wyoming. For days, weeks, months, the horses and cattle plodded on.

The early excitement among the pioneers had been given a quick death by the O'Toole family's loss. Now it faded to dull drudgery as each day stretched out the same. The only break in the sameness came when terrible storms whipped across the plains. Then they longed for the boring sameness to return.

Finally, the mountains began to rise up in the far distance. The land began to break up with outcroppings of rocks, increasing stands of trees. Still they rolled on, the rocks and trees becoming their own kind of drudgery.

Any little towns they drew near to, Beth and her family avoided. Few in the wagon train bothered to go into town, having so little money to spend and knowing the dreadfully high prices would ruin them, leaving them penniless in Oregon.

Then word reached Beth that at last Fort Bridger was just ahead. Oscar and Beth had planned this as their final place to stock up on supplies. Beth and the family needed some things she hoped she could get in Fort Bridger, but she couldn't go there—none of her family could. She needed help. She needed Jake.

She waited until he made one of his usual passes the length of the wagon train. They'd taken to talking together nearly every day, Beth full of questions, and Jake full of answers.

"Would you help me, please?" she asked him.

~

He swung down off his horse. They were approaching Fort Bridger at last. He felt his heart lift as they checked off another long passage of the journey.

145

The hardest part lay ahead on the trek through the mountains, but the prairies were finally behind them.

Beth's eyes shone when she asked for his assistance, and Jake had to wonder why. "What is it?"

"My family has a few important things it needs in Fort Bridger." She drew in a slow breath, watching him carefully.

He could tell this mattered greatly to her. "You've never gone to town during the journey." He knew why, but he wasn't sure how to tell her he knew.

"And we don't want to go into this town. The help I'd like is to give you a list of things to buy. We can afford to buy them, but none of us wishes to go to Fort Bridger.

The wagon train would stop outside the fort. Anyone with purchases to make would walk in. Fort Bridger was a bustling place and well stocked, but prices were known to be high. The pioneers avoided anything other than bare necessities.

He opened his mouth to reply, then hesitated. Now was the time to tell her he knew. Then he looked into those pretty blue eyes and didn't speak. Not yet. Soon. What he really wanted was for her to tell him herself. "I'd be glad to pick up whatever you need," he finally said.

"I wonder if you'd take our cart, the small wagon we've been pulling? We can hitch up the cart horse. We would like chickens if they have any. And a few pigs. Crates to carry them in. Well, I've written it all down." She pulled a rather long list from her pocket and handed it to him.

His heart sank because he knew what it all meant. And he could see she wasn't ready to talk yet. Maybe never. "I'll get what you want if it's possible." He studied the list. "You want a dog?"

"I'm sure it's unlikely there'd be one that anyone would part with. But yes, we would like a dog and a couple of cats. We'd like so many things, but I realize how hard it might be to find a lot of it."

Carefully, he said, "You can get all these things once we're in Oregon, you know. And some of them you'd be better off buying there."

Pink rose on her face. She'd kept her bonnet on mostly, but with the long days in the endless sun, she was tanned. But not so tan he couldn't see her blush.

"We'd like them now if we can get them." She handed him a coin purse, very heavy.

"I'm going in to fetch the things Sebastian ordered." Jake leaned close, glanced around, and said, "At least I'll know a cat and dog when I see one. I have no idea what Sebastian ordered. It was all gibberish."

Beth shrugged. "I never saw the list, but he seems almost desperate to get these supplies. I hope they came in."

"I'll get what I can." He nodded, his heart twisting to think of what lay ahead. He tucked the list and money into his pocket. "Let's get the cart hitched up."

17

J ake found chickens!

If Beth had her way, they'd tuck into the mountain valley Oscar had scouted and never emerge. Not as long as her father was alive. That wasn't really how she wanted it. She fantasized about facing her father. Shouting at him. Demanding respect and independence. But she was a practical woman and knew she didn't have the power in any confrontation with her father. So she'd set out to find a hiding place and she'd done her best to bring everything they'd need.

Her father was ten years older than Ginny's forty years, so she probably needed to find a hiding place and not emerge for twenty years. She grimly intended to succeed at just that.

To that end, when Jake had returned in the cart, she found he'd purchased a small flock of chickens in Fort Bridger and half a dozen piglets. He'd also brought along a rather ragged dog, undersized and thin as a rail, as if he'd found it stray somewhere. The cat was an unexpected treat. And he'd found a collection of wooden crates that, with some stacking, had fit in the cart. He'd lined the bottom of the cart with canned goods and nearly every other thing on her list.

She looked at the stack of crates. Wished she could pull the skinny pup out. Its white coat had brown patches, its feet oversized. It looked at her and whined through the bars of its prison and gazed with pleading eyes. She reached for the small door in the crate.

"Don't let her out. Give her time to calm down."

"It's a girl?"

"Yes. A stray I found being chased by a pack of little boys. I caught her by buying a roast beef dinner at the town diner and using the beef to lure the poor, skinny little girl in. Then I crated her. I asked around, and it appears she'd run off, possibly from another wagon train, and made a pest of herself around the fort. Chewing on clothes hung out to dry, chasing horses. She might be a pest for you, too. But the other dogs in the fort, of which there were only a few, weren't for sale."

"So you had trouble catching her?"

Jake grinned a little, then shrugged. "Others had tried. Dogs are scarce out here. But no one objected or claimed her, so I got her."

"And the cat? Was it a stray, too?"

"No, the cat is one that belonged to the man who runs the bakery for the fort. But he had two and agreed to part with one—for a hefty price."

"I expected the prices to be high. Thank you." Beth turned from the appealing puppy to Jake and saw someone else who appealed to her. Then she noticed his sharp, assessing eyes.

"I wouldn't leave them penned up like this all the way to Oregon. But then . . . you're not going to Oregon, are you?"

He knew. It was frightening, but she wanted to tell him what was going on so badly, it was also a relief. Her stomach sinking, she said, "Jake, I-I think it's time we had a talk." She saw something in his dark eyes. He seemed relieved.

"Let's hitch the cart back to the wagon. I can tell you're worried, and I'm here to help."

Beth called out for Oscar to stop.

She worked alongside Jake in silence, then told Oscar she was done, and the creaking wagon rolled along, now pulling the loaded cart, leaving them to follow on foot.

"This way, Rutledge." The arrogant tone, the man as good as ordering Thaddeus around. Dr. Horecroft needed to be humbled, in Thaddeus's opinion. But now wasn't the time, as Thaddeus had finally managed to secure a visit with Horecroft's madwoman.

Horecroft led the way to a strange sort of place apart from the rest of the asylum, unlocking a gate in the fence, then locking it behind him. He went straight to the front door of a small wretched-looking house. It was two stories. It had been whitewashed at one time but was now mostly worn down to the gray of unpainted lumber. It must have been a home at one time, and Horecroft had come to possess it when he bought the property for his asylum.

The only windows Thaddeus saw had bars. As they approached, he heard singing. Odd, off-tuned singing. He couldn't make out the words, but they sent a chill up his spine.

They stepped inside. The singing grew louder. Mournful, he decided, and foreign. French maybe?

Horecroft went straight to an inner room. Walls had been torn out to make space for what looked like one square room of stone. An iron door with a heavy lock was the only way in. The walls were unpainted, and the rest of the house was filthy. A track in the dust of the floor showed that anyone who came here walked straight to this door and didn't turn aside.

With the keys jingling, Horecroft reached for the lock.

"I had men in here to clean her up and take out the slop bucket. She'll be unpleasant to see, so be expecting it." He twisted the key, then the knob.

The singing cut off.

A blur of motion inside the room was noticeable only because Thaddeus was taller than Horecroft.

"Doctor, you came." The voice rang with joy.

A scuffle and a thud, then Horecroft stepped inside, and Thaddeus followed him to see a woman, skeletally thin, lying on the floor.

The woman, with blond hair in snarls and her face as white as powder, huge brown eyes, made bigger because she was so terribly thin, flickered from Horecroft to Thaddeus. It was impossible to know what the woman was thinking, but she was most assuredly thinking something.

Unlike Eugenia, whose madness was cloaked in her insulting contrary opposition to everything Thaddeus believed, this woman's madness was clear as day, shining out of her face.

"You've brought me company?" The woman, trembling like an autumn leaf in a windstorm, pushed herself to her feet. Her eyes looked back at Horecroft with adoration. The woman seemed to be utterly in love with the man who was starving her. Who'd just knocked her to the floor.

Horecroft reached into his pocket and produced a chunk of bread and held it out to her.

"Oh, thank you, sir. So kind of you." She reached for the bread, snatched it out of his hand, and began to gnaw on it. Much like a starving woman would act. Or a starving animal.

Thaddeus felt only chilled contempt for the woman, for Horecroft, for this house, this whole situation.

The room had a single table in it. A single chair. A chamber pot in one corner.

"Sit down, Yvette," Horecroft demanded.

She obeyed instantly.

"This is the man I told you about, Yvette."

"The one who knows my friend Eugenia?"

"Yes. He needs to find her, and you said a few things that made me believe you have some idea where she is."

The open, adoring expression faded, and a sly look took over the wretched woman's face. "I know exactly where she's headed. I read a note she walked away from." She shoved the rest of the bread into her mouth, fast, as if to keep it from being taken away. Talking around a mouthful of bread, she looked at Thaddeus. "I will help you find her."

"Excellent." Thaddeus, revolted by the woman talking and chewing at the same time, decided Horecroft's methods had indeed worked. "Where is she?"

"I will take you to her."

"Just tell me where so I can go get her."

"No, you have to take me along."

18

I do need help, or maybe advice is a better way to put it." Beth trailed behind her last wagon. Her wagon mates had gone ahead, giving her a chance to finally talk with Jake.

She, Mama, and Oscar had discussed it over and over and agreed they had to leave in the proper way to avoid making too much of a stir among the pioneers. The O'Tooles had kept quiet about their own plans, so when the Collins family left, it might be less noticeable if the O'Tooles came along.

In this sparse land, away from the grass of the prairie, dust kicked up behind the wagon, and she liked to lag back so as not to breathe in the worst of it.

Jake swung down off his horse and walked alongside her. "Is something wrong?"

He sounded so concerned, so kind. So completely capable of handling whatever troubles she had.

She looked around, knowing the women and children from every wagon were mostly walking. She didn't want anyone to overhear her. As always, she didn't want her actions to draw any more attention than was necessary. "My family is leaving the wagon train in about four days."

Jake's hand shot out and grabbed her arm to stop her and turn her to face him. "I figured that had to be it when you asked me to buy such things as chickens. They won't live long crated up. What's going on?"

She had no intention of telling him what was really going on. The less anyone knew, the better. Yet she wanted it all to be easy when they turned aside, and that wouldn't happen if it came as a complete surprise. "The main thing you need to know is that we have always, from the beginning, planned this. Oscar's family . . ." She cleared her throat, thinking fast. "That is, most of our family grew up out here. Not me. I was born back east."

She hoped that covered for her slip, talking of Oscar's family as if she weren't part of it.

"For reasons of our own safety," Beth went on, "we needed to leave the east and hopefully leave no trail behind us. We have an enemy back there. The reason we joined the wagon train late—me, Ginny, Kat, and Sebastian—is because we were doing our best to disguise ourselves, and that went all the way down to talking differently and dressing differently than we normally would. Taking the train would have been dangerous. Our enemy has a long reach and could keep watch of train stations and steamboats. He could send wires and get ahead of us no matter how fast we moved. And he could send out agents to ask questions, and even if we got ahead of them, they could track us." Not all of the boats, though. Not cattle boats. She hoped anyway.

Jake's brow lowered. "Tell me who your enemy is. I'll go straighten things out."

That teased a smile out of Beth. True hero material abided in Jake. She was really going to miss him.

Really.

"Thank you, Jake. But no. We've made our way out here but want to stay in a remote area, and Oscar knows the way. He, Joseph, and Bruce know the area and have a place in mind for us. One of the reasons we brought such a ridiculous amount with us is that we hope to go to the place we have planned and not leave it, at least not very often. So we brought with us everything we'd need. That includes chickens and pigs. Our goal is to set up and let our herd grow. To build a cabin, or maybe one big cabin would be a mistake. Maybe two smaller ones?" Beth shook her head. "We'll probably just see how the building goes and make changes later."

Jake scowled at her. "You're going to find out you need to go to town for supplies. I resupplied you at Fort Bridger, but things like flour run out. You'll want coffee. You'll need to buy fabric. Tools break and need to be replaced."

Nodding, Beth said, "That's all true, Jake, but we'll be discreet about it. I'll send Joseph and Bruce, maybe Sebastian into town. The trouble surrounds Ginny and me, but Oscar is afraid he might run into men he knows."

She and Jake had stopped walking, and the wagon was leaving them behind. But a private talk was best, so it didn't matter. They'd catch up.

"You've known from the beginning this was your goal?" Jake crossed his arms, still frowning.

"Yes. I know you've had questions about us. I appreciate your not asking them."

The wagon train ahead curved slowly around a rising trail, one wagon at a time slipping from view up the heavily wooded slope.

Beth looked into his kind eyes, so different from Father's. As strong, competent, and hardworking as him, but in all other ways so different. She had to tell him this one truth: "I'm going to miss you. Thank you for all the help and kindness you've shown to everyone on this wagon train."

The last wagon rounded the corner. Beth knew they had to get moving. Jake had his horse, but she was going to have to walk fast to catch up. And even though the way west was far safer than it used to be, it wouldn't do to be out alone.

Jake turned to study the trail. "It's time we finally have a talk."

"It is?" Beth's heart sped up. She'd noticed how handsome he was, how attractive. Maybe, while she'd been noticing him, he'd been—

"I found these in Kearney." He drew a small packet of papers out of his pocket.

"What is it?"

He unfolded the papers and turned them so she could see.

"What did you—?" Her words cut off as she began to cough. Still almost strangling, she clawed at the papers. The top one showed a picture of her. A wanted poster with her picture on it. Not a sketch either. A photograph. One she'd had taken when she graduated from finishing school. It read,

━━━━ **WANTED** ━━━━

Elizabeth Rutledge

$10,000 cash reward
Wanted for theft, kidnapping,
and attempted murder

───────────────────────────────

"A ten-thousand-dollar reward?"

Jake didn't speak. She saw that number and looked wildly at him. Kearney, Nebraska, was over a month ago.

"A lot of men would have seen this poster and immediately taken me into custody. Turned me over to the sheriff, collected enough money to live very comfortably, and headed on west."

Jake didn't bother to state the obvious. That he wasn't most men. "Look at all of them."

Beth didn't want to. Her hands were trembling until she fumbled to flip to the next sheet of paper. Another poster with her picture. Then another and another.

"They were all over Kearney."

Beth felt the bulk of them.

"I was relieved so few of our wagon train members went to town. I got the ones near the trading post before anyone saw them, then I walked around."

Beth was still flipping. And then she flipped over one that had Ginny's picture on it. She read, *Wanted, Eugenia Rutledge, for theft and assault.* She lifted her head and snapped, "My mama never stole anything in her life. Nor has she ever assaulted anyone."

158

"Your mama? Ginny isn't your sister—she's your mother?"

Beth nodded.

"I took down the posters. I did ask one man, a loafer who didn't seem much interested in what anyone did, who put them up."

Beth held her breath. Father wouldn't do it himself, would he? The thought that he was there, ahead of them in Kearney, well, of course he would be ahead. He'd take the train. "He's lined the entire railroad with these. Why didn't he leave any in Fort Bridger?"

Jake reached into the front pocket of his blue denim pants and pulled out another stack. "I saw them in every town I rode into. I was tempted to take them, but I was afraid whoever put them up would find out and know you, or someone helping you, had been around."

"And what did that loafer say about who put them up?" Not Father. No, he'd never do this himself. But she felt that hot breath on her neck, like she did in her dreams.

"The man said he'd met a real live Pinkerton agent. He'd heard tell of them, but he'd never seen one before."

"Just as bad as . . . as . . ." Beth continued flipping. She held a dozen posters now. And that from two towns. Father had as good as wallpapered these towns with pictures of her and Mama.

"Just as bad as what?"

"Just as bad as . . . as . . ." She looked up at him.

"Your secret is safe with me, Beth. I think this moment right here proves that, doesn't it?"

Ten thousand dollars for Beth. Another ten for her mother. Yes, he'd passed through town after town where he could have hauled them before a sheriff. At Fort Bridger he could have had the whole cavalry hold her.

"My father. Those Pinkerton agents are just as bad as my father. He kept my mother locked away for three years. I helped her escape."

"Escape from where? Was she in jail?"

A wretched mockery of a laugh escaped Beth. Mama in jail! The thought was ludicrous. "No. Let me tell more of it before I tell you that."

19

Go on." Jake fought down a dozen questions he wanted to bombard her with. Or maybe one hundred.

"Oscar, Joseph, and Bruce are brothers and old friends of my family. We agreed to all use Oscar's last name and head west. Father will never stop hunting for us. We needed a hiding place he'd never find. Oscar grew up in the West, as did Joseph and Bruce. They know the area they want to claim. It's not near where they lived before. But the three of them wandered some when their parents died, before they decided to go back east."

Beth turned to look west. "Back then, they found a place they really loved. It's a mountain valley that no man has ever trod upon. Oscar came west on the train a year ago. The rails were finished far enough that he had only a short distance to ride to find his valley. Still isolated, unclaimed. He bought it, and we're moving there. Father has no call to search for Oscar, which I hope is enough to keep us safe. I have no doubt that he will tear this country apart looking for both of us, simply because Father does not accept failure."

Beth reached out with both hands and grabbed his right forearm. "We have to keep calling Mama Ginny until the rest of the wagon train goes on without us."

"I'll remember." His arm kept her steady when she looked as if her knees wanted to buckle.

"And you said Oscar, Joseph, and Bruce. So who is Sebastian? Who is Kat?"

"Honestly," Beth said, inhaling slowly and shaking her head, "I'm not completely sure who either of them are. When Mama . . ." She punched herself in the forehead. "When *Ginny* escaped, Kat saw her slipping out and came along. We didn't know how else to handle things than to take her along. She seems to have been locked away by a cruel family just as Ginny was, and she seems sensible. Nothing about her that would deserve being locked in an asylum."

"An asylum?" Jake's eyes went wide. "That's where she was locked away? An insane asylum?"

She nodded. "And we found Sebastian wounded in Independence. He thought he was going to die from his wounds—"

Jake interrupted, "I just realized that from . . . from I'm not sure what Oscar said, but I expected two sisters. And he said someone was escorting you. I don't know if he said two, though. When three sisters showed up with a wounded man, um . . ."

"Oscar told me he tried to be very vague about any details."

"He was that, all right. When three sisters showed up,

you said it was a last-minute change of plans. Your brother and sister-in-law came along, and Sebastian had broken ribs. I wonder who was after him and why? And if they gave up. And if anyone is after Kat."

"Anyway," Beth said, "we couldn't just leave a wounded man to die. We scooped him up. I expected him to heal and, at some point, his head to clear, and then he'd find a town, hop on a train, and go somewhere else. But he's feeling fine, and he's had plenty of chances to leave the wagon train. Instead, he stuck with us. I'll give him another chance to leave when we split off. He can have one horse and the cart and enough supplies to get to Oregon, but I doubt he'll leave. My guess is he's going to settle near our land for a while until he decides to move on."

"How was Sebastian wounded?"

"He was shot. I know very little about the man except he's afraid that whoever shot him might try again, so hiding suits him. That seems to fit with our family well. If you want to try to get information out of him, be my guest." She made a rather grand gesture in the direction the wagon train had gone. "I've talked to him any number of times and still I know nothing beyond those strange things he ordered."

Jake followed her gesture with his eyes, then turned back to look at her.

Then he bent down and kissed her.

She froze.

He tilted his head slightly to the side, and his arms came around her waist as the kiss fully became a wonder and the shock eased.

Then he pulled back a bit and said, "I've been expecting

you to do something, though I couldn't quite figure out what. But turning away from the wagon train might be a good idea. I will admit that I had hopes for us."

Beth, her eyes wide, asked, "You had hopes? For us?"

"Yes. This is my last time making the journey back and forth across this great land. With the railroad open, wagon trains will soon be a thing of the past. Oh, a few more will go, I'm sure, but it's not a great job anymore. The supply of wagon train scouts will far exceed the demand. I had planned to find where you settled and come calling."

Beth didn't respond. Instead, she kept taking long glances at his lips. So he kissed her again. Longer, deeper. Her arms went around his neck. He pulled her close. No words were necessary.

She turned her head aside only a bit and slid her arms down from his neck to rest her palms on his face. "It's been so long since I've had any hopes. My only hope, in fact, was to find a good enough place to hide."

He pulled her close again. No kiss this time. He just held her.

"Jake, I have an idea."

He looked down into her eyes. "I have one, too." Wouldn't it be a wonder if their ideas were the same? "You go first."

"When we turn aside from the wagon train to head for this mountain valley, come with us. Stay with us in that valley for a time. We can get to know each other. See where our hopes lead us." She paused and smiled. "Was that your idea, too?"

"Nope."

And the hope faded. She couldn't say it died. There had been some sweet kisses after all. "Then what is your idea?"

"Marry me."

"D-don't you think this is rather sudden?"

"My ma used to say, 'Take too much time, and time will take you.'"

"I'm not sure what that means, but somehow it sounds very wise."

"The truth is we've been getting to know each other for months. Now, with thoughts of making a life together, it might be better to spend more time getting to know each other in a different way. But it sounds to me like you're not interested in going to town very often. Once we leave the wagon train and Parson McDaniels, towns are few and far between. Many of them have no parson or even a justice of the peace to perform a wedding ceremony."

"Getting married later could be difficult," she agreed.

Nodding, Jake said, "I've walked alongside you, watched how hard you work, all of you, and I think you're a fine family—even if you're not quite related. You're a woman I admire and respect. And I am powerfully drawn to you. I know enough to be sure I'd like to work at your side, join my life with yours." He added quietly, "Once you're married, you're beyond your father's reach. Your ma— that is, Ginny—is still in danger, but he can't come and press his will on you with the rights of a father. Not if you're a married woman."

"How can we make Mama safe?" She asked it more of herself than of Jake.

"Will you marry me, Elizabeth?"

She moved as if by reflex and pressed her fingers to his lips. "Please, call me Beth."

He smiled behind her hand, then nodded.

"Yes, Jake. I'll marry you."

He gently pulled her fingers away. Their eyes met. He thought how different they were. He was untidy and wore the clothes of a westerner. She, for all her disguise, had a polish about her that matched the sound of her voice.

Both had skin tanned from the long days in the summer sun.

But his hair had grown overly long. He combed it with his fingers and kept it out of his eyes with his Stetson.

Unlike most of the men heading west, Jake had kept his face shaved. His eyes were dark. Hers a sparkling blue and so full of hope, a different look than he'd ever seen in her eyes before, and the look held. The moments passed.

A gentle breeze blew around them. The scent of pine trees wafted in the air. There were mountains rising all around. A wonderful land. A wonderful moment. A wonderful future.

This time she moved first. She stretched up and kissed him. He drew her close, held her tight.

Her arms wrapped around his neck. Her fingers touched his hair. When the kiss ended, after far too long and not nearly long enough, he whispered, "Let's catch up to the wagon train and tell your family what we've decided. Then we'll see about Parson McDaniels performing a wedding."

"I'll have to tell Dakota I'll be riding off. We've talked of quitting the wagon trains together. I claimed a homestead last fall and lived in it over the winter to start my years to prove up. I'll lose that. But better to lose my homestead than lose you. He'd talked of claiming property near me. I'll have to tell him my plans have changed." He looked down at her, deep into her eyes. "We'll leave—" he cleared his throat—"um . . . *married things* for a time after we've separated from the wagon train."

Talk of *married things* made pink rise in her cheeks. He enjoyed the pretty color under her tan.

"Let's go tell my family that you're joining us," she said.

Jake smiled, then drew her toward his horse. "Come ride with me. We let the wagon train get so far ahead that catching up with them on foot would take a while."

He swung up and then bent down to lift her into the saddle. Her slender waist was one of the nicest things he'd ever held. She sat sideways in front of him on his lap.

Their eyes met as they rode toward the wagon train.

"Beth, I . . . uh, that is . . . I've lived a strange life for a long time. I'm used to having no family. Mine is either dead or far-flung. My ma is in North Dakota. She's buried two husbands and had a third last I heard and had young'uns with each of them. I don't know where any of my brothers and sisters are, nor even how many I have. And the way I've lived, well, I help these folks, get to know them, then they leave and I never see them again. I'm out of practice at feeling a strong connection to anyone. I may need help learning how to belong to a family again."

She gave him a kindhearted smile. "I've been more alone than you can imagine the last few years. I may need help, too. But I think we'll enjoy learning to be a family together."

He leaned down and kissed her as they rode along. When the wagon train came into sight, they were both sitting up straight in the saddle with no sign of any carrying on they'd been doing.

⁓

"She won't say another thing." Thaddeus crashed into Horecroft's office, furious. That woman, who'd eaten little but bread and broth for two months, and precious little of that, had a spine that was made strong by her madness. She sang in that odd off-key way of hers. She watched Thaddeus with those huge brown eyes, and she said, "I will take you to her."

"Her mind is broken." Horecroft tossed his quill pen onto his desktop.

Thaddeus went to see Yvette weekly, waiting for her to break. Waiting for her to say something else. She'd stopped acting like she was in love with Horecroft and switched that adoration to Thaddeus. It would have embarrassed him if he took time for such foolishness. He rarely bothered with anger either, but Yvette did tend to infuriate him.

"I'm taking her out of here. I feel certain she knows something, and I want to see where she takes me."

Horecroft glared at Thaddeus with sharp eyes. "You can't trust her. She'll need to be bound. She'll need guards. She might be dangerous—to herself or to you."

"Get me a straitjacket then. I'll arrange the guards. I'll tell her we're taking her and see where she says to go. If she says we need to fly to the moon, I'll know she's been a raving lunatic with no idea where Eugenia is. All this time wasted."

But it wasn't wasted, not really, because his Pinkertons were searching.

"I've got straitjackets on hand. She can leave with you whenever you're ready."

"I have to settle a few affairs before I leave. But I hope to head for . . . well, for wherever a madwoman tells me to head, and within the week." Thaddeus caught the smirk on Horecroft's face as he pivoted and stormed out.

He slammed the door behind him with plans that would wipe that smile off Horecroft's face for good. But not yet. He had an errant wife to find. And when he found her, he had a much more secure, and much less comfortable, asylum that would take her.

"We're taking the train?" Thaddeus hadn't put his mad companion in a straitjacket. She wasn't going to look like a prisoner. Horecroft advised as much. But the woman seemed eager to stay close to Thaddeus.

In point of fact, she seemed to think he was her husband, and she was devoted to him. He'd learned quickly not to touch her. She tended to scream. He'd only made that mistake once when he'd tried to hand her up into his carriage as they left the asylum grounds.

"Yes, we're headed west," he replied. "Taking the train seems like the best way to travel there. The Transcontinental Railroad was completed just this spring. We'll take my private car. We'll have to leave it behind in Council Bluffs, Iowa. There's no way across the Missouri. But I'll wire ahead, and the Omaha station can arrange comfortable cars for us to continue on."

So Eugenia was headed for the West. Oregon. Yvette had read a letter passed to Eugenia secretly. It seemed there were attendants at the asylum who could be bribed into passing notes.

Eugenia had foolishly left it out, though how Yvette had seen it was suspect. She might have gotten through a locked door somehow and rifled through Eugenia's things.

It was disgusting to think of Eugenia's possessions being searched by this strange woman. But then, if Eugenia hadn't been willing to face such indignities, she should have kept her senses, and kept her mouth under better control and handed over hers and Elizabeth's trust funds.

That she couldn't control her words or obey her husband was all the evidence Thaddeus and Horecroft had needed to be satisfied that Eugenia was insane.

Thaddeus had needed to make extensive arrangements to be gone for so long, but Yvette wouldn't tell him the whole of what she knew. She insisted she'd *take* Thaddeus to Eugenia, and she'd only go if he went along.

His Pinkertons had been searching for months along the railroad line, and he had all their accumulated notes with him. Blayd was coming along, and a few of his crew besides in case Thaddeus needed assistance in restraining his wife and child.

That Elizabeth had plans to go west made sense.

Each bit of the information he'd amassed added up to a woman learning skills that fit with the West. Or perhaps a woman learning to take care of herself. He couldn't quite make sense of all of it. But Yvette said to go west, so they would, even though the Pinkertons had no luck scouring the train stations and papering the western towns with wanted posters.

It took him a week, but now it was time to set out. He

had his private car hooked up to a line of cars. He had a second car for Blayd and his men. A third car for dining that was outfitted with sleeping quarters for his cook and a maid. A fourth for luggage and to haul along the carriage he would need outside of Chicago, and a fifth with horses to draw the carriage, as well as to haul feed for the horses.

Yvette was thrilled with the whole situation and hinted that she knew much more.

Thaddeus was tempted to beat what she knew out of her. But Horecroft hinted that it'd already been tried. All she'd done when Horecroft, in his words, "demanded she talk," was to curl up in a ball on the floor.

Horecroft said harsh treatment made her go away inside her head, and he'd had no luck breaching that hiding place she'd created inside herself.

Now she had turned her love away from Horecroft and wouldn't even acknowledge his existence. Instead, she'd turned her devotion to Thaddeus. Except she hated being touched, which suited Thaddeus fine. He had no desire to touch the woman. For now, he'd go along with her wild notions.

So they headed west. Whatever Elizabeth and Eugenia thought of their great plan to run away, he'd find them, and he'd make them sorry they'd been so foolish as to ever dare to defy him.

20

Ginny clamped her mouth shut and kept it shut. She knew this was largely a surge of pure snobbery, and she of all women, an escapee from an insane asylum, had no claim on believing herself above others.

But never in her life had she envisioned her daughter getting married to a rough western cowboy. Honesty forced her to admit that she, Ginny, had married a man exactly to suit her parents.

And Thaddeus had been a disaster almost from the first.

Her parents had seen his true colors in time to change their will, lock all their money away from Thaddeus, who had plenty of his own, and leave the bulk of it in an unbreakable trust, very carefully invested, to Beth.

There were details in that will that allowed Thaddeus some access to Ginny's money, but it was very limited. Thaddeus had tried everything short of beating her to get the money from Beth. In fact, being locked up was, she fully knew, punishment for defying her husband. He was fond of saying he knew so much better than she did about how to handle money. Nothing he ever said, no cruel insults, no financial deprivations he imposed on Ginny forced her hand to turn over Beth's money or most of her own.

Ginny had never told Beth that the asylum was punishment for not turning over Beth's money, because Beth would have given every penny of her money to Thaddeus to buy Ginny's freedom.

Climbing up on the wagon box, she sat beside Oscar and didn't talk about the wedding. Oscar was delighted to have Jake along to help them tear a living out of a wild land. Ginny was too, mostly. But it wasn't how she'd envisioned her daughter's future.

"We're almost to the turnoff, my old friend."

Oscar turned and smiled at her. He had a full beard now, after months on the trail. But it wasn't so bushy she couldn't see him smile. There wasn't a trace of gray in the beard or his hair. He wore good-quality clothes, though they were of course western in style. Blue denim trousers. A broadcloth shirt—he had a black one on today. She'd seen three shirts, and he wore one for a week or so, then traded them off. A black vest. He wore a gun on his hip and a Stetson on his head. His hair hadn't been trimmed in a long time. A barber was one of many things they'd had to give up because they didn't want to risk going into a town.

"We've almost made it, Ginny. I'm starting to believe."

Ginny didn't know if she'd ever fully believe, but she wanted to so badly. "Can you imagine Beth and Jake getting married? I had no idea such a thing was in the air."

"Nor did I. But he's a fine man. He'll make her a good husband, and having him along will make a big difference in how successful we are. He knows the West."

"So do you. Joseph and Bruce grew up out here, too. And I know how to obey orders."

He grinned. "Never noticed you being an obedient woman particularly, but if you say so, that's good enough for me."

"I'll take orders if they're good ones. And since I have no idea how to live out here, I'm just going to have to trust the rest of you. I'll do as I'm told and learn as fast as I can." She gazed across the expanse of grass to the north as the wagon train rolled along.

Beth and Jake were even now talking with Dakota and the parson. They'd wed tonight and reach the turnoff before the end of the day tomorrow.

"My daughter is getting married." The bite of tears had her stop talking before she made a cake of herself.

Oscar got free of the reins with his right hand and patted her left. "It's a good thing. She's marrying a man who'll treat her well."

"And once she's married, she's safe, assuming Thaddeus doesn't have Jake killed."

"Not an easy man to kill. I'd almost like to see Rutledge try."

Ginny would not.

"As a married woman, Beth is free of her father for good. He can't compel her to come with him or force her into marrying a man of his choosing."

"He had Lindhurst lined up. The man wanted her."

"Gerald Lindhurst?" Ginny pictured the young man.

Handsome enough, but a shallow, money-wasting, gambling, drinking fool. As the son of one of the scions of Chicago industry, his money-wasting could go on a long time, so he'd be no fit husband for Beth.

"Nope, the old man, Walter."

Ginny gasped. "No! That horrid man? No." Then she thought again. "What happened to his wife?" Constance Lindhurst had been her good friend, but of course she hadn't seen Constance since she'd been locked away.

"Mrs. Lindhurst died a year ago. She fell off her horse while she was out riding with Walter."

Ginny probably should keep her mouth shut, but she knew. "They never went anywhere together. They lived almost completely separate lives. He killed her."

"There were some who suspected just that, but no one dared to accuse him out loud. And the police didn't much question him, leastways that's what I heard. I've been gone from Chicago for the last three years."

"Since Thaddeus locked me away."

"Beth and I concocted our plan, and it included a lot of work that took me away. We had to make some solid plans if we were to get you out and keep you out."

Silence stretched as the cattle plodded along. The Angus had lost weight. Their horses were gaunt. Ginny understood why people brought so little west. And if their group was going all the way through the mountains, they'd have to get rid of many things.

But their journey was almost over. And they hadn't brought luxuries. They'd brought things they'd need if they never went to town again.

The loneliness of that hurt her heart. She used to be

a social woman with many longtime friends. Those days were gone forever. She especially hurt for Beth to be driven to such an isolated life.

Once she was married, Thaddeus wouldn't be able to take Beth away, but he'd be able to take Ginny. And if he got her in his clutches, he'd make her regret every moment of her defiance.

She certainly regretted every moment of her marriage, except for her beloved daughter. To wish away her marriage meant wishing away her daughter, and Beth was the light of her life.

Ginny running and hiding ought to be enough for Thaddeus. He wanted to be rid of her, and now he was. But he wasn't a man who accepted defeat in any form. It was the secret to his success. It was also the thing that made him a terrible human being, and that most definitely included as a husband and a father.

She'd never really understood the man. So cold. So ambitious. So wealthy yet never satisfied, as if what lived inside him was nothing but hunger. Winning, earning, owning the finest homes, the finest horses, the finest clothes—it was all a game to him. A showing of his power and pride.

She had been his pride at first. She knew her own father's wealth and knew she'd been very sought after as a debutante. Thaddeus had chased her with such relentlessness, Ginny thought it was love. It was only after they were married that she realized he was in the market for a wife and considered her the best.

Yet his pride in marrying her had seemed like love for a while. His insatiable hunger for the finest of everything included her, and that was flattering. And then when he possessed her, she found out he aimed to control what he possessed—including her and Beth. That strange, relentless hunger for control had driven them to having to run for their lives. And it was going to drive them all into hiding forever. Or maybe only for as long as Ginny lived.

A cold satisfaction reminded her that, no, not as long as *she* lived, But as long as *Thaddeus* lived. Until then, all of them needed to find a place in this world that didn't roll along on wheels.

A true hiding place.

21

Before supper they had a wedding.

Jake stood there saying goodbye to the pretty homestead he'd built on and lived on. He'd told Dakota about it, and maybe Dakota would step in and work it, take it over. Jake had given him a note with permission to do just that. Dakota would have to start over and do his own five years, but he could have the cabin.

A pang in Jake's heart to give up on his land was quickly squelched; it was still there, but he wasn't going to tell Beth about it. The trade, to marry a woman like Beth, was more than even.

Jake didn't want Beth to say her name, but he could think of no way around it. Still, Parson McDaniels arched one brow but otherwise carried on when Beth quietly said a different name than the one she'd gone by during their journey.

Beth took Jake's elbow, turned him to face forward, and the parson took his place. The members of their wagon train stood in a half circle around them to watch. Most everyone was grinning.

"Dearly beloved, we are gathered here today . . ."

The familiar, beautiful words caused a lump to form in Jake's throat as he focused on his soon-to-be wife and the solemn vows he was taking.

"Do you, Jake Holt, take Elizabeth Rutledge to be your lawfully wedded wife? To have and to hold . . ."

Jake listened with his heart and soul wide open, taking in the moment, determined not to be distracted by anything. "I do." He made his promise before God and man, and he truly felt it and believed every word. It struck him that this was the most important moment of his life, a turning point. And he intended to make this turn and do everything in his power to start this new journey with Beth and build a fine life together, dedicated to each other and to God.

The parson asked the same promises of Beth. She turned her head when her time came to speak and smiled at Jake. It was close to blinding, and he liked thinking such a special woman, in the midst of such upheaval in her life, was doing something that made her happy.

"I do." She had her hand through his elbow, and for just a moment she held his arm tighter, squeezed, and leaned just a bit closer to him.

The parson then called on Jake to honor Beth, to love her as Christ loved the Church. These were vows he made out loud, yet he also held them deep in his heart. Vows he was proud to make, eager to make.

Judging by the way Beth hugged his arm, he thought

she was making her promises fully and without hesitation, too.

Jake sensed God right there with them.

Bedelia McDaniels sang "Rock of Ages." The parson finished with a prayer.

The ceremony didn't take long at all. Jake shook the man's hand afterward. He noticed Beth shake hands, too, then saw her slip something to the parson. A coin. That probably should have been his job, but it hadn't occurred to him.

Next came pats on the back and words of congratulations. Then the wagon train rolled on just as it always had. Jake sat beside Beth on the high wagon seat of her lead wagon. He'd told Dakota he was leaving the wagon train. Dakota had been subdued but agreeable.

They had good men on this train, hard workers. They'd be fine, and Dakota agreed they would be, but Jake sensed that Dakota wasn't happy about losing his saddle partner.

"Beth, how long before we turn aside from the wagon train?"

She described the land she'd bought and her understanding of where it was. "Oscar knows the details, but he said tomorrow morning most likely. We'll stay with the others until we reach a cutoff. From there we'll head north into Idaho Territory. There's a big lake there, not as big as Salt Lake but nice enough."

"That's Bear Lake. The Oregon Trail passes by it."

"That's where we turn. He said our land is a fair distance farther north, but not all the way into the wildest mountains." She smiled at him. "But maybe wild enough.

Do you know the area? Are there wild mountains where we're going?"

"There most certainly are. I've made this trip with a wagon train many times. I rode back on horseback with other scouts and trappers. It's a much faster trip home, and we're always pushing to beat the winter. But a few times I've gone with men who wanted to wander. I've seen some majestic peaks for a fact."

"I'm not sure how far we're going, but Oscar talked about the Snake River Valley. He said it's a beautiful, fertile stretch, although we'll be going north of it. It's a bit too settled for us to stay in that area. Oscar found us a high mountain valley with shelter for our cattle to survive the winter."

"I look forward to seeing it," Jake said. "Now, we've talked about our plans for the wagons. What about us, Beth? Are we going to have our own home, or is the whole Collins family going to build one large structure?"

Beth smiled and gave a shrug. "I have no idea. I hadn't pictured us all in one structure. I figured Oscar would be in a cabin with his brothers, myself in a cabin with Mother and, well, Kat, and Sebastian would stay with Oscar."

"How about me, Beth? Do I get to stay in this house of women you're thinking to build?"

A pink blush rose on Beth's face. Jake couldn't take his eyes off her, as it apparently struck her that, yes, she should live with her husband.

"I, um, that is, we . . . I mean, yes, of course you'll stay in my cabin. *Our* cabin." Her blush deepened with every word. She had her eyes fixed on her hands, which clung to the reins. Then she glanced up quickly at him, then looked away.

"Beth, look at me." His heart sped up as his courageous little wife, who'd faced so many dangers to get her mother to safety, turned shy. And she'd given up a fortune to do it. But now she turned into a timid, blushing . . . well, a blushing bride. That no doubt explained everything.

She seemed to have to force her chin to lift. Her gaze met his. She didn't look away. "Yes, Jake?"

The very image of an obedient woman. Jake found it very alluring and knew he'd better get that part of himself under control. "You know what it means to be husband and wife, don't you?"

"I-I . . . well, maybe. No. No, I don't know what it means exactly. I think Mama said she'd need to talk to me."

"I think it would be best if we put off the more . . . personal things of marriage until we reach our destination." He didn't want to, but he wanted his wife to himself when the time came.

Her sigh of relief pricked his feelings, and he clamped his mouth shut. It didn't matter what expression he made because she was back to studying her hands.

"So there's time for a talk with Ginny. But I would very much like to lie next to you in the night. Would that be agreeable to you? Maybe a good-night kiss?"

She looked like he'd ordered a stay of execution. "That sounds fine, Jake. Yes, I think it would be wise to wait." She looked up again and met his eyes, her cheeks blazing. She spoke the next words as if they were torn out of her. "I may not understand exactly what's involved in a wedding night, but I know I want to be fully married to you—in all ways. I hope we reach our destination soon." She smiled, and his heart sped up again.

"I hope for that, too. Let's go talk to Dakota, make sure he remembers we're turning off in the morning. I've already spoken to him, and he's sorry to lose me, but our train has almost made it through. He's a knowing man. He'll make it."

She nodded.

When they neared their night's stopping place, Jake left Beth driving the wagon. Ginny, walking along as usual, climbed up and rode beside her. It was easy now to recognize a mother's love in Ginny's eyes.

And he saw tears.

Beth drew Ginny into a hug so tight, he wasn't sure how either of them could breathe. When the hug ended, Beth looked at Jake.

"I'm going to talk to Dakota." He tugged the brim of his Stetson. Both women smiled at him, and he found he liked the idea of having a ma again. He galloped along the line of wagons until he caught up with Dakota.

The two of them rode side by side at the front of the train, looking ahead to the daunting Rocky Mountains.

"This has been a hard trip across the countryside." He thought again of Shay O'Toole. "I'm glad to be giving it up." Jake rested his gloved hand on the top of his hat and settled it more firmly on his head. "You'll be taking this crew on alone. You shouldn't have any trouble."

"There's always trouble, but I can handle it. Some tough men in this group."

Several of them had taken to riding far afield to hunt for fresh meat. Dakota was right. They were tough.

"We'll get through."

"I made my decision to turn aside after I was sure there were men enough to handle it. We'll head north around Bear Lake."

Dakota nodded. "Been a pleasure riding with you. I reckon the wagon trains are about done. Makes a man feel a mite foolish to ride beside a train track and see that iron horse race on past, leaving us far behind. I plan on getting this group to Oregon and then I might come calling on you, Jake. I suspect there's land enough near you, and I like the idea of living near a friend."

"My homestead is there if you decide to move in on it. It's got a nice cabin. Another set of strong hands would make everything go more smoothly, I reckon. And you could hop on the train part of the way, crawl through the mountains before the snows come. I'd like having you, Dakota, but I can't tell you where we'll end up." He could have told Dakota more, but he hesitated, thinking of Beth's worries about her pa finding her. He wouldn't say more without talking it over with her.

"I can read sign, so I can find you if I decide to hunt. Maybe I can scare up a herd of cattle and head north of Bear Lake, build up my own place."

A loud crack sounded from behind them, and they turned to see a wagon cover flapping loose. Jake said, "I'll get it."

He turned to help, and Dakota went along just in case

he was needed, too. The two of them and Parson Mc-Daniels, who drove the lead wagon, got the cover tied back down while Bedelia kept driving forward without stopping.

Dakota was right. They'd get through.

22

Jake sat at the Collins family fire that night. He made a point of sharing a meal with Dakota as a rule, and then the two of them would usually sleep under the open sky. They had their saddles to use for pillows and bedrolls that served as blankets. On rainy nights, someone would make room and give them shelter.

Tonight was different. Tonight, Jake would still sleep outside, but he'd sleep near his wife. His lawfully wedded wife.

He'd left it to Beth to explain that they didn't plan to act married quite yet. Yet he couldn't bring himself to sleep so far from her side. The fire, the family, his wife, it all made him smile. Beth sat down beside him and leaned her shoulder into his. "What's making you smile?"

He took her hand in his. The campfires were spread out to the extent it was possible, but it was a fairly small group.

"Was Dakota upset that you're leaving your job?"

"He took the news without much fuss. I've been on a few trains where the pioneers weren't suited to hardship.

A few men didn't want to do their share or had a taste for whiskey. A few women liked to complain about the harsh conditions. But this is a good group. They'll all throw in to take up any slack left in the rope when I leave. And with your three wagons and the O'Tooles turning aside, it's not such a big group to watch over. He'll get the train through, I'm sure of it."

Beth nodded and leaned against him again.

The chores were done. The stew, made with a nice-sized elk roast, was bubbling and would be done as soon as the meat, potatoes, and carrots were tender. Ginny had done the cooking. She who had lived all her life with a cook and housekeeper, maids and butlers, was learning under the guiding hand of Fiona O'Toole.

They'd eat, wash up the dishes, bring in their animals, set up their tents, and this day, their last day with the wagon train, would be over. Tomorrow would begin their own personal journey home.

"I haven't had a home in so many years, I can't remember what it was like."

"I lived in a luxurious home with two parents and plenty of money and food. I'm not going to miss it one bit. Love doesn't always come along with your home."

Jake nodded. "My folks were a loving couple. I always knew I had that."

"Tell me about them. Are they still living? Do you want to visit them? I'm not sure how that could be arranged."

"I mentioned my pa passed on. He lived a hard life, and there was nothing comfortable about it. Probably shortened his life. Ma's on her third husband; she buried a second one just before I left home."

"Where did you live?"

"I grew up in North Dakota, raised mostly by Ma's second husband. I hired on with some fur traders and floated down the Missouri with them as a hired man. Then I rode west with my first wagon train when I was thirteen. I was good in the woods and a crack shot, so I could carry my weight."

"Thirteen? You were on your own so young."

"There wasn't much money or food at home, so finding my own way in the world was a good thing. I came back from my first trip west and found Ma alone with two youngsters and her second husband off fighting in the Civil War for the South."

Beth patted his forearm. He had his sleeves rolled up to his elbows, and he liked the way it felt to have her hand on his arm. "From North Dakota?"

"Her husband was from Missouri, a slave state. So I reckon it made sense he'd fight with the South. But I had no liking for slavery and was too young, though there were boys my age who signed up. Her second husband died in the war. Ma's third husband has a homestead in North Dakota. I never met him and haven't seen Ma since she remarried."

"She lost two husbands?"

"Yep, and my little brother, Billy."

"So much loss. So much grief."

"It's a hard world for a fact, Mrs. Holt. We'll hope for better things for ourselves. Good health and a long life." He rested his hand over hers, and enjoyed the life and warmth of her.

"I'm excited to finally stop moving. I'm looking forward to having a place in this world I can call home." He looked down at her. "And a wife in that home. I want us to build our own cabin. Your ma . . ." He lifted his eyes and saw Ginny watching them. Listening. He smiled. "Ginny can live with us. Kat too, I reckon. Two women can't be living alone. We'll build a cabin that's a good enough size we can be comfortable, but not so large we'd struggle to heat it."

"The nights are already cool up here. Will we have time to get a cabin built?"

Oscar joined their conversation. "Don't you worry none about the cabin. I already figured it'd be one for the men and one for the women, close enough for protection. Now with Jake in the same house with the women, I'll feel even better about things, and we can spread out a bit."

Jake nodded. He looked at the Collins brothers. As alike as three peas in a pod. Stocky, dark-haired. Calm, intelligent men who struck him as capable and hardworking. Good men to have at his side.

"We can round up some mustangs," Jake said. "Maybe find cattle that've gone wild. We'll get a good start with the livestock you have at hand and build a herd. I usually high-tailed it back to the east to catch on with another wagon train, as fast as we got to Oregon. But twice I wintered out there. I've worked a cattle ranch. Busted some broncos. We can make a nice life out here."

Oscar opened his mouth, then closed it. Jake could see the man had a lot to say but didn't want to say any of it. He had a flicker of regret that he'd told Dakota even the little bit about where they were going.

Moving briskly, Ginny tasted the stew. "It's ready. Let's eat and then get settled for the night."

After finishing their meal, they went to fetch the cattle and horses to spend the night inside the wagon-train circle.

23

Jake?" Beth glanced behind her and Jake. They were leading the last two of their saddle horses back from the stream.

Walking side by side as the sun dipped behind the mountains that loomed ahead of them, Beth heard the hoot of an owl cutting through the quiet night. Two coyotes exchanged howls. A third joined them. They sounded so close, it made a chill rush up her spine.

Jake rubbed her arm. "Are you cold?"

She stopped leading the horse and moved so she was close to Jake, facing him. The horses kept going for a few steps until she and Jake stood between them. It felt private. She was confused about all she felt for her husband after such an unexpected change in her plans. She decided to stop and enjoy the present moment, to forget the world and all its troubles and just be with Jake.

And give him some bad news.

"No, it's a lovely night," she answered. She swallowed, then added, "After a lovely day."

Jake's eyes flickered to her lips, and he leaned down and kissed her.

She let herself enjoy the honorable kiss of the only man who would ever be given leave to kiss her. It made what she needed to tell him even harder.

Once the kiss ended, she whispered, "Jake, I know we talked about sleeping side by side, but Ginny—"

He pressed his finger to her lips, cutting off her words. It was a gentle touch, but she had to wonder if he was going to be upset. They'd talked about this. She'd agreed to sleep beside him.

"I realize you need to sleep next to your ma tonight," he said.

She nodded. He watched her. She saw the shadow of disappointment in his dark eyes.

"She has nightmares. You've heard her screaming."

"I have," Jake said. "They're terrible. How do you stop them?"

"I've just learned, when she wakes me up, to immediately shake her. I don't exactly stop her from having them. I just help her escape them once they start is all."

"I want you near me, but you need to help Ginny get through the night. Waking up to her screaming is mighty upsetting."

Beth slid her arms around his waist and hugged him. "Once we turn off from the wagon train, I'll risk letting her sleep through the whimpering and moaning. Every dream she has that makes her stir might not lead to terrible nightmares, but until we split off . . ."

"Could Kat learn to help Ginny with her nightmares?"

Beth reached up and kissed him. "That's a good idea."

His sigh made her feel both wanted and needed. It lifted her spirits.

"So tonight," he went on, "we'll leave things as they are, and then maybe tomorrow night we'll try and sleep near each other. I do think we should still share a good-night kiss, though."

Beth looked past Jake's shoulder to see if they were still alone.

"No one around?" Jake had a glint in his eyes, like he wasn't overly worried about witnesses.

Beth stretched up again and kissed him. His arms went around her waist and lifted her to her tiptoes. As he tilted his head, the kiss deepened, turned warmer. Her arms wrapped around his neck.

She lost track of things for a bit.

A horse swatted at a fly with its tail and whipped Beth enough to let go of Jake. She smiled at him. He smiled back.

"Let's set up camp now." He took her hand, and they led the horses to green grass. They'd stake them out to graze until the camp was ready for the night ahead.

It wouldn't be the wedding night of Beth's dreams, but it was still enough to warm her heart.

Jake slept outside. He was used to it, and the three tents were full enough, the night fine enough, that he didn't need shelter. When his turn came to stand watch in the late August night, snow sifted down on him. It wasn't alarming—he'd been snowed on plenty of times when on high ground—but it was a reminder. They needed to get settled, build a cabin with a solid roof, and do it without delay.

If they were turning off tomorrow, the Collins and Rutledge clans would be stopping in Idaho with its cold winters, beautiful river valleys, and towering mountains. Jake trusted Oscar, and it sounded as though he was the only one who knew just where they were headed. Jake suspected the man had chosen well.

Thinking of the last kiss he'd shared with Beth made him lonely for her. Sleep eluded him. He stared at the stars, so bright it was like someone had cast bucketsful of diamonds into the sky.

The cattle and horses slept, some standing, some lying down. A few grazed quietly on what grass was left within their circle. The animals were gaunted but not dangerously so. They were the first wagon train to have rolled out of Independence this spring, so the trail wasn't grazed down. But this early on, the spring grass had been young and sparse.

Long days of hard work had worn them all down. If the Collins family wasn't turning aside before they reached the steep mountains, he'd've told them they would have to lighten their load. Instead, he thought they'd make it without throwing things away, and since Beth intended to hide, they'd probably chosen carefully and needed to keep what they had if possible.

He heard a wolf howling in the night. The lonely sound made a shiver run up his spine, spooking him a little. Just enough to make him careful around the predators when he had cattle to watch, especially that young calf.

It reminded him of the wanted poster and the dangerous man pursuing his wife and mother-in-law. Most likely someone was hunting Kat, too. Jake didn't know, and neither did any of them. And maybe the pursuit wasn't as intense as that of Beth's pa, but that didn't mean if they found her, she wouldn't be hauled away.

And what of Sebastian? Who was he? Why did he just tag along west with them? What man let himself be attached to a family the way Sebastian had? A man who was leaving something behind maybe. A man who was hiding from someone or from something . . .

Beth and Oscar hadn't planned for such a crowd—including him.

Yes, he was another mouth to feed, but he could feed himself and hoped to lift burdens rather than add to them.

The wolf howled again. Jake knew wild places, and the wolf was a fair distance away. A dangerous animal if a man wasn't careful. But Jake knew the most dangerous predators in the world didn't have four legs. They had two.

Thaddeus's temper turned to ice. He turned to look at the madwoman beside him, who smiled at him with pure adoration.

He wanted to slap her face. He was good at covering his thoughts and did his best to do that now, but the cold fury that boiled within him when he dealt with Yvette was unlike anything he'd felt before.

He remembered how comfortable he'd been at first with Eugenia. Yes, he'd held her in contempt right from the beginning. He recalled their wedding day, how she'd glowed with happiness as she spoke her vows—sealing her fate, and the fate of her inheritance, for a lifetime with him.

Her parents had smiled and served a delicious wedding feast. Their clothing was of the finest design, the church banked with flowers. The most powerful, influential, wealthy people in Chicago had been there, most of them associates of Eugenia's father and grandfather.

Thaddeus had considered that wise old man to be a dupe. An elderly dupe who hopefully wouldn't have long to live.

Old Grant Wyse didn't boast of his connection to the Founding Fathers, but somehow everyone knew of it. And his wife, Christina Wyse, had roots going back to the *Mayflower*. They had relatives who'd been senators and governors. They were devout Christians, honorable in all their dealings, and they had a genuine warmth that Thaddeus did his best to imitate, at least when they were watching.

Eugenia had considered Thaddeus, an up-and-coming business mogul, to be the finest catch in Chicago. He'd thought she was just as fine, so he'd let himself be caught.

She was a fool not to have noticed how calculating he'd been in marrying her. But Eugenia, most unfortunately, hadn't been a fool for long. Neither had her parents or grandparents. She'd taken exception to his membership in a church that supported slavery. He'd done business with slaveowners and profited handsomely from that. He'd accepted hefty financial earnings from men in the South who didn't want their slaves taken from them.

And he'd owned property in Chicago that housed the poorest of the poor. He never quit buying and never quit getting richer and richer. Eugenia hadn't known about those tenements, but her grandfather soon found out. He'd gone to Thaddeus and tried to convince him to improve the lot of those "hardworking, deserving poor," as Grandpa Wyse liked to call them.

Thaddeus called them peasants.

They'd rocked along poorly, he and Eugenia and her family, until the day came when she quit the church they belonged to and joined one devoted to emancipation. She'd spoken publicly about freedom for all. He'd found her public rejection of him humiliating, but he endured it because the war had begun and all the slave-owning men he'd known were losing their wealth anyway.

She'd never trusted him again, despite his efforts to convince her he now agreed with the new ways of freedom.

And he'd left those peasants to dwell in squalor because doing so made him a fortune.

Her grandparents had died, leaving a fortune to their children, of which they had six. But even divided six ways, that had added vast wealth to Eugenia's future inheritance, which of course meant it added to Thaddeus's wealth.

Her parents had just one child, Eugenia, so she'd get everything. But those two pious folks kept living and living and living. Meanwhile, he'd made his own money, and Eugenia had come in with a dowry that helped launch him into the upper echelons of Chicago society.

And now she'd run away. One of the few bits of pleasure Thaddeus found in this mess was picturing Eugenia when he got his hands on her. He thought of Walter Lindhurst and the convenient death of his wife, Constance. This might end in the same way for Thaddeus because he was fed up with his wife's defiance.

His daughter's as well.

And picturing that day, when Eugenia would regret all she'd done to him, with that smug smile of hers wiped away forever, made him endure Yvette's mad ravings.

As they sped along the rails, the mountains ahead loomed nearer. He rarely left his private train car, though he'd step outside at each stop to give his staff a few minutes to clean. He'd never been out west before, but he'd heard of San Francisco and wondered about buying up lots out there.

"Thaddeus, look at that string of wagons." Yvette pointed out the window.

Thaddeus saw the silhouette of a wagon train. What a miserable way to travel that would be. Then he saw something in Yvette's eyes, something sly as she focused on the train of covered wagons . . . and he had an idea.

Here they were speeding across the West, with Yvette claiming Eugenia and Elizabeth had gone west, and yet Thaddeus's agents had found no trace of them. He'd had them search the docks and question those working on passenger ships. They hadn't found even a hint of the presence of two wealthy women traveling together.

Was it possible? Could his pampered wife and debutante daughter have traveled that way?

He stepped up beside Yvette as the wagon train was lost, left far behind by the speeding train. "That's how they got out here, isn't it?"

Yvette gave him a startled look, then turned away.

He grabbed her arm and spun her back to face him,

and she screamed. He drew back a fist to shut her mouth, thinking of how long she'd known this and the time he'd wasted.

Blayd rushed into the room.

Thaddeus wasn't worried about what Blayd thought. The man thought what Thaddeus ordered him to think. But behind Blayd came the chef, carrying a butcher knife. Obviously ready for a fight.

It was a heroic instinct for the man, but since the one he'd need to fight was Thaddeus, the chef decided to relax his hand and let Yvette back away.

It didn't matter.

Thaddeus had seen her startled look. He had his answer. And now he had a whole host of other questions, none of which required Yvette's help.

Had any wagon trains reached Oregon yet? Did they all go to Oregon? Of course, he'd heard of the Oregon Trail, but there was the Mormon Trail, too, and the California Trail. Which one was his wife traveling on?

And how long did it take? It was early September, but he thought it took an entire season to cross the prairie. He knew they usually left in early spring, but might he beat the first train across the country?

Maybe if the trains all followed a similar route until they divided to head to Utah or San Francisco or Oregon, he could find where they split off and be standing there, watching each wagon train roll through, ready to greet his runaway wife.

24

Beth, riding beside Fiona on the O'Toole wagon, saw the huge pine tree about a hundred yards ahead. It was just as Oscar had described it. The top lay on the ground, dead; the bottom, a massive trunk bristling with branches, looked as if it were still fighting for life after something, lightning most likely, had tried to knock it down.

She'd been watching for it. So had Jake. She waved at him. He was watching for her signal and gave her one firm nod before turning back to talk to a young couple who had a spot near the middle of the train.

Beth watched the wagon train rolling along ahead of her. They were on a narrow, steeply uphill trail that wound between rocks and trees. The way was getting harder, the climb steeper. Beth had already seen things that had been tossed off earlier wagon trains, some of the objects years old. If she was going on toward the majestic mountains ahead, she'd be lightening her load, too.

But she wasn't going on.

One by one, the trail ahead swallowed up each wagon. When the wagon ahead of her disappeared from view, she drew her wagon to a halt just as Oscar had instructed.

Driving the lead wagon of the four wasn't much use when she didn't know where they were going.

Oscar came to climb up the wagon box and sit beside her.

She headed to the back of the four wagons and found Sebastian walking alongside the one nervous Angus cow. They'd taken to having someone with her most all the time. Strange, jumpy critter.

"Sebastian, it's time." The Collinses' wagons and the O'Tooles' wagon were all stopped now. The Angus seemed happier when receiving attention, so she went to stand at its head and scratch the animal between the ears while Sebastian patted the cow's neck.

Kat came up to them carrying the puppy. It yipped and wiggled, but she held on tight. They didn't want any of their precious animals taking off alone into the wilderness. "I've told you, Beth, I'm coming along. Now that I've got the order, I arranged with Jake. I need time and a safe place to be. I'll do my share of the work. Besides, I have nowhere to go. If I can just stay with you for a time, I promise you won't regret it."

Beth saw a sharp intelligence in Sebastian, a trait he possessed that was connected to all the strange things he'd ordered. He was not a man who would *accidentally* agree to a four-month, three-thousand-mile journey that he was free to turn aside from anytime they drew near a train station, which was almost weekly.

"You're welcome to come," she answered, "but if you

have any doubts about joining us, I'll let you have the cart and the horse that pulls it and enough supplies to get you through to Oregon. I'm not sure you understand that we intend to go deep into the mountains now. And we'll be there for a long stretch without running into any towns." By *long stretch* she meant forever, but Sebastian didn't have to stay.

"I know you had trouble back in Independence, but surely that trouble won't have followed you all the way out here."

"I'm not all that sure." His blue eyes flashed with fear. "I just don't know who I can trust."

She saw no danger in the man, just secrets. Well, she had a few of her own.

"You seemed to want to be away from trouble, too," he added. "Did that trouble follow you all the way out here?"

Her lips pursed. She stared at him through narrow eyes. She most certainly did not want to talk about that. "My plans weren't made by others as I lay mostly unconscious. We are going exactly where we planned to go. You had no such plans. We'll be even farther from the railroad. Going with us isn't a decision to be made lightly."

"I am coming with you." He sounded almost patronizing, like he thought she was stupid and was trying to use small words so she'd understand.

She understood exactly how that felt because she was thinking the same thing about him. Nodding silently, she stared at the man. His skin was tanned after months on the trail. He'd been thin when they found him, but now from the days of walking, the hard work, he was much sturdier looking. His short hair had grown long, and it had bleached to a whitish-blond.

"I just had to be sure, Sebastian. Come along home with us, then." Beth walked to the lead wagon just as Oscar took her seat.

"He still going?" he asked.

Beth turned to her friend. "He certainly is."

Oscar tipped his head in a way that encapsulated all their confusion. "You ride with Joseph now. Fiona and I will blaze a trail with her wagon. Just ahead we turn off. I've ridden this trail a few times. It's a rattlesnake of a trail for a fact. The wagons ahead won't notice we're gone for the next hour. Then Dakota will tell everyone we left by choice, to prevent anyone insisting they come back for us." Oscar paused, then said fondly, "Some good folks in this bunch who would do it. Jake hopes Dakota handles things so it seems simple and forgettable."

Beth felt a warm breeze flutter the hair that hung around her face. "The folks on this wagon train were kind. I would have liked to tell them a decent goodbye. I hope they all find homes they love." She hoped she did, as well.

"Fall in with Joseph, Miss Beth. I know where to go. It's a fairly long ride. We won't make it today to the land I bought, nor tomorrow. I reckon we'll be most of a week reaching the place. We're headed north toward the most beautiful mountain range you've ever seen."

"Is your land near where my children and I homestead?" Fiona managed a smile, though her usual boisterous personality had faded when Shay died.

"We're on past you a ways, Mrs. O'Toole, but the directions they gave at Fort Bridger when you filed were clear enough. We'll get you settled and a roof over your heads before we move on."

He flicked the reins, and the well-trained livestock plodded on for a bit before Oscar turned north on a trail Beth hadn't noticed until Oscar took it. That didn't mean it was hidden; it just meant Beth was that bad at tracking. Yet another skill she was determined to learn.

They'd been riding a while when Jake caught up to them. His shoulders were square, his head lifted as if he didn't want to miss a thing. He tipped his hat at Beth and gave her a very special smile before riding on to meet up with Oscar.

"I'm looking forward to what's ahead, Oscar," Jake said. "I'm hoping you've picked us a fine spot."

"I have for a fact."

Jake nodded, then turned to see how the other wagons were faring.

The day went on as all the others had. Then the next and the next.

In the middle of the fourth day, Oscar stopped and shouted, "Hold up! We're there!"

Fiona jumped down from where she sat beside Donal on the second wagon. Oscar had taken over the lead. "This is it?" Fiona's eyes lit up. It was indeed a beautiful place.

"The land agent sent along a map." Oscar descended from the wagon. "That line of aspens there on the rocky outcropping"—he pointed to the spot—"is the far north side of both your land and Maeve's. Donal?"

The young man climbed down, looking at the craggy mountain range to the north and west. Groves of trees. A stream running across a grassy meadow. "This is our land?" Donal's voice was hushed with awe. "I've the Irishman's love of the land. It's been a dream of mine, along with Da, to own me own piece of the old sod. But never did I dream of owning such beauty as this."

Oscar came up and rested a hand on Donal's shoulder. "It's a good place to settle. Your property line is right across that stream and up to the first fall of rocks. Your ma and Fiona are on this side. We'll have to build two cabins. Fiona and Maeve can put theirs on the boundary line, and you'll need a cabin all your own." His eyes met Donal's.

Jake saw the young man stand straighter, as if he were growing an inch or two right before their eyes.

"My own cabin?" Donal said.

"Yes, but close enough you'll be right on hand to help out your family." Oscar's voice rose a bit. "Fiona, does that suit you?"

"Yes. It's good and right for me boyo to have his own place on his own land. Maeve, will you be wanting your own cabin, too?"

Maeve's freckled face beamed in the fullest smile Jake had seen since Shay died. "I'd be lost in my own cabin, Ma. I'd be glad to share, and maybe when Conor is acting up, we'll just send him over to sleep with Donal."

Donal laughed. "I'll be glad for the company. But to start, I'm building a house that's easy to heat, and that means small. Ma, you'll need a bit more space in your cabin." He turned and smiled at Oscar. "It's only midday. Can you stay long enough to get me started before you go on to search for your own home up the trail?"

"We won't be far. Maybe we can stop in now and then just to hear different voices."

"Dakota said more settlers all the time are turning aside rather than go all the way to Oregon. And Boise, Idaho, the new capital, has gold mining nearby. I expect a train will go to Boise before long. You're here first, so you get the pick of the finest land, but you'll have neighbors before you know it. Now let's build a fire and make a noon meal. Then we'll start chopping down trees for two cabins—one large, one small."

When the Collins family pulled away a week later, the O'Tooles had a roof over their heads, and Bruce had been persuaded to stay a while to finish up the doors and shutters.

Beth felt a twinge of worry when Oscar said Bruce would help finish the cabins and Oscar would return soon with a crew to put up a barn. The whole idea was for them to hide and stay hidden. Now they had plans to go visiting? And did that include trading work? Because to trade work meant bringing the O'Tooles to the canyon Oscar had found. A canyon so remote that Oscar was calling it "Hidden Canyon."

Well, it wouldn't be hidden if the neighbors knew where it was.

The Collins-Holt family rolled on north. Maeve shed a few tears as she waved goodbye, and Beth decided going to visit such fine people would be well worth the risk.

Mountains loomed ahead. They drove through rich-looking land with a good amount of grass. Beth was impatient with the trip, for she was tired of traveling. At the same time, she didn't think they could go far enough, fast enough. She wondered if the land ahead would be truly hidden from others.

She talked with Jake about Ginny and Kat. Both women would be staying with them. He kept to sleeping on his bedroll outside.

The group set up their three tents. It was more difficult to graze their animals because four wagons, even with three tents between them, made a mighty small corral. But then the oxen and horses the other pioneers had needed to pen up were gone now, so they didn't need as much space.

Jake, along with the Collins brothers, strung rope between the wagons because three didn't really make a decent circle. The men always stood watch. There'd been no sign of trouble. No bad weather. No renegades or bears or cougars. It was a time of perfect peace.

And yet Beth couldn't quite believe her life would always be this peaceful. In fact, knowing her father as she did, she was certain he was still hunting for her.

25

Beth, honey, can I talk to you?" Jake asked after they'd finished their supper.

She smiled at him and nodded. He took her hand and led her into the night, away from the others.

As they walked under the starlit sky, his heart rate picked up and his breathing became shallow, but Jake forced himself to ask for what he wanted. Once they were out of earshot, he began, "It's a pretty night. Not too cold, no rain. Oscar said we'd be home in another short day. Um . . . have you talked with Kat about your ma? Do you think it'd be . . . what I mean is, I'd like for you to sleep beside me—tonight and every night. Not for . . . uh, reasons of marital, well, knowledge. We can wait for that until we reach our destination and get a cabin up. But just because I'd like to hold you close."

Beth turned to face him. His breathing almost stopped. They still held hands, but she reached her free hand up and rested her palm against his cheek. They stood facing each other.

"I'd like that," she said softly. She took an unsteady step forward, and he took it as permission and kissed her.

Once the kiss ended and Jake's head cleared a little, he spoke. His voice rasped, and he quickly cleared it, then tried again. "I'm longing to share a home with you."

Now Beth rested both hands on the sides of his face. "I absolutely want that, too. I had a cabin pictured with two bedrooms. One for me, one for Mama. And a second cabin for Oscar and his brothers. When Kat joined us, well, I hadn't really thought beyond the two bedrooms. I've tried to talk to Oscar about building plans, but something always stops us from discussing it. I'm sure I'm imagining it, but he seems oddly reluctant to talk about how we're all going to live."

"I've tried to bring it up, too." Jake frowned. Oscar was usually talkative. Maybe not so much about plans, especially before they'd left the wagon train, but he seemed quieter now. Worried maybe? "We'll need a bedroom of our own," Jake went on. "A second one for Ginny to share with Kat. Three bedrooms would be best, but cabins this high up in the mountains are hard to keep warm, even with plentiful firewood." He looked around at the forest. Firewood wasn't the problem. Getting heat to all corners of the house was another matter altogether. "Yep, smaller is better."

"It's so odd to speak of a two-bedroom house. Our home in Chicago had ten bedrooms on the second floor, with ten more for the servants on the third floor. And three apartments on the ground floor, which were for the housekeeper, the cook, and the butler—the hired help who handled the other servants. Mama's so-called *bedroom* had a dressing room, a sitting room, and a bathing room with hot-and-cold running water. Father had a similar set of rooms. I've always counted their suites as one bedroom."

"Each room possibly bigger than the whole cabin we'll build."

Beth suddenly looked grim. "There's not much about my life in Chicago that tempts me to go back to it. Father provided that home through ruthless business practices, cruel treatment of folks who rented rooms in his tenement houses, and no interest in the people he crushed or the small businesses he ruined, all to fatten his already fat pockets. If you want to build a one-room cabin, that'll be fine with me. I won't fuss if you want us to keep sleeping outside."

Jake grinned. "In October, when a foot of snow lands on our heads, you might fuss a little."

Beth laughed. "Maybe a little."

Jake kissed her again, longer this time. Afterward, he said, "We will have our own room. We'll make it two bedrooms, or three if Ginny and Kat don't want to share. But tonight we'll sleep out under the stars together. We'll leave married things until we can have true privacy. Still, I'd like you near me. I'd like to hold you while I sleep."

Beth touched his lips with her fingertips. "I'd like that, too."

"Is your ma adjusting to the idea of your being married to a wagon-train scout?"

A furrow appeared on Beth's smooth brow. "What did she say to you?"

He shook his head and gave a half smile. "She hasn't

spoken one unkind word. But I can see she had dreams for you, dreams your father stole."

"Father stole dreams from both of us."

Jake hadn't heard all that Ginny had gone through. Beth had told him of her escape from the asylum and Beth's part in it, and Oscar's and his brothers' parts, yet he had few details. "That you ended up married to me puts an end to those dreams, and she's not very good at masking it."

"I think you fit into my dreams much better than any man I was likely to end up with. My father had no intention of allowing me to pick my own husband. You should have seen the awful old business associate of my father's he had planned for me to marry."

He felt her shudder under his hands and looked into her pretty blue eyes. He saw the liveliness in her and was glad she'd managed to survive her growing-up years without having her spirit broken. "Your father and his crony are doomed to disappointment." He kissed her again. "You are officially taken off the marriage market."

With a firm nod of her chin, she said, "I certainly am."

"And what about Sebastian? What do you think he wants all those odd supplies for?"

Beth shook her head. "Is he going to accept living with the Collins brothers?"

"If he doesn't want that, I suppose we can help him put up his own cabin." Jake, thinking of all that took, added, "I'll help him get a roof up, but I'm not chopping wood for him all winter."

"He has to go back eventually, doesn't he? Who shot him? Why doesn't he want to ask the police to find and arrest the man? And what in the world is in that packet he keeps tucked inside his shirt all day and night?"

Jake patted her shoulder. "I reckon he'll tell us about it when he's ready. If he's ever ready. My real worry is how he'll act the first time he sees a wanted poster with your face on it. And sees the reward that's offered. He wants to stay with us, but is that the same as loyalty? Can the man be trusted beyond ten thousand dollars?"

"I'd like to shake the man until I get some answers. It looks like you're going to have to be the patient one in our family."

He smiled as he drew her into his arms. "I don't feel all that patient waiting for bedtime."

They stood holding each other, surrounded by the scent of pines. She was slender but strong and felt perfect in his arms.

Beth gave her head a little tilt. "I think that's now."

He took a step back, held out his hand. She took it, and together they walked back to the campfire.

⁓

"Mama . . ."

Ginny gasped and shook her head quickly. "Hush now. I'm Ginny to everyone."

"And I say now that it's just our group, I'm going to call you Mama. I've missed saying the word."

Ginny stopped and turned to face Beth, her eyes swimming with tears. "And I've missed hearing it."

Ginny flung herself into Beth's arms, and the two of them stood, Mama sobbing, and Beth crying quiet tears of joy.

Speaking into her mother's soft bonnet, she whispered, "I want to talk with you, Mama, about Horecroft. I want to know everything you've been through. It seems as if we're never alone, and I don't know if you want to talk in front of everyone."

Mama nodded quietly, but then Jake rode up and once again they weren't alone. "Is something wrong?" he asked.

Ginny managed a watery smile. "No, nothing in the world is wrong. Beth has just decided it's time to resume calling me Mama. These are happy tears."

Jake arched a brow at that, as if he very much doubted there could be such a thing as happy tears. He shifted his eyes to Beth and looked just the littlest bit alarmed, as if wondering if unexpected tears ran in the family.

Which got a smile out of her. "This whole crying moment began because we were discussing how much farther we had to follow this lumbering row of wagons."

Jake swung down from his mount and walked between them. "Oscar says we'll sleep in your valley tonight."

Beth said, "*Our* valley."

Jake nodded. "I have no idea where we're going, and Oscar seems to enjoy being mysterious, but it sounds like soon we can stop rolling."

Beth and Mama resumed walking. Jake swung down to walk alongside them.

When the sun was just past its peak at midday, Oscar leaned around the corner of the last wagon and shouted, "Just ahead!"

He pointed to his right, and all Beth saw was a wall of rock. They'd been climbing for days. They'd left the fertile grasslands behind, with the ground becoming

213

increasingly rocky and wooded. Right now, maybe a hundred yards ahead and slightly to the right, a solid rock wall stretched overhead, too sheer and too far to ever hope to climb, let alone get their cattle, horses, and wagons up and over. Joseph veered to the right, following some trail Beth couldn't see.

The going was ever steeper. The wagons found their way, but they seemed to be rolling over untouched land. Rocky and studded with scrub brush. Trees growing sparsely enough, it didn't speak well for the fertility of the soil.

"Do you see a way across that mountain right ahead of us?" Beth glanced at Jake.

They had fallen behind the wagons as the way grew rough. Mama seemed to be worn clean out, so Jake slowed his pace even more and offered both women an arm.

"There is no way across I can see." He shook his head. "I trust Oscar, though, and if he's somehow found a way to make an Angus-drawn covered wagon fly, I guess I'll just follow along."

So the three of them followed along.

The rear wagon had the smaller cart still rolling behind it. The saddle string of horses stretched out behind them. Beth, Jake, and Mama were behind the horses, except for Jake's horse, which he was leading. Onward they plodded, nearer and nearer to that gray rock wall. Then suddenly, just as the lead horses were about to bump their noses against rock, or so it looked from where they walked, the horses vanished—two, then four of them, then the wagon they pulled.

"What in the world?" Mama gasped.

Jake grinned and said, "I've got to see this." He swung up onto his horse and trotted forward across the rugged ground on what no one would ever call a trail. Beth, watching ahead, saw the same thing with the second wagon. Two Angus, then four vanished, followed by the wagon. Jake, riding behind the second wagon, disappeared next.

"I hope I didn't just lose a husband," Beth said.

"Oscar calls it Hidden Canyon." Mama hugged her around the waist again. They were close enough now that they saw the lead Angus on the third wagon turn just as they reached the rock wall. When the team and wagon with Kat pulled by their nervous Angus went around whatever lay ahead, then the cart, then the saddle string, it was left for Beth and Ginny to walk boldly into solid stone.

Except, of course, it wasn't solid at all.

26

Jake went from worrying about the stony soil feeding the livestock to being delighted.

Carefully, Jake rode his horse through a narrow-necked canyon that was sheer rock beside him and underfoot. The ground sloped upward, with the snow having turned to ice in the little crevices. Soon the rock walls that stretched high overhead on both sides fell away as he moved into a mountain valley, one that made him catch his breath.

Jake guided his horse to the side of the entrance because a wagon was coming—he could hear its rattling wheels. He swung off his horse, pulled the saddle and the bridle free, and slapped the pretty quarter horse on the rump. The horse meandered down the side of the strange-looking bowl: a beautiful valley lush with belly-deep grass, its canyon walls lined with quaking aspens. Jake's horse grabbed a mouthful of grass, ripping it free, then began to walk faster, then trot, and finally ran down toward his home. The horse even kicked up his heels and bucked as he galloped into the grass. It was as if the chestnut knew the thousand or more acres of beauty around him was home.

Out of the trees along one of the canyon walls of the vast bowl, a spate of water came out of five or maybe six places, gushing down from higher ground, bubbling into a stream that started before the waterfalls combined and joined it. He watched the joyful gush of water flow across the valley, coming in from the north and disappearing into a woodland on the south side.

At the far end of the bowl, a herd of elk lifted their heads and turned to stare. Jake spotted a bull halfway up the side of the valley. Massive and regal, his antlers larger than any Jake had seen before, the bull watched the chestnut horse that dared to intrude on his kingdom.

The bull elk didn't run

They were far across the valley, and Jake wondered if any of the wild critters had ever seen a human being before.

"What do you think?" Oscar rolled his wagon up beside where Jake stood.

"I think I've come home."

A gentle breeze coasted down the sides of the bowl. It ruffled the spinning leaves of the aspen trees and swept along the grass, as if the hand of God were brushing across the valley.

The two men stood there staring, enjoying the moment. The lead wagons rattled and rolled along, down the side of the bowl on their way across the valley.

Jake thought of the hidden entrance to the canyon. "How did you find this place? How did you ever see that hole in the wall that led to this valley?"

"Joseph and Bruce and I wandered around these parts when we headed back east. Must be fifteen years ago now. We were barely grown boys. We started out just wanting to get closer to the mountains."

Sebastian and the third wagon came through the narrow canyon entrance.

"Follow the others," Oscar called out and made a sweeping gesture toward the two wagons moving toward the bottom of their beautiful valley.

Sebastian grinned and rolled on.

Huge mountains loomed in the distance, visible over the top of the canyon walls. Part of the Sawtooth Range. They seemed to be right in front of them, pressing close, but Jake had a lot of experience with mountains and knew they were still a long way off.

"Before we got into the peaks," Oscar said, "I saw a bird swoop into that canyon neck in a way that looked like the bird should have crashed into solid stone. I walked up here to see what happened to the bird, and I found the opening. My brothers and I spent two years here. This canyon is sheltered somehow. It gets cold all right, and the snow can be heavy at times, but the wind blows the snow up against the canyon walls and the grassland stays open enough that a herd can live through the winter months. A herd of mustangs came in once when we were here. The water never freezes. I've missed it ever since, like the valley was another brother I'd left behind. When Beth said she wanted to get her ma and leave her pa, that she needed a good hiding place, I knew exactly where I wanted to take them."

Oscar pointed to a clump of trees about halfway to the

cascading waterfalls. The bull elk had moved on a bit but was still focused on the new strangers, wary. "We built a cabin all those years ago, and it's still standing. I was afraid someone else would have found it by now."

Jake scanned the valley before him. "I can see rocks stacked, but I don't see a house."

Joseph drove past the stack of rocks. Bruce aimed his wagon toward the cave, then called out something to Sebastian, who was following Joseph.

Oscar chuckled. "It's built across the mouth of a cave. We made the cave livable. There are a few rooms inside it, and one has a hot spring. In fact, there are several hot springs around here."

Oscar rested a hand on Jake's shoulder and pointed to a smaller grove, where Joseph was heading. "And when I was out here a year ago with my brothers, we built a cabin for Miss Elizabeth and Mrs. Rutledge." He paused and smiled. "That's the last time I'll use those names for the ladies."

Jake looked to where Oscar pointed. Almost swallowed up by the woods, he saw the front of another cabin.

"It's nothing grand, not like the house where the ladies lived in Chicago. But we did a fine job of making a home for those ladies we admire so much. I wouldn't claim it has three bedrooms, but it has a front room and a sitting room, and there's another hot spring close by. We enclosed that and put a pump in it with a pipe to carry the water, so the women can have hot water for cooking and washing up anytime they please."

Jake was impressed by all that Oscar and his brothers had done to start the homestead.

Oscar continued, "That sitting room will make a likely room for you and Beth. Ginny can share with Kat. The bedrooms are good-sized, so if they don't want to share, we can put in a wall to give each woman privacy. There's a loft if one of them wants that, but it's not a true second floor. Or we can always build on."

Jake thought of how much easier it'd be to add a single room to the already standing cabin than it would be to start from the ground up.

"My cave is much more rustic," Oscar said, "but it's warmer and easier to heat because the cave stops the wind better there. It's cool in summer and warm in winter. But the cabin for the ladies is well built. Sturdy."

"I thought you were acting mysterious whenever we'd talk about what to build here. It was because you'd already built it." Jake watched the wagons roll on toward the second house. "And there's room for me in Beth's house?"

Oscar smiled at him. Jake could see the man was pleased that his Beth had married a two-bit scout, and Jake felt the pleasure of it because Oscar treated Beth like a daughter. "I reckon it'll be a bit more crowded with Kat and you in there. And ours will have Seb, but we'll fit all right. Something else I did when I was out here a year ago, I—"

Beth gasped, and Oscar stopped talking to turn and grin at her. She drew Jake's attention. Ginny clutched her hands under her chin and beamed. Then the two ladies emerged fully from the narrow canyon entrance, moving forward to face the valley.

"Oscar, this place is beautiful!" The two men parted a bit so Beth could come stand between them. She gave one of her bright smiles to her old stable hand.

"I'm mighty glad you approve, Beth, because we're here to stay." Oscar tugged the brim of his hat, then turned to Ginny. "I hope it suits you, as well."

"More than I can say," she answered, her eyes brimming with tears.

The wagons had reached the stream and stopped. Joseph and Sebastian had climbed down and were unhitching the team. Bruce had his animals turned loose already and was working in the back of the wagon. As each draft animal was set free, they headed straight for the water to drink deep.

The four of them stood watching it all. Jake knew they needed to get down there and help unload the wagons, but for just a few minutes he watched his horse, dropping to the ground and rolling in the soft grass.

Soon the Morgan horses and Angus began cropping grass.

The bull elk bugled in the distance. Maybe he was trying to warn them away, but the poor old guy was going to have to learn to be neighborly because they weren't going anywhere.

Jake saw an Angus calf come charging out of the far woods, followed by another. He remembered Oscar had started to say something and was cut off by Beth's gasp. Jake had a feeling he knew what Oscar was about to say. Or maybe Oscar had done a whole lot to get this valley ready to be a comfortable hiding place, and he had a whole list of things he wanted to say. It looked like that bull elk had sure enough seen a man before, for Oscar had spent some time here.

A bald eagle screamed overhead and drew everyone's

eyes upward. Jake watched the magnificent bird swoop down toward the stream that flowed away from the waterfall. It dove straight for the water, skimmed the surface with its talons, and came up with a fish. It looked like a trout.

"I've never seen anything like it," Ginny said, her voice reverent. "Oscar, you've found us what must be the most perfect home ever created by God."

Oscar's ears turned slightly pink with embarrassed pleasure. Hard to tell, Jake thought, with the man's over-long hair, battered Stetson, and dark tan. But Jake still had to control a smile.

Beth said, "We need to get to work. We'll need a roof over our heads before snowfall, which comes early out here. I've been reading up on the weather conditions in northern Idaho. Then we'll need to—"

"Beth?" Oscar interrupted her, and she fell silent. He looked at Jake, then at Beth, and finally at Ginny. "I've got a surprise for you. In fact, I've got several."

27

So far, the wagon-train trip had been mostly routine, except for that nightmarish day when the O'Toole family tragedy occurred.

Beth had a lot of time to think, brood, worry. And pray. The prayer had helped her manage the rest.

Now there weren't enough hours in the day.

Unloading the wagons was a big job. The men threw into it with such goodwill that Beth and the rest of the women had to hustle to help at all.

Oscar surprised her endlessly. He had established a small herd of Angus cattle in their canyon. The house he'd built for her and Mama was lovely, made of log and stone. And there was plenty of room for both Kat and Jake.

With the men carrying the heavy contents of the wagons, the women had scrambled to clean the dust off the furniture. The different pieces were basic and homemade, yet they were all a delight to Beth.

Once the wagons were emptied, the women began heating water to wash clothes, a task made so much easier by the hot spring that piped water right into the cabin. The water wasn't dangerously hot, but hot enough for washing clothes and dishes. If they needed to boil water for cooking, it only took a few minutes.

Oscar said if the women wanted to, they could put out a warning for the men to stay away, then bathe in the little hot spring. The water flowed up from deep beneath the ground and then into the stream, so the water was always clean. Beth had longed for a hot bath. She could barely keep from ignoring all they had to do and jumping in.

A line had been strung between two oak trees on which to hang everyone's clothes to dry once they'd been washed. Beth had convinced Oscar to let the women do this as the men worked to get their things carried into the cave, the cattle and horses settled, and mark off a place where they'd build a barn large enough to hold four wagons, a cart, and a few horses.

Jake was going hunting while some of the men went to see how Oscar's herd was doing.

Beth felt a softness in her heart for all the men. Except for Jake, it was both a spark and a softness. And Oscar, well, he was the kind of father she'd never had. These strong, hardworking men made this more than a hiding place.

It was a sanctuary.

"I'd like to sleep in the loft, Beth, if that's all right," Kat said as she wrung out a newly cleaned dress. "Ginny can have the second bedroom. I think after so much time spent together, a little space between us might feel like a luxury."

The cabin had a large front room. A fireplace and two

rocking chairs on the south side, a rustic but sturdy table and four chairs on the north. Above the fireplace was a small loft, not even space to stand upright, but tall enough they could build a bedstead when time allowed. It would probably be the warmest space in the house.

A hallway divided the rest of the house right down the middle.

To the south was the sitting room, across the hall from the kitchen. The kitchen had a stove that included a baking chamber, a dry sink, and cupboards Oscar and his brother had built, now filled with supplies.

Beth had expected to cook over a fire in a fireplace and haul in cold water from the creek, but the hot spring piped right inside.

On past the kitchen and sitting room were two bedrooms. These had bedsteads and empty mattress ticks. Oscar said they'd cut prairie grass and have them filled in time for sleeping tonight. He was afraid vermin might move in if he stuffed the mattresses and then left for a full year, as they'd done all this last summer.

"I think the loft will make a fine bedroom, except . . ." Beth looked at Kat and asked, "Do you think maybe you could stay with Mama for now?"

"Oh, that's right." Kat smiled slowly, and it was a sad smile. "She hasn't had any nightmares since we turned off from the main trail."

"Can you tell that? Do you sleep lightly enough to be sure? Because maybe we should give her a chance to sleep alone."

"Let's let Ginny choose," Kat said. "Yes, I'd be honored to stay with her if she wants that."

"I'm hoping the dreams don't torment her much longer. I'm hoping now that we've come home and can settle in, things will be all right."

Even as she said the words, Beth felt that hot breath on the back of her neck. What she always felt when she thought about being safe, being in a hiding place her father couldn't find.

Was there such a place? Would he give up? Maybe he already had. But they would never know until the day Father, or some of his men, came into their canyon to drag his wife and daughter away. Or until Mama had the courage to go face a judge and jury and fight to be declared sane.

Thaddeus disembarked from the train. He'd had time to question the folks in each railroad town and found where the main westward trains split. When he reached the right spot, a town with a hotel and a second row of rails so he could pull his private cars aside, well to the west border end of Idaho but before the worst of the mountain passes, he stopped his journey and turned to wait for the first wagon train. And if necessary, he'd wait for the second and third and however many he had to inspect until he found his wife and daughter.

The side rails were located deliberately at a few spots so trains could pull aside if they needed repairs, and this town was a good place to wait.

Thaddeus had Blayd and his crew of men, five in total. Blayd suggested they contact any Pinkertons in the area, assuming a few were nearby, thanks to their traveling the rails and putting up wanted posters. Thaddeus had sent out wires from the first town he'd come to after realizing a wagon train was his wife's hiding place.

He'd wired Chicago with the orders from several towns back once he'd decided where to set up. He expected to see a few men arrive shortly, though they'd be coming from San Francisco probably, or even as far away as Denver or Omaha. They should arrive in time to question the folk rolling through on the wagon train and get a good look at every single person traveling in such primitive conditions.

He knew Eugenia and Elizabeth might well see him and beg to go home with him. He'd love to hear those fool women beg.

He descended to solid ground. Though his private car moved smoothly and the hotel in this town didn't look promising, it was nice to be standing still. He walked down the steps from the train station, leaving Blayd to arrange for their luggage to be transported the few short blocks to the hotel.

Yvette came along beside him. She didn't seem to remember screaming when he'd grabbed her. Or remember that he'd been furious and ready to land a fist in her face. All was forgiven, it seemed, and she now walked beside him, calm and cheerful, chatting inanely about the weather and the town and her dress being travel-stained.

He'd taken about ten steps when a man wearing a black suit with a white shirt and a string tie came up to him and tugged on the brim of his black Stetson. "You must be Mr. Rutledge. I'm John McCall. I was told to meet you here."

McCall held out a Pinkerton badge, and Thaddeus nodded. "Yes, I'm Rutledge. I'm glad to see the Pinkertons got someone here so quickly." Thaddeus's eyes slid past

McCall. He saw a tall woman with dark hair. She wasn't in such fine clothes as McCall, but decent enough to pass as the man's companion.

McCall gestured to her. "And this is my wife, Penny. She's a Pinkerton, too. There's a third agent in town, as well. Rachel Hobart is her name. She happened to be visiting us and rode along on the hunt when the agency told us they wanted everyone possible working on this."

"How did you get here so fast? No other trains have come through." Suspicion colored Thaddeus's tone, and McCall's eyes narrowed a bit, as if he'd picked up on every bit of that suspicion and didn't like it. A smart man. That suited Thaddeus.

At the same time, he had to wonder what the Pinkerton Agency was coming to with their having women agents. Thaddeus was all too aware of the weakness of the female mind.

"We live in Nevada, near Carson City. We have been questioning people along the train route and wiring in our location to receive further instructions, hoping to be told the hunt was concluded. We received word you were stopping in this town in hopes of intercepting the women you are after, thinking they're on a wagon train. The agency said you needed help, and since we were the closest agents, we came as soon as we could."

"The wagon trains don't pass through this town." Penny McCall stepped forward. Thaddeus saw a coarse woman, which to his mind meant none too intelligent. "The railroad route follows the Oregon Trail generally, but the Union Pacific, due to surveying and newly discovered trails, sometimes chose different routes not followed by the wagon trains. If you're wanting to see these ladies on your posters, and believe they're on the wagon train, we need to ride to the north about twenty miles. There's a town there—Alton, Idaho—that has a roof for all of you. We've been able to verify that the first wagon train of the season hasn't pulled through town yet, so you should be on time."

Thaddeus looked past McCall and saw a town so new that the boards weren't yet weathered, so it was most likely built in the last year or so by the railroad. But Thaddeus was smarter than most anyone he ever met. His mind added and subtracted information as quickly as it did numbers, and he didn't accept anyone's opinion without confirming it. He also took into consideration the quality of Mrs. McCall's thinking. If she said they needed to ride north, they'd ride north—but not until he got a few questions answered first.

Blayd came up behind him. Thaddeus said, "Excuse me for a moment." He turned to Blayd. "Come this way."

He led Blayd aside a good distance and repeated what the McCalls had told him. Blayd wasted no time but headed into the nearest business to verify what the Mc-Calls had said.

Meanwhile, Thaddeus went back to the McCalls. Neither of them had the look he liked to see in his employees. Neither seemed to understand that they worked for him and should show him more respect. A little fear wouldn't be out of place. He turned to Mr. McCall. "Can the road we're traveling take a carriage or will we need to ride horseback? We have supplies, but they can be left here if necessary. I'd prefer to take with me members of my staff and a few other things along, and that requires my carriage."

McCall nodded. "The trails can take a carriage. Let's load up what you need and head out. We can be there before dark if we push hard. And the first wagon train could be coming through anytime. Best to stay ahead of them."

"I'm going to need a wagon. I have a carriage and two horses to pull it. Find a wagon for sale in this town and a team of horses. And get back here with them as soon as possible."

McCall tilted his head a bit as if he might object, then didn't. Maybe the man had some sense of caution, after all. At last he nodded and said, "We'll need money to make those purchases. And you may be asked to rent the wagon, not buy it. I'm not sure there's a spare one in this town. The horses will cost you one hundred dollars apiece, and no one's gonna take your word for it that you're good for the money. They'll want cash money, and now. Do you have it?"

Thaddeus reached into the inner pocket of his black suitcoat and pulled out the pouch of gold he always carried with him. He poured out twenty-dollar gold pieces until he had three hundred dollars in his hand and thrust the money at McCall. "I'll expect an accounting of every penny when you get back with the wagon and horses."

"Will do, sir," McCall replied, his expression blank. No smile.

He sounded polite enough, but still, Thaddeus didn't like him. Any man who looked at a pile of gold and didn't know he was dealing with his betters was a foolish man indeed.

McCall turned to his wife. "C'mon, Penny. We're going shopping for Mr. Rutledge." He took his wife's arm and had to tug a bit to get her to turn away with him. The couple strode toward a barn on this end of town and began talking as soon as they were out of earshot.

Mrs. McCall glanced back in a way that told Thaddeus he was the subject of their conversation.

Thaddeus needed their help in getting to Alton to the north or he'd have fired them on the spot.

28

Jake woke up with a woman in his arms.

He'd done that twice now since luring Beth into sleeping beside him a few days after they'd turned off from the wagon train.

But not like this. Not in a bed, in a house, and not after spending the night learning what it meant to be fully married.

Beth's head was resting on his shoulder, her eyes closed, dark lashes against her cheeks. His arm was wrapped around her back. It was daylight, and he hadn't slept past the sunrise since leaving Missouri back in May.

Now here he lay. Rested. Happy. Stunned by how wonderful it was to be married.

Then Jake heard the soft click of metal on metal and recognized that someone was up and about inside the house. He was torn between pleasure and embarrassment because whoever was moving around out there was trying to be quiet and leave the newly married couple undisturbed.

He should get up. He should get dressed and get to work. They had a lot to do before they were ready for winter. Chopping firewood alone might take two or three men working hard all day, every day, until the deep snows came and buried all their heat.

Beth shifted, and her dark curls, escaped from the braid she'd worn to bed, brushed his cheek. The silky-smooth hair, the warmth of her skin, the smell of her, he couldn't think of anywhere else in the world he wanted to be more than right here with his wife.

The outside door to their cabin opened and closed. Whoever was in the house—maybe starting coffee?—had slipped outside. He looked down at his wife and saw her eyes flicker open. They focused on him, and she smiled.

A smile that warmed places in his heart he hadn't known were cold. A man would do most anything if he could get a woman to smile at him like that. And here he was, getting just such a smile.

Jake hugged her a bit closer. "Good morning, Mrs. Holt."

Her smile widened. "Beth Holt. I like that name. It's much improved over the name I had before."

"You were perfect with the name you had before. But I think now you are even better. That makes you better than perfect, which sounds just exactly right to me."

Beth reached up toward him as he bent down toward her. Their lips met. His heart trembled a little.

Then their cabin door opened again, and Beth's eyes went wide. Her thoughts were plain on her face. She was remembering where they were. Noticing it was fully daylight. Noticing just how married they were.

Jake grinned, snagged another quick kiss, and said, "Time to get on with the day, Mrs. Holt. And a fine day it is."

He tossed the blankets aside. She snatched them back and pulled them up to her chin. Modest. He didn't mind that, within reason. He pulled on his newly washed clothes. Beth and the other ladies had worked hard yesterday.

"I'll leave you to dress," he said.

"I should say you will." She sniffed at him, but a smile stole across her face as she let go of the blanket with one hand and shooed him out of the room.

It was a fine start to this new chapter of his life.

"This is Alton." John McCall made a grand gesture with his arm. He rode his horse alongside the black carriage Thaddeus had brought west with him. Blayd sat up front and drove the rig.

Yvette was beside him. Dressed perfectly, as she always was, from several trunks of clothes Horecroft had sent along.

Thaddeus had to wonder just who she was. Her clothing was expensive and plentiful. No doubt some family was paying a hefty fee to keep her locked away. A fee Horecroft was now pocketing without telling her family she was gone.

Today, Yvette wore a blue dress with cream-colored lace along the neck and cuffs. She had a parasol made with matching lace and looked in all ways lovely. Yet she was, Thaddeus concluded, a madwoman.

Two wagons rattled along behind them, carrying the

rest of his staff, supplies, and luggage. He hadn't been able to fit everything and had to promise to return the wagons, this after being charged a hefty rental fee. But he planned on returning to the station, wife and daughter in tow, so returning the wagons was no big inconvenience.

Thaddeus peered ahead and saw the words *Alton General Store* painted on the nearest building. He glanced at McCall and wondered if all the Pinkertons he'd hired were of such low intelligence. No wonder they'd never found Eugenia or Elizabeth. With a smirk, he said, "Alton's likely to die without the wagon trains and the railroad picking a different route. And considering its rundown condition, no one will miss it much."

"Very possible," McCall replied, then kicked his horse toward the hotel, leaving Thaddeus behind. His wife and the other Pinkerton, Rachel Hobart, rode along with McCall.

Thaddeus looked around at the ragged town and frowned. There was a two-story hotel. On the first floor were three windows on each side of the front entrance; the second floor had seven windows. He hoped there'd be enough rooms available for his group. He itched to be surrounded by the comforts he'd become accustomed to: cleanliness, a soft mattress and pillows, silk sheets. He wondered what kind of food they'd get in this town. He'd carried what he could from his train car, and he'd demand they allow his chef in whatever passed for a kitchen around here, but even then it would barely suffice.

"This is the place we'll find her, Thaddeus." Yvette clasped her hands together under her chin and beamed at him. "I just know it. At last, you can ask her."

"Yes, yes. At last." Thaddeus had learned to never, ever touch her, not even to offer her a hand up to the carriage. And if he couldn't ignore her completely, then to agree with whatever she said. The woman hadn't thrown a fit in days, and Thaddeus would like to keep it that way.

He also knew he had a straitjacket included with the things he'd packed, but he hoped it wouldn't come to that.

Thaddeus said to Blayd, "Drive us to the hotel. We'll get rooms and then you and your men can haul our things in and find a stable for the horses." He turned as the wagon pulled up close behind him. "We're staying at the hotel. Chef Toussaint, I may need you to take over a kitchen in town to prepare decent food. If you need assistance, let Blayd know."

The chef nodded firmly. Thaddeus had no doubt the man could handle the bumpkins in this town.

Blayd got the team moving.

The entire hotel was empty, and the manager, a weary-looking, overly thin, older man, who'd admitted to his hotel being empty, was agreeable to whatever Thaddeus wanted, including renting the entire place exclusively to him and giving his chef run of the kitchen—all for a price. The man's wife did the cooking normally, but she'd be glad to give way or stay and assist, whatever Thaddeus wanted.

Whatever Thaddeus wanted. He liked the sound of that. That's how McCall should be talking to him.

29

After two weeks settling in, it was time to go help the O'Tooles. Not an easy decision. They were settling in well, and Beth had begun, just barely, to let hope grow that they'd found a place where they would be safe. That Mama and Beth, all of them, had a real chance to create their own lives. To live in freedom, not hiding away like scared rabbits. To have a comfortable life away from the tyranny of Thaddeus Rutledge . . . and to thrive.

They'd built a fire outside the cabin and had roasted a haunch of elk. They'd got it with a bow and arrow. Joseph was skilled with the weapon. He said he didn't want their herd of elk to learn to fear them, and a gun gave off a loud, frightening noise.

Oscar had built a stone chimney of sorts that he called a smokehouse, and he'd use it to turn the rest of the elk—a nice-sized chunk—into jerked meat. Jake was busy tanning the elk hide. Joseph was sharpening each point of its antlers to fashion tips for arrows.

Kat had found a mound of fabric Oscar had brought

into the canyon last year when he'd driven a small herd of Angus in, hoping the herd would thrive and grow to give them enough beef to live on forever.

Beth was peeling potatoes as Mama turned the roast, cooking in the cast-iron oven, and Kat was sewing warm winter clothes for everyone. After the food was cooking, they all stepped outside and settled around a campfire as they did for most meals. Oscar had dragged in stumps and set them on end for chairs.

Gathering around a fire reminded them all of their travels west and seemed to be the place they were all most relaxed.

Beth thought Sebastian seemed on edge and tried to get him to join their group more completely.

"You said you're an inventor, didn't you, Sebastian?"

Sebastian nodded eagerly. He was a secretive man, and Beth had respected his secrecy, considering her own. Now she wondered if he could use his inventive mind to help the group. "Inventions can be used here, though maybe not the one you have in mind."

"My invention will save money, save lives, save the world," Sebastian said with conviction.

His eyes gleamed with something that scared Beth but also excited her a bit. Whether right or not, the man believed his invention would make the world a better place, and he had an almost fanatical need to see that it benefited as many people as possible.

His voice rising with every word, Sebastian added, "And the people trying to stop me are willing to kill to keep my invention from being released into the world. It will be worth my life to go on with it. But it must be done.

The materials I had Jake order, that we picked up in Fort Bridger, will help advance my work. I have found a room in the cave I plan to use as a laboratory. I have enough of what I need, but only for now. I may need more supplies. And I'm never sure where my work will take me."

Silence fell over their circle. The fire crackled, sending sparks up into the sky. The sun had set, and the night birds called from the treetops, as if signaling to Beth that danger, even death, lay in Sebastian's hands.

Mama said quietly, "I believe I've mentioned, at least to some of you, why we are here. Sebastian, maybe you don't understand why we're here—not fully."

"Mama, you don't have to—"

Mama held up a staying hand to Beth. It almost made Beth smile because the gesture was so familiar. Something her mother had done when she wanted to finish her point and expected a talkative little girl to wait for her turn to speak.

Beth poured hot coffee while Mama settled onto a stump. The campfire was surrounded by them, with places for everyone to sit.

"Thank you." Sebastian took a sip of coffee from his tin mug.

"Sebastian, I am an escapee from an insane asylum."

Sebastian spit coffee into the fire. The sizzle of wet on embers hissed, and more sparks flew upward.

"I take it you haven't heard that before now?"

Sebastian stared at Ginny. "No. I knew you or Beth, maybe Kat, had something bad you were running from, but that's all. And I figured that is why we came to live in such a remote area."

"Well, that's what I'm running from. Did you know that laws have been passed that protect people from being locked away by spiteful or greedy relatives? It used to be common to send a wealthy grandfather to an asylum so his younger relatives, impatient for him to die, had access to his money. They passed a law that says no one can be locked away without a judge ruling on their sanity. That law applies to everyone—" Mama frowned and drew a deep breath—"that is, except for wives."

"But why exclude wives?"

"Why indeed? My husband was angry at me for having an opinion and speaking up about it. He was angry that I changed churches to one that had abolitionist sympathies. And the final offense was refusing to give him access to the money my parents had specifically shielded from him. Money for me. For Beth. When I refused to give him that money, he had me locked up in an insane asylum. I was there for three years before all the planning and scheming got me out. I can promise you my husband is not a man who accepts defeat. He is right now out there, turning over every stone in this country, maybe in the world, to find me and take me back to that awful place. And when I go, he'll drag Beth along. He's got plans to force her into marriage with one of his elderly cronies . . . plans I hope are now thwarted by Beth's marriage to Jake."

Mama looked from Beth to Jake, then back to Sebastian. "That asylum is what gives me nightmares."

"But, Mama, we talked about laws in different states, laws where you can fight Father."

"Yes, insane until proven sane. Guilty until proven innocent. I haven't heard of these laws."

"They were passed just recently—after you were locked away. We are safe here." Beth sincerely hoped so, anyway. "But there may come a time when you're ready to fight."

Sebastian took a long drink of his coffee.

Mama nodded but looked very doubtful. "I haven't talked much about it these past long months. I was afraid I'd be overheard, that I'd give away I was going to leave the wagon train to find a hiding place. But I think I need to talk about it. The only reason I haven't had nightmares lately is that first Beth, then Kat have slept beside me and helped get me through it when the dreams begin. Maybe if I can talk about it a little, the nightmares will end completely. I pray they do, though I hate adding the burden of my memories to any of you. You can walk away, get out of earshot. I'll understand if you do."

"Go on with it, Ginny," Sebastian said. "And I won't leave the canyon, I promise. Not yet." He then whispered more to himself than to them, "Maybe I can wait until spring."

Mama nodded, remaining quiet for a while. Beth could see she was sorting through memories, trying to think of where to begin.

Finally, with a sigh, Mama said, "This happened after I'd been committed a while. I was moved from a smaller dining room with nice ladies eating together. Ladies like me—rational, trapped, trying to remain calm and to act in all ways as if we were sane." She gave a sad smile. "I'm afraid I was too bold in my protests about the injustice of being locked away. I got transferred to a different section, one with more . . . troubled women.

"The first night in the larger dining room, they seated

me beside a woman who seemed calm and silent. I tried to talk to her. She didn't respond. Something about the way she stared at her food worried me, and I was afraid she was ill. I touched her arm, and she erupted from the bench we sat on, screaming. She grabbed the tin plate she had in front of her and threw it in my face. The bench was tipping, the food shocked me, the screaming all added to it, and I fell backward onto the floor. The woman leapt on me, beating me with her fists.

"Two attendants came. One dragged her off me, then knocked her aside so hard that she fell to the floor, still screaming. She staggered to her feet and dove at me again. She was shouting that I should keep my hands off her.

"I guess that meant, at least in those attendants' minds, that I'd started it." Ginny shook her head. "Maybe they didn't need any reason to include me in their punishment. The attendants dragged us both out of the dining room. I was bleeding and covered in food. I was crying in pain and shock, trying to keep up with the woman who dragged me along. The other woman was fighting and clawing. The orderly who had ahold of her hit her every few steps. I did my best to cooperate, not wanting that treatment. I knew that they had to separate us, but surely they could see she was mad and I was sane and harmless.

"We were taken to a room with five bathtubs, all full of cold water, and they threw us in. The orderly that had me held my head underwater. I swung my arms at her, fighting to get above water."

Kat came to sit on the ground beside Mama and held one of her hands. Beth saw that Mama's hands were clenched so tight, her knuckles had turned white. Kat held one clenched fist and murmured words Beth couldn't hear.

Beth had heard none of this before, but Kat was clearly familiar with the ill treatment in the asylum.

Mama continued, "The orderly was a huge woman, one I learned later took great pleasure in torturing others. She held me underwater for a long time, then dragged me up by my hair, let me gasp in a short breath before shoving me under again. I became exhausted enough that I went limp, which seemed to satisfy her. She dragged me out of the water. I could hear the poor madwoman still being dunked, still screaming.

"I was then dragged to my private room. I could only assume somehow Thaddeus had arranged one for me because many of the rooms were filled with bunkbeds. I was thrown to the floor. The orderly left, locking the door behind her. Some hours later, the door was unlocked, and Dr. Horecroft, the head of the asylum, came in to tell me what a shame it was that I was so furiously mad. The asylum was the best place for me until I came to my senses, if I ever did."

At the mention of Horecroft, Beth saw the terror flicker across Kat's face. Mama hadn't mentioned anything about Kat being there, and Beth wouldn't either. It wasn't anyone's story to tell but hers.

"I had gathered my wits in the time I'd been locked in. I'd changed to dry clothing. Made myself tidy. I'd even gotten some sleep, though I woke up screaming in the middle of the night. Screams in the night were common enough in there."

Mama stared at her hands for a time before looking up

at Sebastian. "The rest of our group hasn't heard these details. This is the first I've spoken about them. But the main reason we don't want anyone to venture from this place is my husband. I've been married to him for twenty years, and in that time he has never accepted failure. Never taken no for an answer. He will not accept that I got away from him and defied his wish that I be locked up. He will hire the best detectives, trackers, and mountain men to find me. He will never give up, and anyone who stands in his way will be dealt with severely. I believe, if he finds me, one of us will have to kill him to keep him from taking me because that alone will stop him. And I won't ask anyone to do such a thing for me. If he arrives, now that Beth is safely married, I'll go with him rather than allow one of you to put such a scar on your soul. But maybe he won't find us now that we're here . . ."

"So you're not Oscar's sister?"

"No. Oscar used to work for us at our estate. He was the man ordered to drive the carriage the night my husband took me to the asylum. I didn't know where we were going when we left home. Oscar protested and was fired. He got word to Beth about what had happened. All she knew was that I was gone. The two of them began to plan. He and his brothers knew of this place. I hope and pray I can be safe here."

Sebastian looked confused. "You're meaning to stay in this canyon for the rest of your life? All of us staying here?"

"Thaddeus is quite a bit older than I am. Maybe I can come out in twenty years." Mama's sad smile peeked out again.

"Sebastian," Beth said, "If you want to go, you can go.

I tried to be clear what we were doing, but I'm sure you couldn't quite imagine the extent to which we planned to be hermits. If you do leave, please go a different direction than the wagon-train route, and please never speak of us to anyone."

Sebastian shook his head. "I'm not going. But if I ever do, I'll talk things over with you beforehand. I might feel different after spending a winter here. We'll see."

Oscar came to Sebastian's side and gave him a pat on the shoulder. "Thank you. Now, the roast is done, and I'd say the potatoes are tender. Let's all eat."

Beth shuddered to think of Mama's story. Jake's hands remained steady on her shoulders. She stood and hugged him. Mama still wasn't safe, but maybe, at last, Beth was.

30

"Fifty-two head of cattle." Oscar looped his rope across his saddle horn and sat on horseback beside Jake. Jake on his chestnut, Oscar on the gray Morgan that showed talent as a cow pony.

Oscar's brothers were on the far end of the immense valley, looking closely at the edge of the canyon for bolt holes, where a cow could get into a cave or hung up on rocks while trying to climb out over the walls. But these were Angus, a mild-mannered breed, at least compared to longhorns, which were as tough and agile as mountain goats. The Angus wouldn't attempt to bust out if they had plenty of grass and water, as well as shelter from the winter winds.

Oscar had left them here for a year, and they were still roaming this same valley.

"Your goal was fifty head?" Jake asked.

Oscar nodded, scanning the placid herd, comfortable already with the new cattle. "I brought in twenty head last summer. I didn't dare drive a big herd in. I'd be noticed. I hope I didn't draw attention even with twenty.

There was one bull among them, though a few were spring calves. Now they're almost as big as their mamas. Most of the adult cows among the twenty had another baby last spring, and we've brought in the animals that carried us west plus the milk cows and the calf.

"My brothers and I figured that with a herd of fifty, we'd never want for meat. We saw the elk herd here and knew we'd have meat there, too. There's also a flock of turkeys roosting in the trees. Fish in the stream. Plenty of jackrabbits, raccoons, grouse, ducks. Mountain goats up in the highlands. Beaver have dammed up the stream toward the back of the canyon—they'll give us furs plus there's good eatin' on a beaver. Together with the pigs and chickens, every day will be a feast. I even planted a garden with things I hoped would grow, reseed themselves, and provide fresh vegetables this year. Then, riding away, I just had to hope I'd find things in order when we returned someday." Oscar glanced at Jake and added, "If we returned."

"And there are apples on those trees." Jake pointed to a nearby grove of trees. He hadn't noticed the apples at first because they were still small and green, but now he saw the fruit had ripened. He didn't think apple trees grew in the wild.

"Yep." Oscar nodded. "A couple of them are cherry trees, some walnut trees, mulberries and such. I planted potatoes and onions, parsnips and garlic. And horseradish because it's real tough and likely to survive. It looks like they all came back, too." He gestured toward some ferns. "Those there are asparagus plants. My ma always had asparagus."

Shaking his head, Jake said, "I've never heard of it."

"We won't get any of it until spring. But it comes early, and we'll be thankful for anything green by then." Oscar pointed to a bramble at the edge of his garden and grove. "I also planted raspberry bushes, strawberries, plums, anything I could find and haul here. Appears most of them lived, as well."

"Considering I've been eating jerky and trail dust for most of my life, it sounds like a man can thrive in this place."

Oscar gave Jake a genial clap on the back. "Men *and* women. If we got away clean, that is."

"If Rutledge wanted to be rid of his wife enough to pay someone to lock her up, why would he chase after her when she ran off? He has to know she's not going to be a nuisance to him, I mean with all her foolishness about daring to have opinions and ideas and speak them out loud." Jake snorted. "He sounds to me like a prize fool."

Oscar shook his head. "Rutledge made it in Chicago by never accepting defeat. Never turning aside when someone told him it couldn't be done or shouldn't be done. He's been a law unto himself for so long, he thinks it's his right to give orders, no matter how evil, and have them obeyed. He won't let Ginny get free, nor Beth."

"Well, I'll be standing between them, and I'm not an easy man to get through."

Oscar was silent for a moment, his expression grim. "Trouble with that is, neither woman is going to want us to die for them. We'll have to handle it just right when Rutledge arrives. And I fear he will come, and Ginny and

Beth might just walk right out of here with him to save our worthless hides."

Then Oscar turned to Jake and looked hard at him. "You're going to be a problem, for I heard tell that Rutledge is stretched way out on a limb with his investments. He was getting paid well to marry Beth off to that foul old man, Walter Lindhurst. Now he's spending a fortune to hunt down his wife and daughter just because he won't accept defiance from them. Which means he needs Lindhurst's bride price, and access to the trust her grandparents set up for her."

"Lindhurst is doomed to disappointment."

"He must be in his seventies, same as Rutledge."

"Rutledge is that old? How old is Ginny? She looks young enough, I believed she was Beth's older sister without doubting it."

"She probably isn't forty yet. She married young, had Beth young. I heard there were some babies lost, but I'm not sure about that. Not a single one was born alive after Beth."

"That must've broken her heart," Jake said.

Oscar nodded. "Lindhurst had one son, and that boy's given over to betting on horses, chasing women, drinking until dawn and sleeping until sunset. Lindhurst got it in his head he could find a young wife and start over, try and raise up a second family. So he ain't gonna like the fact that Beth is a married woman. Not one bit. And that could make your life real fragile for a while."

Jake almost hoped the old man came. Both old men. He would enjoy teaching them the word *no*. But it was doubtful they'd ever find this canyon. It was too well hidden.

Tomorrow they'd leave this place to go help the O'Toole family. A chill rushed up Jake's spine. A warning to not be sure of anything.

～

Thaddeus sent his staff to work, making sure his room was bearably clean before sending Yvette to her room to rest. She looked near to collapsing. Though he didn't need her anymore, he wasn't sure what to do with her. If there weren't witnesses, he might well have Blayd just knock her in the head and toss her behind a pile of rocks out in the wilderness. For she'd become more trouble than she was worth.

He went outside, considering all that lay ahead, and found McCall approaching the hotel from across the dirt street. He had a look of purpose on his face.

"There haven't been any wagon trains through yet," McCall said, "but word came from someone who rode in recently. He'd passed one, and according to him, they should be here in the next two or three days. A wagon train moves slow. We can wait for it, or if you'd prefer, I can ride east with my agents and any men you'd like to send along and talk to them. Find out if the women you seek are among them."

Based on the dates Horecroft had told him, Thaddeus expected his wife to be on the first or one of the first wagon trains of the season. He could very possibly end this nonsense as soon as tomorrow or the next day.

"I've got a room for you and your wife, and one for Miss Hobart. Join me in the dining room. It's been a long day, and it's time for a meal. I'm eager to be done with all this.

Going out to meet the wagon train will speed things up. We'll plan on leaving town at first light."

Thaddeus wouldn't be sending McCall and his squad of female agents out alone, though. Oh, how he wanted to be there to see Eugenia's face when he stopped the wagon train and dragged her away. Just to see her tremble. Terrified and guilty and furious. He almost smiled to think of it. But McCall was close by, and Thaddeus didn't like the way the man studied him.

Mrs. McCall and the other agent, Hobart, approached McCall from behind, all of them watchful. How difficult was it going to be to take Eugenia with these three looking on?

McCall said, "We'll take our things up to our rooms and be right down." He looked back at his wife and Hobart, a woman with sharp eyes and little to say. Both nodded.

The three of them walked past him, swung the screen door open, and let it slap closed as they went inside.

Thaddeus stared into the middle distance of the hick town. A gust of wind blew a tumbleweed across what might laughably be called the main street.

Tomorrow.

Something hot and eager flared inside him as he imagined Eugenia's face when she saw him. When she knew all of her running and hiding had come to naught.

He wondered if she'd scream and fight him. Oh, how he hoped she'd fight him.

Then he thought of McCall. Blayd needed to be ready for trouble because nothing would stop Thaddeus from reclaiming what was his.

31

T here's no point in branding the cattle." Oscar waved off his brothers like they were talking nonsense.

"It'd be good practice for us. We need to learn cowboy skills. We even brought along a forge. We can make the branding iron, then fashion shoes for the horses."

"We can't register the brand, and even if we could, it wouldn't hold any legal power. And a shod horse is necessary for long, hard rides. But there won't be many of those out here. The shoes they're wearing now will eventually fall off. After that, we'll let the horses go without like a wild mustang."

"We should learn to rope. If we start on the spring calves, we won't be risking our necks." Joseph leaned forward to talk across his big brother. "Jake, you know how to rope a calf?"

Jake tugged the brim of his Stetson low over his eyes, maybe to hide a smile. "I do indeed. But I could help you learn to rope without the branding. It's hot work, dangerous for a man, and painful for the calf. Why do it if it's not necessary?"

Joseph looked disgruntled but didn't respond.

It struck Beth how completely ready Oscar was to live here for the rest of his life. He'd willingly given up the rest of the world to help Beth. She'd needed help, and he'd thrown right in, eager to save Mama. But he might not realize how much he'd have to sacrifice. Maybe none of them had quite realized that. His brothers might be figuring it out even now.

Sebastian seemed to accept that he couldn't go to town. But he wanted to work on things that interested him. He wanted to invent. And for that, he needed materials they didn't have. Pipes and such things like that. Beth hadn't paid much attention because her focus was in keeping the man inside the canyon.

Kat had yet to speak of her life before escaping Horecroft and what had led to her being locked away there. And she'd yet to admit to the group that she'd been there with Mama. Beth didn't blame her, but if she didn't talk about it, how much harder would it be for her to heal from that dreadful experience? Maybe that worked for Kat. She wasn't tormented with nightmares, after all. But Beth wondered what all Kat had been through, and it worried her.

That left Jake, a man who'd traveled almost nonstop for the last decade, back and forth across the country. He'd explored huge swaths of this beautiful nation, and yet now he'd agreed to never leave this canyon again. How long would it take him to get restless?

"Wagon train straight ahead." John McCall came riding back. He, his wife, and the other Pinkerton rode ahead. McCall called it *scouting the trail*, which Thaddeus assumed was just an excuse to ride off so they could gossip about him.

But here came McCall back to where Thaddeus and Yvette rode in his carriage to report that they'd caught up with the first wagon train. Thaddeus's heart sped up as he considered whether he'd get his hands on Eugenia only moments from now.

"We have to take her quickly and without fuss. Elizabeth too. My wife isn't fully rational, though she can put on the appearance of it for a time. And Elizabeth defends her."

"Wait a minute." McCall pulled two sheets of paper out of the breast pocket of his shirt. "You said Eugenia was wanted for theft and assault. You've got attempted murder on Elizabeth's wanted poster. Are they wanted for crimes or not?"

Thaddeus hesitated. He was a good negotiator. He could read people quickly and most often correctly. He sorted through what he needed to say to make McCall cooperate.

"Where are you from, McCall?"

McCall's eyes seemed to penetrate Thaddeus deeper. He wanted an answer to his question, and Thaddeus had responded with another question.

"Nevada. My wife and I have a ranch close to Carson City. We have family nearby, and they can pick up any work we abandon at the ranch when our Pinkerton duties call us away."

"But where from originally?" Thaddeus asked. "I think I heard the Midwest in your voice. Or somewhere back east at any rate."

"Pennsylvania originally. A case brought me west, before the train came through. I found it suited me, and I've been out here ever since. But the wanted posters—"

"Yes, yes." Thaddeus waved away McCall's concerns. "Simply put, Eugenia is a danger to herself. I put on those wanted posters words I hoped would get action. The rewards are real, however, and you'll stand to profit from it if we find my wife and daughter today. Perhaps to divide with your fellow agents."

McCall's eyes narrowed. The man was weighing his options.

Thaddeus glanced at Yvette, whose attention was riveted on him, her jaw as tight as a miser's fist. It occurred to him then that the woman thought herself in love with him. Did she understand that Eugenia was his wife? Surely it had been mentioned in the many hours he'd spent with her, both when traveling west and when he and Horecroft had questioned her back in Chicago. Still, it might be best to discuss this away from the woman.

"Can we walk a bit, McCall? I need to stretch my legs. And some of what I have to say is private business." He swung down from the carriage. "Yvette, please remain here."

Thaddeus didn't give her a chance to object. McCall dismounted, and the two of them walked some distance away. When they were out of earshot, Thaddeus stopped and glanced back to assure himself she'd stayed behind. "What I'm going to tell you is confidential, especially concerning Yvette. You can tell the other agents, but it's . . . well, it's shameful and an embarrassment." He did his best to sound sincere and genuinely worried. "As I suppose you've deduced, Eugenia Rutledge is my wife."

McCall crossed his arms and looked straight at him. "I'd figured as much. Or a sister or relative of some kind, what with the name Rutledge. I considered that she'd stolen from you, and I believe assault is one of the crimes she's wanted for?"

"The crimes she's wanted for *happened*. But I'm not looking for Eugenia and my daughter, Elizabeth, to have them arrested and jailed. My wife . . ." Thaddeus looked behind him at Yvette, who'd remained in the carriage. He was a bit surprised. "My wife was in an asylum. She's lost her mind. My running across the country searching for her, and getting you Pinkerton agents involved, well, I'm afraid she'll harm herself and perhaps others. She mostly acts fine. I am making this desperate search in the hopes she hasn't fallen into trouble or attacked anyone." Thaddeus thought of Yvette and how rational she acted, except for her obsession with him and her hysterical way of behaving if someone touched her. He lowered his voice. "Just as Yvette does."

McCall looked over Thaddeus's shoulder. "She was in an asylum, too?"

"Yes, and she's usually as rational and calm as can be. If you don't believe me, try touching her. She goes utterly mad. Very strange. But she knew where my wife had gone. She'd overheard talk of a wagon train, so here I am chasing after my wife. I want her safe, back in Chicago where she can be properly cared for and even, hopefully, cured.

"My daughter was very much opposed to how I handled things, and she's taken her mother's side in this. When we find them, as I sincerely hope to do today, I am afraid they may object to returning with me. I've carried a straitjacket with me if it becomes necessary to restrain Eugenia. I want to get her to the train and return to Chicago. I can only hope she hasn't done anything dreadful to herself or to my sweet Elizabeth or to anyone else on that wagon train. You can see why I handled this as I did, can't you?"

McCall glanced at Yvette again. "She really reveals her madness if you touch her?"

"That's how she acts with me, and I'm talking something as simple as offering her a hand up into a carriage. If you want to see it for yourself, you're welcome to rest your hand on her arm, but honestly, I'm afraid of setting her off."

McCall seemed to let some of the rigid tension go from his shoulders. His eyes weren't so suspiciously narrowed anymore. "I can't imagine why a man would spend as much money as you have to chase after a wife who'd run off, not if he wasn't concerned about her. Not unless he wanted to take care of her."

"I'm glad we talked. If we find her . . ." Thaddeus strengthened his voice. He had great skill in handling people, and it looked like McCall wasn't going to be an exception. "If we find my Eugenia, she may try to run or fight."

He gave a deep sigh. He did his best to sound sad when,

in truth, Thaddeus felt very few emotions. And those he did feel were coldly felt, so a soft emotion like worry or sadness wasn't that easy for him to fake. "So, shall we go see if my wife is on this wagon train?"

McCall nodded. "Yes, let's go see."

32

Beth loved exploring her new home. She and Jake found time every day to ride to one corner or another of the canyon. She'd found the turkey flock, the beaver dam, and today she found an enchanting cave. She knew tomorrow they'd leave to meet up with the O'Tooles, so today she'd convinced Jake to wander with her a bit.

"Jake, come in here."

Jake, who was only a few paces behind Beth, came fast. "What is it?" He rounded a curve in the deep cave and bumped into her. His arms went around her waist and picked her up so he wouldn't bowl her right over. "Another hot spring like the one in Oscar's cave?"

Just over her head, water poured out of the side of the cave. "Have you heard of Yellowstone?"

"I've read a dime novel about it."

"Those are usually exaggerated. A lot." Beth, still in his arms, looked over her shoulder at him in the dim light and smiled.

"I know. It sounds impossible, but I read a newspaper article that said they're planning to send an expedition to explore the area. I've never seen the place, but I've heard talk of the hot springs there and other odd water features. We're a fair distance from Yellowstone, and yet we have hot water springs around here—one in Oscar's cave, one behind our cabin. You know, this cave might be a good place to store supplies. Some rooms will be cold enough to preserve things, some warm enough that cans of vegetables and such won't freeze and explode. And we've got years' worth of goods stacked up in the cave house. It'd be wise to spread them out."

They were in the far west corner of the canyon, probably a mile or more ride from their cabins. As Beth emerged from the cave, she saw their dog, barking wildly at a rock. "Here, girl! Come."

The dog, not an obedient critter most of the time, turned and raced for Jake. Seconds later, they heard the rattle. Jake swept the dog up in his arms. "Mount up, let's move."

Soon they were galloping toward the cabins. The dog squirmed, but Jake held on tight.

"Rattlesnake?"

Jake reined his horse into a trot. Beth felt her heart pounding as they slowed.

"I've never heard that sound before. But I knew what it had to be the moment I heard it."

"It's like a wolf howl. Nothing else like it in the world." Jake slowed again until they were walking. "Settle down, girl. You know, it's time we named this dog."

"Yes, let's name the dog and talk about the cave and

260

debate whether a shower bath is worth risking a snake-bite."

Jake chuckled. "I'm going to take a bunch of our supplies and store them in that cave. It'll give us more space in the cabin. We've already got Oscar's cave packed full. We can put canned goods in the room with the hot spring and they won't freeze."

"Good idea," Beth agreed. "Once it's colder, maybe we can hang beef in there. Block off a cold room so that no varmints can get inside.

"Let's head back—it's time to ride for the O'Tooles." Jake paused and looked at Beth. "I don't want you to go."

"I know, but I'm going all the same. Mama can stay here with Kat, Sebastian, and either Joseph or Oscar. Such a small group to come and help. I hope no one's found our trail yet. I'd like to believe I can venture out at least a little."

Jake frowned, then nodded despite his obvious unhappiness. "Let's go then."

They arrived back at the cabin to find Oscar alone. He'd planned to accompany them and wasn't happy about Beth going either. Shaking his head, he reined his horse around and rode for the canyon mouth.

~

"Why sure, it's Ginny Collins." A redhead. Irish folks were flooding this country, and if Thaddeus had his way, they'd be exterminated like vermin. Of course, they worked in a few of the factories he had part ownership of, and they filled up his tenements and made him good money. Even so, everyone knew the Irish couldn't be trusted. Even this one standing there smiling with his Roman collar on looked shiftless.

Thaddeus had folded his wanted poster so the reward didn't show. He suspected she'd've won loyalty from these folks. She was always fussing over unworthy people. "Which wagon is she in?"

"They left the wagon train a week back," McCall stated.

Thaddeus's hunger to get his hands on his wife deepened further. He jerked his chin up. "A week! Where did she go?"

McCall reached across from his horse to Thaddeus's carriage and gripped his arm tight. "Stay calm."

The man said it like he was being friendly, yet the grip on his arm hurt like fire. He'd be bruised tomorrow. Still, Thaddeus clamped his mouth shut.

"Where did they turn off, Parson McDaniels?" McCall asked politely.

Thaddeus couldn't quite manage acting polite right now. He'd come so close, only to be thwarted. He'd been preparing himself for the look on Eugenia's face when she saw him approach her.

"We need to find them." McCall, still calm, finally released Thaddeus's arm.

The Irishman looked sideways at his wife, who answered, "The Collins family turned off when we were on the north side of that big lake . . . Black Bear Lake or Big Bear Lake? Something like that. I heard they had a place to the north. Our wagon master said it's not uncommon for folks to not go all the way to Oregon."

"Yes, thank you." McCall tugged at the brim of his hat.

Collins. That would be Oscar Collins. Thaddeus re-

membered this fool who'd insulted him, demanding that
Eugenia be brought home. Thaddeus had fired him and
blackened his name all through Chicago. As far as Thaddeus knew, he'd left town. But instead of accepting defeat,
Oscar Collins had brought Elizabeth in on his plan to
break Eugenia out of the asylum. Oscar and Elizabeth
working together, plotting against him when Thaddeus's
money had provided both of them with everything they
had. The betrayal burned in Thaddeus's gut.

The Irish trash were in the lead wagon. Thaddeus saw
a filthy man in western clothes riding toward them.

"Is that enough information, McCall?" Thaddeus
didn't want to talk to anyone else. "Can you find where
they turned north and track them?"

"My wife's one of the finest trackers on the frontier."
McCall smiled at his wife. "I reckon she can figure out
where a wagon turned off this trail."

"Four wagons," the parson piped up. "And before they
left, I presided over the wedding of Elizabeth to Mr. Jake
Holt, our wagon-train scout. He went along north with
them. It was a fine thing to see."

Married? Elizabeth had married a scout? Thaddeus
clamped his jaw shut and said through gritted teeth to
Blayd, "Drive on. Head for the lake. Come along, Mc-
Call."

"I've a few more questions I need answers to. I'll catch
up with you later, Mr. Rutledge. They said it was a week
ago, but a horse moves a lot faster than a wagon train.
Even with your carriage, we can find where they headed
north—probably today still."

Blayd slapped the reins across the horses' backs and set

the carriage into motion while Thaddeus fought to not kill someone. Everyone. He fingered the folding knife he kept hidden in his pocket, which he always carried with him. He pictured himself using it on Elizabeth. Or better yet, on her husband. Maybe on both.

He carried it, but he'd never had to use it. That's what Blayd was for.

Blayd and this blade. The worst of his fury died as he let himself be amused by that twist of words. For the first time ever, he thought he could kill. In fact, he wanted to. Hemler Blayd might well have to step aside and let Thaddeus handle this one. He was, after all, in the Wild West. Such things happened in the uncivilized countryside. Thaddeus had heard all about it.

Blayd drove the carriage down the line of slow-rolling wagons. Thaddeus noticed Yvette had pulled out her handkerchief, and she waved it delicately at each wagon they passed.

A lot of folks were walking alongside the wagons. Some were on horseback. Had Eugenia and Elizabeth trudged all the way across the country?

Both of them had truly lost their minds.

And Thaddeus intended to lock them up right where they belonged—if they were alive when he was done with them.

33

The O'Toole homestead came into sight. It was heavily wooded, with cabins built on both sides of a stream.

Bruce was dragging a log toward Donal's smaller house. Donal stood on the end of one log while cutting a notch in the corner. Both men looked up from their work and waved.

The cabins looked about finished. The shutters and doors were all hung, and smoke billowed up from the chimney of the larger cabin. Bruce's stack of logs was sizable, all they'd need to build a barn and add a floor to each cabin.

"You really came back." The voice with the Irish lilt turned them all toward the door of the larger cabin, nearly swallowed up by the trees. Maeve stood there waving. Her eyes skimmed over them, and Jake knew she'd noticed their small crew. Yet it made sense that some of them would stay behind and work on their own land.

"Maeve!" Beth called and ran toward her.

Jake watched the two of them hug for a few moments before he realized he had a foolish smile on his face. Turning to see if Oscar noticed, he saw what he suspected was the same smile.

Oscar caught him looking, and the two men shook their heads and started forward—Jake on horseback, Oscar driving their cart.

As Fiona emerged from the cabin, both her youngsters wriggled past her to greet them. Donal and Bruce left off their work.

Jake noticed a row of flat rocks crossing the stream that hadn't been there when they'd left the O'Tooles. Donal and Bruce walked across the shallow stream easily over the stepping-stones.

"What's all this you've brought now, Oscar?" Fiona plunked two fists on her hips, frowning. "We'll not be accepting charity, not even from good friends."

"Not charity, Mrs. O'Toole."

"It's Fiona, and well you know it. You're just taking that fancy tone hoping I'll go along with whatever daft plan you've cooked up."

Oscar had the cart loaded with supplies. He was leading four head of Angus cattle, including a bull. He also had a plow in the cart. They really needed a wagon for it all, but Jake had agreed with Oscar when it was decided the O'Tooles would be hard-pressed to accept the supplies and animals, let alone anything added.

"Fiona, I worked hard all last summer dragging supplies to the canyon where we live. Then we hauled more along. I've got a garden planted with things that come back year after year, besides getting a start on a fall garden. Doubt it'll yield much, it being September. But we're hoping for radishes and greens and maybe peas to add to the menu. Well, I outsmarted myself, and that's a fact."

Fiona tilted her head and didn't look one bit persuaded.

"I also had a small herd from last summer and a calf crop that's a wonder to behold. We're set up where we are—more than set. I know we left your family with scant supplies. Donal's a good hand with a rifle and can bring in fresh meat, but you're sure to be short on other goods."

Fiona shook her head while she watched her two young-sters charge at the Angus cattle. Because they were so unusual as draft animals, everyone on the wagon train knew of them.

"And, Fiona," Oscar said, "I brought along that nervous Angus cow. You'd be doing me a favor by taking her."

Beth released Maeve and went to hug Fiona. Fiona's hands left her hips to hug Beth back.

"Let us share these things with you. It'll help you and your family get a good start."

Fiona patted Beth's back. "It will be welcome. Thank you, Oscar."

Donal and Bruce came up to the group.

"It looks like you've been loafing here, Bruce." Oscar slapped his brother on the back. "Good thing I came back."

Bruce laughed. "I gotta long list of chores for you, Brother."

They threw themselves into the work in high spirits. Be-fore they started in on the barn, they put up a chicken coop because, among all the supplies, they'd brought with them ten chickens. Which was enough to keep the O'Tooles in eggs for the winter, and maybe with some chicks in the spring, a flock would grow enough for the occasional meal of fried chicken.

When Fiona saw those chickens, she broke down and wept.

~

"I should have made Sebastian come." Oscar slammed a post into the corner of the corral. "That boy needs to learn building."

Jake carried one of the split rails to Oscar's line of posts. "We'll work with him come winter. Look how fast Donal is learning."

They paused their work to watch Donal, who grabbed the piece of timber Bruce handed up to him to frame the barn roof.

"How old do you figure Donal is?"

Beth and Fiona were putting together a much smaller building for the chickens so that, together with the new coop, the birds would be sheltered for the winter. And Maeve was cooking a noon meal outside.

"He's sixteen if he's a day."

"But he homesteaded."

"As the head of his household. It's all legal." Oscar lifted the rail Jake had brought and lined it up. Oscar had drilled holes in the rail and the post, lined them up, and tapped a wooden peg through both pieces of wood.

"Where'd you learn to build like this, Oscar? Did you really grow up out here?"

"My pa was a hand at it," Oscar said. "He taught me and my brothers the way of building, handling cattle and horses, and tracking. You know, I wish I'd brought some of our nails. It's a faster way to build, and we've got a good supply of 'em. I wasn't generous enough." He looked at the horses, grazing in the pasture they'd fenced off, and the oxen, eight from the O'Tooles' two wagons. Somehow the animals had all survived, even if one of the wagons hadn't. Another pasture held the Angus cows and a milk cow.

"Turn them loose." Beth waved at Bridget and Conor, who carried a crate out of the barn, a clucking crate. The two children giggled as they brought the chickens to the open door of the coop.

"We should've brought more chickens. Ten hens aren't enough."

Jake smiled at Oscar as he straightened from finishing the last corner of the corral. "You're a good man. You want to take care of everyone. But the chickens you brought, along with the milk cow, will get the family through the winter just fine. You've given them plenty of potatoes, too, and those along with the eggs and milk and Donal's hunting will be enough. And Fiona knows how to turn an ox into a pile of steaks once winter arrives."

Maeve called out, "Dinner is ready."

Oscar nodded. "We'll head home tomorrow. I hate leavin', but we must go. One good snow and we could be locked out."

Jake slipped his hammer into the leather belt he wore. "Really? That canyon mouth snows shut?"

"It never has when I've been there, but we came late in the summer and worked most of a year. When we left there was snow aplenty in the canyon. So yes, I think it snows shut."

The two of them walked toward where Maeve had prepared the meal. Donal and Bruce weren't yet finished with the barn roof, but they were close. They still needed to put up a fence in the yard to keep the chickens safe, but Donal could handle that without any trouble.

Maeve had a covered metal roaster nestled in the hot coals of a fire. The day had been long and warm, so they'd cooked outside so as not to heat up the cabins too much.

Beth and Fiona talked quietly as they joined the others.

When they drew near, Bruce said, "I'm going to stay until the barn's finished and the chicken yard's ready. I'll follow you later. I know you're worried about the snow closing you in, Oscar, but if I'm too late, I'll winter over with Donal. These folks seem to need me more than you do."

Beth looked at Jake. Her forehead furrowed as if she thought they needed Bruce mighty bad. But the man was right. The O'Tooles needed him more.

"If we have time, we might add a room onto Donal's house," Bruce went on, "and there's furniture to build. I can be useful here."

Oscar nodded. It was true. The O'Tooles had need of him right now. "Come home whenever suits you, Bruce. We'll miss you, but you're a fine hand and good with the cattle and horses, the hunting, and most every other thing these good folks might need. We'll probably come over in the spring to help again. You can follow us home then."

Maeve lifted the cover of the roaster to let the steam escape, revealing two cooked grouse and baked potatoes. "Time for supper, everyone."

"We'll head for home in the morning," Oscar finished. "It's time to get on with our own chores."

"I'd like to hit the trail as soon as possible tomorrow," Jake added.

Fiona asked everyone to bow their heads. After a fine blessing, they feasted and talked about the rich soil and the impending winter. The sun disappeared below the horizon as they finished their meal. Then Jake, Oscar, and Bruce followed Donal home.

Jake gave Beth a lingering look before following the other men. He smiled as he remembered her own lingering look. It would be good to be back home.

34

Beth, Jake, and the others hadn't told the O'Tooles exactly where they had settled. "North" and "the canyon" were all they'd shared, and the family accepted that. Being so busy with their preparations to survive the winter, they had no plans to come visiting anytime soon.

Oscar got them up the next morning. Donal and Bruce had built a fire outside and were getting breakfast ready.

It'd taken the group a solid week to build the corrals, chicken coop, and barn. Oscar had used a pair of oxen to plow a patch for a garden where he'd planted a few precious seeds. They'd kept at it until near dark the night before, working hard until all was done.

Beth perked up at the sight of the campfire, a sight she'd seen so many mornings on the trail west. She couldn't smell the bacon and coffee, but she knew it was coming soon, and the thought stirred her senses awake.

The dawn had come fully by the time they emerged from the cabins, so they'd slept past their usual time of getting up. Yesterday had been a day of hard work, followed by a late night. Sleeping an extra hour wouldn't hurt them, and Jake assured Beth he was okay with that, tired as he was from their labors.

The men had stayed at Donal's house, and even young Conor had slept with them. The women had stayed with Fiona. Beth had enjoyed her friends' company, though she missed sleeping in Jake's strong arms. Yes, it was time to go home.

"Good morning." Beth went to Maeve and gave her a hug. "Let's have a meal, then it's time for us to pack up and go."

"No one's going anywhere."

Beth whirled around at the voice she'd feared until it slithered like a snake through her nightmares.

Thaddeus Rutledge stepped out from behind Fiona's house. His henchman, the vile Hemler Blayd, was at his side like always.

"Father!"

"Get your mother out here. We're going home. Now."

Beth's heart began to race. Her father sounded more ruthless and threatening than ever.

Blayd had a knife and a six-gun at his sides, and his hands were balled into fists.

"So you're Thaddeus Rutledge." Jake's voice, low and strong, echoed in the air around her.

Beth reminded herself that she was married. Father couldn't take her. Some of her fear eased at the thought. But what about Mama?

Thaddeus grunted. "And I suppose you're the greedy bumpkin who tricked her into marrying you. That's at an end. She's not in her right mind. I've had her examined by a doctor, and he'll swear in court she's unable to make such a decision as marrying. We'll have it annulled once we're home."

"I'm not going anywhere with you, Father. And Horecroft will say anything if you pay him enough. Go home. I have no intention of interfering with your life. I demand the same from you."

Father took two long strides toward her, his hand raised to grab her. Jake stepped in front of her, and Father, unused to anyone thwarting him, staggered backward.

"Beth is my wife. She's not going anywhere. And neither is—"

Blayd's pistol clicked as he drew it and cocked it. "A widow is as good as an annulment."

Beth's lungs nearly seized working when she saw the gun pointed straight at Jake's heart. "No, no, don't hurt him. Please." She shoved her way past Jake and stood between him and the barrel of Blayd's gun.

"Beth!" Jake grasped her shoulders from behind. "Step out of—"

"What's going on, Thaddeus, dear?"

The light, cheerful voice shocked Beth, and for a moment she wondered if she was still asleep and dreaming. A woman stepped up beside Father. She was dressed in beautiful clothes, her hair so neat she must have a lady's maid following her around.

Beth felt a little dizzy. "Who are you?"

"Get back in the carriage, Yvette. I'll be along soon with my daughter, who'll then take me to my wife."

Yvette? Who in the world was Yvette?

The strange woman whirled to face Thaddeus. "No. *I'm* your wife."

"Shut up and do as you're told."

"Thaddeus, darling, don't speak to me that way. I love you!"

Father backhanded her.

Yvette fell to the ground and began screaming. Beth noticed the wild look in her eyes. Horrible as it was to be hit, it seemed as if the shrieking had nothing to do with pain.

Suddenly the woman leapt to her feet and lunged at Father. She had a knife in her hand—the folding knife her father always carried with him. Yvette thrust the blade into Father's side, then quickly pulled back and slashed at him again and again, all the while screeching like a tormented soul.

Father roared in pain, his mouth agape, his eyes filled with disbelief.

Jake pulled Beth well back from the melee.

Blayd turned his gun on Yvette and fired.

He missed. Yvette's gyrations and Father's efforts to shove her away got her out of the line of fire.

Then Father was between them, and Blayd shoved his gun in its holster and rounded Father just as Yvette stabbed him again.

Father knocked her to the ground, howling and clutching at his wounds.

Someone else crashed into the clearing to see Yvette on the ground. Blayd drew his pistol a second time.

"No, stop." The newcomer drew his own six-gun. "Don't shoot her."

"Stay out of this, McCall!" Father shouted. Crimson

spread on his chest and arms. His side was bleeding, his leg. He'd been cut into tatters.

"She needs to die." Blayd aimed and fired. Then Blayd looked down at his chest. He looked confused, stunned.

Beth could see it wasn't Blayd's gun that had fired, but the newcomer's, McCall.

Yvette clamped her mouth shut and stared at him, probably afraid of being next.

"She was going to kill me. Blayd saved my life." Father raged at the man who'd pulled the trigger. A second later, Father collapsed. "Help me, please. She stabbed me. Blayd was protecting me . . ."

Blayd lay on the ground, unmoving.

McCall gave them all a sweeping look that seemed to take in every detail of the scene before him. His eyes then locked on Beth. "I'm John McCall. I'm a Pinkerton agent. I was hired by your father to find you and your ma." He dropped to the ground beside Father and raised his voice. "Penny, Rachel, get the blankets, anything. We'll need a lot of bandages."

Beth saw two tough-looking women turn back to follow McCall's orders. They weren't overly dismayed by the shooting and stabbing. Behind them, she noticed several other men she recognized as her father's thugs. They all worked under Blayd.

She eased back another step and bumped into Jake. Their eyes met as he urged her to stand behind him. His broad back kept Beth protected from these other folks.

Oscar, Donal, and Bruce rushed forward and formed a wall of men between the women and the Pinkerton agents, who apparently had been hired to escort Beth and Mama back east with Father. Beth stood on her tiptoes to see over Jake's shoulder.

One of the women said to the group, "I'm Agent Hobart." She crouched beside Blayd and lay a hand flat on his chest. "He's dead. We're not wasting bandages on him."

"And I'm Penny McCall. I'm mostly a rancher, but I help John with his cases sometimes."

"You men," John McCall called over his shoulder, "do you wanna dig a hole or should we haul Blayd back with us?" As he spoke, he took strips of blanket from Penny and tended Father's wounds, still bleeding badly.

The men all looked frozen in place. Beth could well imagine they'd taken orders all their working lives but now had no idea how to proceed.

Mr. McCall must've thought the same thing because he started giving orders. "Let's take Blayd's body to town, bury him there."

The men strode away. Returning to their horses maybe? Once they were out of sight, Beth nudged Jake's shoulder.

He turned to face her, a scowl on his face. "You stay well away from him."

"I want to speak to my father, Jake. Don't worry. He can't hurt me anymore."

"They can." He glared at the Pinkerton agents.

Beth spoke past him to the agents. "I'm a married woman. My father has no rights over me. I refuse to go with him, and you haven't got the power to take me."

McCall looked up, and his eyes had a cool look that told her the man would do as he thought right and not much would stop him. He went back to bandaging and said, "Your pa told me he faked those wanted posters. He

277

told me he was worried about you and your ma and put out those posters so someone would bring you in and then he'd be able to take care of you because you were both out of your minds." He raised his cool eyes again. "You seem sane enough to me."

Beth pressed her way past Jake, who allowed it but stayed close. She stood over her father, who writhed in pain. "Will he live?"

Father turned his hateful eyes on her. "You're going home with me. Where's your mother?"

"Mr. Rutledge, your living on is by no means a sure thing. We have to get you to a doctor, and fast. You're losing too much blood. You need these knife wounds sewn up. The cut on your leg is so deep, you might lose it entirely. There's no time to search for your wife. Your daughter is under no obligation to go with you. She's a married woman who seems quite sane and whose husband seems fully able to take care of her. Now, do you want to live or do you want to die?"

"Of course I want to live, you fool!"

Agent Hobart, working on Father's leg, tightened the bandage, possibly a bit too tight. Father flinched and released a groan.

Penny's eyes seemed to suggest just who exactly was the fool around here.

"Fine. Then let's take you to town. If we push hard, we can get to a doctor by nightfall and maybe you'll survive those wounds. By the way, I'm telling Allan Pinkerton you admitted to lying about those posters. He'll refuse to work for you anymore, regardless of how much money you pay him."

Agent Hobart moved to the edge of the clearing and yelled, "Get over here and help us load Rutledge into the carriage, then toss Blayd over his horse! Then I'll get . . ." Her words trailed off as she looked around. "Where'd Yvette go?"

Everyone wheeled around, staring. Beth almost felt the blade of that knife coming right at her, but the woman was nowhere to be seen.

Two of the men came and picked up her father. A third dragged Blayd's body out of the clearing.

As he was lifted, Father's face twisted with rage as he glared at Beth. "I'm not done with you."

"Well, I'm done with you, Pa." She almost smirked—maybe more than almost. She'd never called him Pa in her life.

The men carried him away, and he proved he was hurt bad by complaining every step of the way.

McCall sighed. "The men will drive like mad for Alton. The doctor there will do his best. Afterward, they'll get into those fancy private train cars Mr. Rutledge left at the town down the trail and head to the nearest big-city doctor."

"He may think no one west of Chicago is good enough." Beth looked around, wondering if the knife-wielding woman Yvette was somewhere in the woodlands nearby. Yvette held a grudge against a man she thought she was married to but who had another wife, and now she'd shown herself to be dangerous. "Maybe he'll want to go all the way home."

"I'll suggest it. While they hunt for a doctor, we'll hunt for the woman. We can't leave her out here alone."

He looked at Beth. "Go on your way. I'll spread word of your pa's bad intentions. I apologize for everything. I can't promise no one else will come looking for you, but I can promise it won't be me or my fellow agents." He said goodbye and left the clearing with his arm slipped around Penny's waist. Rachel walked a few strides ahead. All three looked to be on the alert for the possible presence of Yvette.

Beth and all those with her stood still. The carriage and the men riding along with her father tore off to the south. The Pinkerton agents mounted up and rode toward the west.

Finally, when all the intruders were out of sight, Beth said, "I like the idea of calling our new home *Hidden Canyon*. What do you all think?"

"Sounds just right." Jake started saddling Beth's horse while she helped with the breakfast dishes.

"A good name," Oscar agreed as he hitched his horse to the cart.

Before long, they left to head for their Hidden Canyon home.

"Let's make sure we're not followed," Oscar said. "I don't care to add Yvette to our little family."

It was over, and yet Beth couldn't help but feel that somehow her father would survive his injuries. He was stubborn enough to do that. And he wouldn't give up.

He'd come looking for her again, she was sure of it.

Epilogue

Winter came down hard on Hidden Canyon. Beth loved it. It was no colder than Chicago, after all. And not having her father nearby to frighten and threaten her made it a paradise. A rather cold, snowy paradise, but fine nonetheless.

By January she was sure a baby was on the way. Jake was thrilled by the news, Mama eager to add to the family.

They were all settling in—except for Sebastian, who seemed a bit confused. He sat at the table with the whole family gathered around. "If I just had a few more supplies, I could make progress on my invention. Beth, we have good reason to believe your father isn't coming back, at least not until his wounds heal. I'll ride to town fast, order what I need, come back and wait however long it takes until my order arrives. Then I'll go fetch my items. Just knowing they're coming would make life here more bearable."

"What's not bearable?" Jake asked. "This canyon cuts the cold wind like no other place in the West."

Beth noticed the wind picked this unfortunate moment to blow so hard that the front door rattled in its frame.

"Not enough." Sebastian glared at the door as a bit of snow blew under it to whiten the floor.

He'd turned one room of the cave house into a laboratory, but his inventions had a tendency to create clouds of foul-smelling smoke. Oscar had begun building a separate cabin for Sebastian, well away from the cave house, though the winter had slowed him down some. And he hadn't started the laboratory until he'd finished the barn and corrals.

"The slope of the canyon walls keeps the snow swept off the grass in a section large enough for the cattle to graze all winter."

"Yum, grass."

Beth fought a smile. Poor Sebastian. She'd tried to warn him.

"The cattle are thriving," Oscar said with satisfaction. "We'll have a good calf crop in the spring. We've got food enough and warm places to stay. Good friends and family. We're safe. God is with us. What more can a man ask for?"

"Pipes." Sebastian slammed the side of his fist onto the table. "Tools. A supply of hand drills, carbon plates, zinc oxide, a—"

Beth rested a hand on Sebastian's forearm, who sat to her right. Jake was on her left on one side of the crowded table, with the Collinses sitting across from them. Kat was on one end of the table, Mama on the other. Beth said, "It'll be all right. There are books to read and songs to sing, and don't forget, I've got a child on the way."

She caught the gleam in Jake's eyes, and it was possible that his chest puffed out with pride. The two of them shared a private smile full of the joy they both felt.

"Your books are *Jane Eyre* and *Persuasion*. Books full of romance and feelings." Sebastian sounded disgusted.

"Oh, but Mr. Rochester and Jane." Beth pressed a hand to her chest and sighed.

"Rochester is a philanderer, while Jane spends her time preaching little sermonettes."

Mama added, "Well, we've also got the entire collection of Plato's *Republic*. All ten volumes."

"It's in *French*. I don't read or speak French."

Jake laughed. "I'll give you that, Sebastian. I don't speak any French either."

The Collins family all nodded. Not Kat, surprisingly.

"I know it, and I could teach anyone interested," Kat said.

Beth looked at Jake, the Collins brothers, Sebastian, then nodded. "There, you see? And learning French might make the winter pass more quickly."

Oscar arched a brow.

"We've got Bibles, too," Mama said. "Jake and I each have one, and the Collins brothers have one."

"I've read it already—twice since we got here." Sebastian shoved his chair back so hard that it toppled over. "I've *got* to get out of here."

"But you can't," Jake said, looking up at him now.

Sebastian whirled on him. Beth was taken aback by the fierce look in Sebastian's eyes. His reddened face. His grimly taut jaw. Through clenched teeth, he stated, "Yes. I. Can." Then he gave a sigh and seemed to calm himself a little. "I thought this was what I wanted, but it's not. I've got to leave. I have work to do and ideas to pursue."

"I didn't mean you shouldn't," Jake said, holding his hands up, palms out. "I meant you *can't*. I checked this morning, and the passage out of this bottleneck canyon is completely filled with fresh snow. Filled in *tight* all the way to the top."

Sebastian Jones wobbled where he stood. Beth wondered if he might be losing his mind. Then he walked over, grabbed his coat, jerked the door open and stalked outside, slamming the door behind him.

Everyone at the table looked between themselves for a lengthy minute or two.

Jake said quietly into the tense silence, "It's going to be a long winter in Hidden Canyon."

Read on
for a *sneak peek* at

TOWARD THE DAWN

by Mary Connealy

Book 2 of

A WESTERN LIGHT

Available in the summer of 2024

I'm going to tear this canyon open with my bare hands."
Sebastian Jones had endured. He'd lasted the whole
winter trapped in there. He hadn't known just how
much he'd hate it until he found out there was no escape.

"Seb, will you stop? The canyon will melt open when
it melts open."

Seb whirled to face the little woman who had probably
saved his life last spring when she and her friends had
found him, shot, in an alley in Independence, Missouri.
"Kat, just go away. I'm busy losing my mind." Seb tried to
unclench his jaw, his fists, his gut. He'd been doing it for
months, deliberately forcing himself to breathe, remain
calm, endure. "When is this ever going to melt?" At the bit-
ter, dead end of his endurance, he threw his arms wide and
exploded at Kat, who had done nothing to deserve this.

She marched straight at him, her own fists clenched, and
he braced himself to take a blow to the chin. Or maybe
duck.

Instead, she marched right past him and plowed a fist
into the stupid snowdrift that had blocked the canyon
closed since January. "I hate it."

That pulled Seb up short, distracting him from the sense
of feeling trapped. "You hate it, too?"

She yanked her fist out of the snow, stared at her knuckles

for a second, then slugged the snowdrift again. She whirled to face him, fists still clenched.

Once more he braced himself.

"Yes!" She threw her arms wide.

"Why didn't you say something?" And like a trapped rat, he was suddenly clawing at anything to get to the truth. He jabbed one pointy finger into her shoulder. "You've been listening to me rant and complain all winter." He poked her again, hard enough that she backed up a step. "Let me behave like some ungrateful, irrational man." Poke, poke, poke. A poke for each insult he dealt himself. "And while I whined and moaned, you watched me with that tidy little complacent smile on your face." Another poke, but this time she swatted his hand aside. "You did that while you *agreed with me*?" He jabbed her again. "That's just pure mean of you. You could at least have spoken up, divided their attention."

"By *their* you mean the people that took us both in? Fed and clothed us? Saved us, transported us across the country, gave us a home and heat and friendship?"

Seb fell silent, watching her. The wind buffeted them. The beautiful canyon stretched out for miles. The narrow-necked entrance to the hidden canyon stood clotted with snow, up to twenty feet or more over their heads. He couldn't see the top of it.

She stood glaring at him. Blond, blue-eyed, delicate, with doctoring skills that had probably saved his life. A hardworking woman who, he just now realized, he knew very little about. She was quiet. She was with Beth and Eugenia Rutledge when he'd met them. He'd just assumed—

"Us?"

She plunked her hands on her hips.

"How'd they save you? You were with them from the beginning. You, along with Beth and Ginny, saved me."

More silence. He saw something in her, something bubbling, like a pot with its lid too tight. "What are you thinking? You're standing there trying not to just flat-out tell me I'm furiously mad."

She swung her fist.

He ducked. Glad he was ready for it.

"Hey, why'd you do that?" Maybe for all the poking, but it could be for anything. "Now *you're* overreacting."

She threw her arms wide as she shouted, "I did it because . . ." Tears spurted from her eyes.

Seb hated it when women cried. No, not hated it. Feared it. He always felt helpless and stupid, like a reckless, clumsy bull turned loose in a glass factory.

And still she yelled. Tears, yelling, arms moving like pistons on a speeding train. "I did it because I *am* a lunatic. I am *not* a friend of this family, or least I wasn't at the beginning."

Seb stopped thinking about the snow and was suddenly focused on the gyrating woman in front of him. "I'd been shot and was on the verge of death when I met you. I don't know what brought you along to this locked jail cell of a canyon. I don't know anything because you've never *said* anything."

She vibrated in silence like she was fighting not to speak, and then she exploded with, "I escaped from the same asylum as Ginny!"

Seb froze. He felt his eyes go wide. He clamped his mouth shut so he wouldn't say another thing. Just in case it led to more yelling, more tears, more agitation.

Her eyes narrowed, and she glared hard enough to burn the flesh from his bones. "You agree, don't you? You believe I'm a madwoman, just like my wretched uncle did when he locked me away and took all the money I inherited from my husband."

He didn't have the choice now of keeping his mouth shut. Her accusation called for a response. Staying silent would make it seem like he agreed with her uncle. "Really, you escaped from a lunatic asylum?"

She swung again. Open hand this time. But he was ready, and she missed.

"Cut that out." He braced himself to duck again.

"You should let me hit you."

"Why would I do something that stupid?"

"You just seem like a coward is all. Ducking like that. Stay in there and take it." She shrugged, and some of her fury seemed to ebb a bit. She swiped the sleeve of her blue dress across her eyes, then pulled a handkerchief out of one sleeve, turned aside and blew her nose, then turned back.

"Tell me about the asylum," he said.

Kat shook her head. She stepped up to the snowdrift she'd punched and studied the holes she'd left. "Do you remember last September when we came in here?"

An annoying question when he'd already asked one and had been ignored. "Of course I remember it. It's the last time I was in the world outside of this paradise."

Kat glanced over her shoulder at him, her mouth in a grim line. "Me too. Well, when we came through here in September, there was snow on the ground. Not snow like a recent storm—old, melted ice, tucked into the nooks and crannies of this canyon."

Seb remembered. "You think it was still melting in September?"

"Mountains have snow that never melts. We're not on a mountain peak, but we're high up. Yes, I think this will take months yet to melt. If it ever does. You remember this closed up in January?"

"I remember that too, Kat," he said impatiently. He didn't want to talk about that. "About the asylum . . ."

"It strikes me that Oscar came out here maybe early summer."

Oscar Collins was the man who'd helped Beth plan Ginny's escape from Horecroft Asylum. He'd discovered Hidden Canyon a hundred miles from nowhere. He'd bought it. He'd driven in a herd of cattle. He'd built the cabin the women lived in. With Jake Holt now married to Beth, Jake lived in the cabin, as well.

The men lived in a cave near the cabin with an entrance built onto it. They had a hot spring in the large cave that provided most of the heat, and the three men—Oscar, his brother Joseph, and Seb—each had their own room plus a kitchen area and any other rooms they wanted. The cave stretched back a long way.

"I don't know when he came. He said he knew about this canyon from years ago. How it had felt like home to him from the first moment he saw it, but his life drew him back to Chicago. Then when Ginny needed a hiding place, he thought of it. Beth gave him enough money to buy it, and enough to outfit three wagons with supplies to last a long time. They intended to move in here and stay for the rest of their lives—or at least the rest of Thaddeus Rutledge's life." As long as Thaddeus, Ginny's husband, was alive, he had rights over her that included locking her away in an asylum based only on Thaddeus's opinion that his wife was insane.

"I wonder if he survived those stab wounds last fall?"

"How could we ever know when we're trapped in this canyon?" Seb turned to the mountain and sighed.

Kat nodded. "I think we can dig out of here. We have a shovel in our cabin."

Seb's head snapped around. "Admit it, you want out as badly as I do."

"At least as badly," she said.

He moved close enough, his nose was almost touching hers. He wasn't an overly tall man—five-foot-nine with his boots on—but she was a little thing and made him feel tall. He did his best to loom over her. Then his blue eyes met hers and held.

She was a pretty woman, no doubt about it. But only a fool tried to court a woman with no preacher in sight and with a group of men who'd shoot him for anything less honorable than a true courtship.

Her eyes held the same as his. Speaking just above a whisper, he said, "I've known you now for close to a year. You're as sensible and sane as any woman, any *person*, alive. Who locked you up? Who's this uncle that wanted you out of the way so he could take your money? Where is he? I've a mind to go have a talk with him."

"No. You don't dare." Her hand came out and caught the hand he'd just poked her with.

Well, not *just*. It'd been a few minutes before he realized what a terrible thing it was for her to be declared anything but the most rational of women.

They stood locked in combat, her eyes urgent, her grip like iron. Well, very soft, warm iron that he could have freed himself from instantly, except he didn't want to.

"I'm getting out of here. Come with me." The words just popped right out of his mouth, as if his brain were in no way connected to it.

She let go of his arm and shook her head, then closed her eyes and turned back to the snowdrift. "How will you do it?"

Seb's mind went a little wild when he heard something in her question that she probably didn't mean the way it sounded. "How will you do . . . ? Oh, the snow barrier."

"See where you punched your fist in?" He stared at the snow, anything but look at her, just in case she could read his mind.

"Of course I can see it. It's right in front of my face."

"Earlier it was like powder, remember? There was no getting over it, a person would just sink in over his head and flounder. Impossible to make forward progress, and a horse was out of the question. But it's since changed. It rained twice in the last few weeks. I think we can climb it now. We can cut a more gradual slope in it so a horse could walk over."

Kat leaned forward and clawed at the snow. "It's tightly packed and heavy. It's not going to go back to powder. And look." She pointed at the ground near the canyon wall, where a small stream flowed like a spring. "It's melting. It'll take a long time, but it will melt eventually." Crossing her arms, she studied the stream of water, the wall of snow, the fist dents. "You're right. We can do it. It's spring now. Granted, it's early spring, but spring all the same."

She turned, her gaze different now, and studied him. "It's as wrong as it can be for the two of us to ride off together, travel together, an unmarried man and woman."

Seb stared right back. There was no need to read her mind, for he knew exactly what she was thinking. It was the same thing he was thinking.

They both spoke at once. "We have to take Beth along for propriety's sake."

"We need to get married," he added.

Kat's eyes widened when she realized what he'd said. She opened and closed her mouth, not unlike a landed trout. She was so shocked, he almost laughed. Except he was insulted that his proposal had come as such a shock.

"I think we'd better get out of here soon," she said, "because I'm real close to needing to be locked up for real."

Mary Connealy writes romantic comedies about cowboys. She's the author of the Brothers in Arms, Brides of Hope Mountain, High Sierra Sweethearts, Kincaid Brides, Trouble in Texas, Wild at Heart, and Cimarron Legacy series, as well as several other acclaimed series. Mary has been nominated for a Christy Award, was a finalist for a RITA Award, and is a two-time winner of the Carol Award. She lives on a ranch in eastern Nebraska with her very own romantic cowboy hero. They have four grown daughters—Joslyn, married to Matt; Wendy; Shelly, married to Aaron; and Katy, married to Max—and seven precious grandchildren. Learn more about Mary and her books at

maryconnealy.com
facebook.com/maryconnealy
seekerville.blogspot.com
petticoatsandpistols.com

Sign Up for Mary's Newsletter

Keep up to date with Mary's latest news on book releases and events by signing up for her email list at the link below.

MaryConnealy.com

More from Mary Connealy

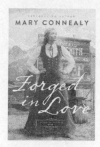

After surviving a brutal stagecoach robbery, Mariah Stover attempts to rebuild her life as she takes over her father's blacksmith business, but the townspeople meet her work with disdain. She is drawn to the new diner owner as he faces similar trials in the town. When danger descends upon them, will they survive to build a life forged in love?

Forged in Love
WYOMING SUNRISE #1

Widowed seamstress Nell Armstrong finds solace in helping widower Brand Nolte's daughters learn to sew. But she's more than a seamstress, and her investigative skills from her late lawman husband come critical when a robbery survivor arrives in town. As danger encroaches from all sides, Nell and Brand must discover why there appears to be a bull's-eye on their backs.

The Laws of Attraction
WYOMING SUNRISE #2

When Becky Pruitt's ranch foreman, Nate Paxton, confesses he's a former US Marshal investigating the notorious Deadeye Gang, she agrees to let the marshals use the ranch as a hideout. But the outlaws won't go quietly, and as danger draws ever nearer, Becky is drawn to Nate and finds both her heart and life in peril.

Marshaling Her Heart
WYOMING SUNRISE #3

◊BETHANYHOUSE